# THE GHOST SONG

**Nothing sings louder than the past**

TOM GALVIN

www.theghostsong.com

Copyright © 2019 Tom Galvin

All rights reserved. No part of this book may be reproduced, stored, or transmitted by any means—whether auditory, graphic, mechanical, or electronic—without written permission of both publisher and author, except in the case of brief excerpts used in critical articles and reviews. Unauthorized reproduction of any part of this work is illegal and is punishable by law.

This is a work of fiction. Names, characters, businesses, places, events, locales, and incidents are either the products of the author's imagination or used in a fictitious manner. Any resemblance to actual persons, living or dead, or actual events is purely coincidental.

Tom Galvin's first book, the travel memoir There's an Egg in My Soup (O'Brien Press), was based on his five years living in Poland in the 1990s. His first novel, Gabriel's Gate, was published in 2007. He worked as a magazine writer and editor before joining Independent News & Media, where he remained stubbornly until the bottom fell out of the newspaper world. He lives in Wicklow with his twins and Polish wife, Asia, happily writing again, performing music and generally watching life go by.

To hear songs featured in this story and for blogs and updates, go to: www.theghostsong.com

# CONTENTS

Prologue..................................................................................5

Chapter 1: A Star is Torn .......................................................7
Chapter 2: Birdsong................................................................13
Chapter 3: For the Record......................................................26
Chapter 4: The First Song......................................................53
Chapter 5: The Puppet Master...............................................87
Chapter 6: When the Deal Goes Down ................................117
Chapter 7: That's Entertainment..........................................129
Chapter 8: The Ghost is Real................................................149
Chapter 9: The Final Song....................................................165
Chapter 10: The Bird has Flown ..........................................180

# PROLOGUE

Jake Green was a hardworking songwriter from an age when people listened to their music on vinyl, on cassette tapes, on the radio and played it for each other on acoustic guitars. A time when they rolled up cigarettes on gatefold album sleeves and discussed lyrics of love and loss and life late into the night. A time when people celebrated their heroes for being the only people they understood and the only people who understood them in return because they spoke to them in the same language. The language of music. Guitar heroes. Vocal heroes. Bass heroes. Drum heroes. Heroes who corralled a generation into herds and dictated the fashion, the hair length, the spirit of the times, the mood of their days and the mood of their nights and even the mood of their dreams. Life is a long march and the music you choose to follow provides you with the beat, the pace, the reason to keep on going until your legs give out and you can't dance any longer. When the music is that good, you don't even need a reason for living and you don't even need God. Your heroes are your gods.

Jake almost made it, back in those days. That was before the tragedy. The one that involved his beloved daughter and broke him like a ballad. So he did something drastic. Vanished down a musical wormhole where time was measured in crotchets and quavers, supplanting the words of the spoken world and the written world, none of which could have adequately eased the pain the way music could. It was down to his best buddy, Smithy, who brought him back to write and play and sing again, find that second chance. But it's a different world now. Things have changed. Except music. And people. They don't change that much because the march will always go on. But for Jake to make his music reach the right people he had to go and do something drastic all over again. Really drastic. But brilliant. Really, really brilliant.

Good stories are like good songs that have been mixed and sieved by producers who have their own take and their own spin. A lot depends on what version you're listening to and how attuned your senses are to the nuances of the narrative. When I was asked to write this story, I began by going down the traditional route – interview the subjects, do the research, get the angles and plot out the path to take you, the reader, down. But I too was a part and had a role to play in Jake's journey as much as the people I spoke to. So I did the most honourable thing I could do and presented everyone's voices exactly as they presented them to me.

This is a story about Jake the singer, songwriter and a loving parent. But it is also the story of thousands of Jakes and thousands of Janes, the ones you never get to hear about or the ones you get to hear about only briefly because 'they never made it'. The music business is two worlds. There is the world of music and there is the world of business. But you don't always have to make it in both worlds to make it. Enjoy the story.

***Andy Kirwan. Music writer and journalist.***

# ONE

## *A Star is Torn*

**Paul Smith (Smithy). Jake's childhood friend.**

Losing my best mate is the only ending to this story that really matters to me, you know. Nothing could have readied me for what happened to Jake. It tore me to bits, so it did. We were like brothers, the pair of us. We go right back. Back to when we were just kids on the streets with very little to offer each other except our love of music and that boyhood bond. It's unbreakable. It should be unbreakable. But this whole thing went and broke it.

Now, here's the story. A lot of different people are going to give their versions about what happened. And I'm not saying they're all liars. But what I will say is they've all got their own versions of the truth. So, it's going to be up to you, when the ending comes, to decide who is really telling it. There's going to be a lot of twists and turns. Me, I think I do know why he did what he did — not that I was entirely expecting it. You were always expecting something out of the ordinary from Jake, but, you know, not that. Not that. Not after all he'd put into his music and not after what people had done for him. And especially not after what I had done for him. So when you're trying to make your mind up, just don't lose sight of what it all means to me. I lost the best mate I ever had. That's what it means.

## *Brian Blake. Promoter and manager.*

I used to love the sound a needle made when it reached the end of the record and just stayed there. Like it had nowhere else to go. This very delicate, almost inaudible sound. WHOOSH. WHOOSH. WHOOSH. WHOOSH.WHOOSH. Do you know what that is? It's the sound of silence. It's over. There is nothing more to give. And when I think about Jake now, that's what I hear. WHOOSH. Just silence. He had nothing more to give. You can talk about talent. Hard work. Commitment. Perseverance. Dedication. Application. Will power. Motivation. Lucky breaks. Don't be fooled by that last one, by the way. Anyone in the business I know who had a lucky break deserved it. And maybe Jake had all those things and maybe he even deserved it. But has anyone ever asked if he really wanted it. Because if he did, why didn't he stick around long enough to prove it?

Here's the thing about Jake. Jake was chasing something elusive. He thought success would liberate him, give him this sense that he was in control. We are all controlled by something or someone. None of us get liberated, baby. We are all heading towards that silent ending, when things just go WHOOSH. All we'll become is the sound we made before. So people think music holds the key to it all. Maybe. Maybe. And you might ask, who out there doesn't want success? Who doesn't want fame? But the problem is, one follows the other in this business and not everyone wants them both. They're the terrible twins. Success is great. Fame is a bitch. But they're two sides of the same coin, baby. Get used to it. And Jake? BANG. He just decided to blow a big hole in his whole world. You want my side of the story? No problem. I've got nothing to hide.

## *Katie Ryan. Girlfriend.*

I had put a lot of thought into helping Jake map out his career after we began seeing each other, like, seriously. So, the fact he'd been keeping this . . . plan, if that's what it was, from me all along is probably what hurts the most. It hurts deep. Because I don't think it was an impulse. I don't think it was this rash decision. And I don't think he bottled it, like some people say. Jake, chicken out? Are you kidding? Jake could handle anything really. He could handle anything because he had this ability to suddenly . . . like, freeze the moment and see it for what it was. A moment. Stripped back and bare and suspended like an object that could be pushed aside so he could move beyond it. Maybe that sounds like bullshit. But he didn't let too many things get to him until . . . well, until he abandoned us all. None of this is easy for me, telling this story like this. Now that he's gone. What bothers me is that I actually thought I was the closest to him in those last few months when things seemed to be falling apart and he seemed to be losing his shit. But in the end he just played me like one of his precious guitars. I'd almost go as far as saying he actually loved his guitars more than me. But guess what? When he disappeared, he left them behind too. So what does that tell you?

## *Donnie Miller. Record store owner, old friend.*

That's all folks! Looney tunes, looney tunes. I think it's going too far to call Jake a tragic figure, because this story for me is really a tragicomedy. I know others don't see it that way. But I'm just this old hippy whose passion for music and records is all I've ever really lived for. Music is all I've ever cared about. And that's what Jake and I had in common. I guess, all he ever wanted to do was play his songs. Right? Strum his guitar. Slow the world down, watch it turn at thirty-three revolutions per minute. Damn. It was never about riches, stardom, fame or any of that shit, man. Nah, he always went in deeper than that. Then, late in his life, he gets this deal. He was tempted and he fell then he found, I suppose you could say, redemption. I'd like to say it could have happened to anybody, but, Jeez, nobody could have done what Jake did. Nobody would have had the nerve to execute something like that. And for me, that's the comic side of it, right there. How he ended it all. Man, it cracked me up. So now, here we are, all of us, coming together like this to spill the beans, hoping it might shed light on the whole damn thing.

Listen, if you want light, go get a torch. Cos this whole story is as murky as hell and if there's light at the end of it, it'll be Jake blazing a trail. And wherever he is right now, out there in the cosmos, up there hanging out with the real stars, man. I just gotta wish him well.

## *Miles and Jenny Adams. Father and daughter.*

So, when it all came tumbling down I was very saddened. Most of all I felt for my little girl, Jenny. It was silly of me to let her get involved with Jake like that. What was I thinking? But she loved him. I loved him. We all loved him. From the moment he entered our lives, we all took a fondness to Jake. He shone. Does that make sense? He had a shine about him, a warmth. He was tall, good-looking, with light hair and light eyes and he moved lightly like he was constantly walking on a breeze. I don't know. As a father, a man his age getting that close to my daughter, I shouldn't have let it happen. But Jake, he was just one of the good guys. You let him in. So why, oh why, did he do that to us? To my little girl? But look, she's over it now. She has moved on. She has a career focus and a life and this chapter is closed. This is why we agreed that I would be giving our account. She wanted nothing more to do with it and besides, I didn't want her involved anymore. She's a bright young thing and she has a bright future ahead of her and this experience will, in fact, stand to her. As for Jake, well, I really think he should have at least had the maturity to honour whatever commitments he'd made to the people who helped him out so much.

Look, it's been a bit of a rollercoaster for all of us and he certainly left his mark, didn't he? And if that's what his aim was, to make some sort of statement, then he achieved it. But you have to wonder what it was all for? I hope in time, I'm going to be able to look back and make some sense of it. But you know when you've just stepped off the rollercoaster, a little wobbly, a little shook, a little queasy and you glance over your shoulder and wonder what possessed you to step on at all. But later you think about it and say to yourself, wow, that was one hell of a ride. So, if you're really intent on reading this story, that's probably the best advice I have for you. Try and enjoy the ride.

## *Andy Kirwan. Music writer and journalist.*

Apparently, all stories can be reduced to one line. Somebody wants something but they have trouble getting it. It's the story of all our lives when you think about it. So where do you begin with this story? A story about this someone — Jake Green — who wants something — to be a musician and songwriter — and, now here's the conceit, gets within reach of it and throws it all away. I mean, we're not talking about someone who gets that little taste of glory, that little glimmer of stardom, that flutter of hope in the belly, then slowly withers under the intensity and glare of the spotlight because they can't cope with the pressure, the fear of failure — or even the fear of success. Or somebody who just wants out and decides to fall apart but on their terms, I mean, self-destruct through drugs or alcohol or just sheer manic anxiety. People who do things like that, they do them because it's the only part of their lives left they have any control over, if you think about it. They've surrendered everything else in their pursuit of this, this, how can you put it, this chimera we call fame, without ever stopping to try and understand what it really is. And what is it anyway? It's just another way of life, that's all. Another way of life that is not going to work for everybody. And people aren't always ready for it and they don't know how to get a handle on it.

But Jake, I mean, he hadn't even reached the edge but it was like, he'd already made this decision he was going to go ahead and jump when he reached it anyway. And if you ask me, the really tragic thing was it was probably all there for him, all there for the taking if he'd just adapted, accepted what had happened and went along with it. And, for the time I knew Jake, I really grew to like him a lot. Aside from what he did and what he was doing, musically, he was just a loveable guy. And although I didn't want it all to end the way it did, it was one of the weirdest – no, the weirdest – exits from the arena of rock 'n' roll I'd ever seen. Completely mad. My take is that he believed, he really believed, he was doing something revolutionary. But maybe he just bottled it and needed a way out. So he found an exit door that nobody else had ever gone through before and out he went. Brilliant ending in one way but very, very tragic in another.

# TWO

# *Birdsong*

### Jake Green Fan Page

*Jake's next Fly-in gig will take place this Saturday (Nov 14) in the wonderful surroundings of Merrion Square park, 11.00 am. Be there early; we can never predict how long Jake will get to play. Please share with friends. Better still, bring a friend along. Preferably someone you love.*

👍 *1238*

### Smithy. Jake's childhood friend.

We're going to start off this story with the day when, fortuitously, coincidentally, slidey-doorsy whatever way you want to look at it, right, the day when almost all of us happened to be at one of Jake's public gigs at the same time. Okay? Think of the story of the Garden of Eden. Remember all that? Well, they were all there that morning just like the set-up in the garden. The whole cast. You had Jake, under the tree there like Adam. You had Katie, who was, you know, like Eve. And you had the cherubs, like little Jenny, the innocent one, sitting at Jake's feet batting her eyelids. Then you had Andy, the conniving schemer, skulking on the sidelines, you know, not really getting his hands dirty. Then, along comes the big fella. The snake

Brian Blake. And what follows is Jake's fall. And there you have it. That's the story. And it might seem like I'm being hard on everyone. But, I'm telling you, you don't even have to read on anymore if you just want the brief synopsis.

I wasn't there but, sure it didn't matter. I wouldn't have been able to save him either way. The big players were all present. And that's why that particular morning has this, whatever, resonance. That was the stone in the pond. Otherwise, Jake was just doing what he had been doing for a good while and, you know, doing it very well. Between himself and Katie, right, they had been working on this plan to help get his music out there because it had been a long time since he had played in public. And it was working. It really was working, against all the odds like his age, his lack of knowledge when it came the whole changed, digital landscape and all that. It was working. But that was the day his music changed his life. Because all these people happened to turn up and, like I said, fortuitously, coincidentally, slidey-doorsy shite, whatever way you want to look at it, right, they all turned up and decided they were going to feature in his story. And his downfall.

The only one who wasn't there was old Donnie. Because he was in his little cave. He was like the hermit, Donnie, so he was. Jake and I had been going to Donnie's basement shop for years. Since we were knocking around on the streets together we'd been going there. It was where we really learnt about this whole world of music and Donnie grew to become an old mate. Actually he became something of a Yoda, especially to Jake, probably because Jake never had a father growing up and Donnie became a father figure for him. He offered a lot of advice to Jake — some he took, some, you know, he didn't. And I wish he'd been there that morning. He would have just told Jake to get outta that garden and probably none of us would be reconvening to do what we're doing. Then again, Jake, like the great man Oscar Wilde — and his statue was sat on a rock right there in that very park just a few feet from where Jake was playing that morning — could resist everything except temptation.

# THE GHOST SONG

## *Miles and Jenny Adams. Father and daughter.*

So we were walking through the park on Merrion Square, Jenny and I, on our way into the centre of town for the day. She had wanted to walk through the park and she seemed pretty insistent. I didn't mind. It was one of those lovely crisp, sort of golden winter mornings in November that would almost make you thankful for being alive and as we went through the gates we could hear this music coming from somewhere. And the next thing, under a tree, we saw this guy singing, playing the guitar surrounded by a fairly spellbound gang of people, most of them standing in front of him but a few had rugs with them too, so they had obviously known what was going down and were sitting at his feet like disciples. I thought it was batshit odd, to be honest. It wasn't a concert, was it? Just one guy?

So we stop to have a look and as we're watching, my daughter takes my hand and squeezes it. Now, there's nothing unusual about your daughter taking your hand. But she'd stopped taking my hand when she was about eight and she's almost 16 now. So this was unusual. Besides, this wasn't meant for me, this squeeze. It was like she had just made a connection to the song this guy was singing. And I look at her and she's beaming. And I look back at him and I'm thinking, he's not a young man at all, is he, with his flowing locks and leather jacket and that red shirt with the frills? Not much younger than myself, all told. But he looks better than me, doesn't he? There's the thought that stopped me still as I looked around at the attention he had. He looked cool. I certainly didn't look cool. In fact it had been a long time since I had looked cool. A long time since I'd worn a red shirt too. Don't think I ever got away with it. And the song? Well, I didn't recognise it. And I take pride in knowing my music.

And he has this audience of 60, maybe 70 people in front of him, all ages, and they're swaying and nodding and some of them are holding hands too. Christ, it's like a religious experience, I think to myself. Then they all start singing the refrain, my daughter included. Little Star, your world is wide, it goes. Nice. So I look around. And you know how you begin to feel really left out of an occasion? And suddenly I want to leave. So I whisper to Jenny, love, do you know this guy, or what? And she glances up at me and shakes her head quickly, letting go my hand. No, I just know the song, Dad. Ssshhh. Listen. Listen.

And I felt my age all of a sudden. You've reached that moment, you don't recognise the songs your kids are singing. But then I look closer at this guy and again, I'm thinking, he can't be a lot younger than myself. And as if to confirm that, he plays this fairly obscure Bob Dylan song. I knew it was a Bob Dylan song but I was struggling to place it. And he even has a harmonica around his neck on one of those brace things which he plays, quite honestly, beautifully at the end. Then, just as I'm beginning to relax and enjoy him, he does that John Lennon song, Free as a Bird and that's it. It's like a cue. And suddenly a few people at the front stand up and they're clapping and whistling in this rounded burst of applause. And he stoops into this eccentric sort of bow, taking everyone in with this slow, steady, exaggerated sweep. And that's it. The little gig, if that's what it was, is over.

And as people are shuffling away I look up, and I remember thinking at the time, he doesn't have a hat, or a box, nowhere to throw a few coins into. But then I see it. The bird cage. One of those old dome-top cages with the little perch inside. And a couple of people on the periphery come up with some change then walk away awkwardly when they realise there is nothing to throw money into except this bird cage, which is closed anyway. Then a park attendant arrives and there's a bit of casual banter and the show comes to a close.

So, suddenly Jenny just says to me, give me two minutes, Dad, and off she runs, pushing her way up through the crowd. And I'm watching her, as she launches herself at this guy and brazenly sticks her hand out. And he takes it. And as he's shaking hands with her, she gets up very close, almost talking directly into his ear, still gripping his hand. And he's nodding away and stroking his chin with his free hand. And I think, oh no, what is she possibly asking him? So I go up and introduce myself. Miles. Jake, he says. And he has this little grin. People grin at my name. Miles. All I can say in my defence is I was given it at birth. So, you understand, bugger all I can do about it.

# THE GHOST SONG

Your daughter tells me she's involved in a musical, he says, after Jenny finally lets the poor man's hand go. That's right, I say, with a drama society. It's in her school. It's a big deal every year and it raises a lot of money for charity. Very professional. Very competent. Very, how would you say — that's okay, Dad, I think you've sold it, Jenny says and slaps me on the arm.

And what is the charity this year, Jake asks. It's the children's hospital, Jenny says, staring at him. So he looks down for a moment and he's stroking his chin again, like he is pondering one of life's great unponderables. But then something changes. Like a cloud had passed overhead and just darkened his already dark eyes, sounds strange but you could see this change in him. A sadness or something. Children's hospital, he says quietly.

Think about it, Jenny says suddenly. You play anywhere, everywhere. That's your thing. Music has no limits. That's your maxim. Is there something wrong with playing at a school? Think of this as, like, a blessing. Karma. If you help with this maybe some good will come out of it for you.

And he smiles at Jenny again only this time he shows his teeth and he glances awkwardly at me. Karma is mostly one-way traffic, he says then. And a school does present a lot of problems. But I will think about it. Then he takes his phone out of his inside pocket and there's jewellery jangling around his neck as he does so and I really can't take my eyes off that red shirt with the frilled collars. Could you give me an email — if that's all right with you, and he raises his eyebrows at me. So I just shrug at him. I'm totally confused but surrender to whatever is going on. And as Jenny is giving this guy her email, I notice this girl, young girl, younger than this guy, maybe in her twenties, who was standing under the tree behind Jake, watching. And I do mean watching. And suddenly she marches over to us and she's looking as baffled as I am.

Hi, she says. So what's going on? And I have to just shrug all over again. Don't ask me. And Jake is tapping the email into his phone and as he puts it back into his pocket, without looking at this girl, he just says, Jenny here, she needs a favour. So this girl, and I have to say, she is stunning. Stunning. Flaming red hair, toppling down in front of her, and these great big emerald green eyes. And she's wrapped herself into this flowing, knitted robe and there's a fairly intense pause until suddenly a hand appears from beneath it.

My name is Katie, she says, and she forces a smile as we all introduce ourselves. Then she turns quickly to Jake. What kind of favour, she asks him. And he does that bit of chin stroking again for a third time then he looks directly at Katie. She wants to borrow a song, he says. And Katie erupts with laughter. It's like a howl. Borrow, she says, scowling at Jenny. Borrow, she says again. And are you planning on giving it back? So Jake suddenly puts his arm between them and says to Jenny in this calm, very pleasant voice, I'll be in touch, Jenny.

Then I just pull Jenny away and, to be honest, I'm happy to be moving on. It was getting quite intense. This girl, Katie, was giving her daggers. And as we walk off I look behind and the two of them seem to get into this fairly heated argument. It all looked a little too out there. Too out there for an early Saturday morning.

What in the name of God did you just do, Jenny, I ask her. Apart from giving some complete stranger in a park your email address. And Jenny gives me another one of those annoying tuts. Some guy in a park, Dad? He's, like an up and coming musician, a songwriter, he's an artist, Jenny says.

Hmmm. Up and coming, I say. Well, he's taking his time about it, isn't he? The guy is nearly my age. And Jenny just shakes her head. No, he's not, Dad. Don't be so bitter. And it doesn't matter, he looks great. Thanks, I'm sure he does, I say to her. But Jenny love, you don't go asking some busker for a song, I say. That's just insane. And giving him your email address? He's not a busker, Dad, she tells me. Oh, precious as well, is he, I ask her. So you know him then? And she doesn't answer. But there was something between them. I mean, this Jake guy and her. Or her and this Katie girl. But she ignores me and I just drop it. Look, I didn't want to make a whole lot of it that morning. We were going out for the day and I wanted to enjoy the time. In another year or two, she wouldn't be seen dead by my side. Besides, Jenny was always this brash sort of child with no fear and no shame. It wasn't totally out of character. And she was so passionate about her music and her drama work that I wasn't going to go and put her down about it. Anyway, I didn't expect she'd hear from him, Jake, ever again. I hoped she'd never hear from him again. But remarkably, she did.

## *Brian Blake. Promoter and manager.*

SSSSSHHHHHH. Someone tipped me off about this guy, Jake Green, who had been doing these little impromptu performances around the place. Fly-ins, he called them. Actually it wasn't a big secret but this was something new to me. He'd post a location up on his Facebook page just a few days before and turn up and just play to whoever was there.

And the novelty factor was the locations of these gigs. A beach shelter. A park or some green space somewhere. Top of a hill. Bottom of a mountain, who knows where. Sometimes he'd manage to get a café or a bookshop to accommodate him. An art gallery. But the outdoor ones were usually a bit wackier. You never knew where he was going to be next and although he'd invariably end up getting moved on from the public spaces it was an impressive way to build up a bit of a following and get some traction. These gigs would be shot on video, edited, posted online and anyone who had been there would pass them on because, well, that's what we all do now, don't we? Share wherever we are and whatever we're doing and whoever we're doing it with, we can't help ourselves. So that was the nuts and bolts of the whole thing.

And yes, I admired his nous. I liked the innovation of it all. Plus he was just one guy with a guitar – and a harmonica too, fancy that? How long has it been since someone played the guitar and harmonica together, like Woody Guthrie, Donovan or Bob Dylan? So I got down to the park around 11 o'clock and there was a healthy crowd there already, 60 or 70 people, who had formed this tight circle around him. Some at the front were lounging around on rugs. And it's not easy when you've got people looking right up your nose. All he had for sound was a small PA. He could have made things more convenient for himself by using better amplification, like the kids do on the streets with all the latest gear. Give himself some room, create a bit of distance between himself and the audience. But he had them gather right in front of him and that was a brave decision. But he seemed as comfortable as if he was back in his own living-room. And that level of comfort either comes from the confidence of youth, which is very often misplaced, or years of experience. And Jake, as I could see, fell into the latter of those two camps. And that was a good thing. So I lingered.

Just as I get there, he begins playing this infectious little song which I didn't recognise, although a lot of the people in front of him did because they're singing along with him. Shine on, say you'll shine on, too beautiful to fall. Little star, your world is wide, that was the refrain. And they were nearly all singing along with him so I tap the nearest shoulder to me and it was a girl, mid-twenties somewhere, and ask her what the song is. And she looks at me without batting an eyelid. Little Star, she snaps and turns away. So I lean back in and whisper to her, I've gathered that much, darling, but whose song is it? And she turns back and snarls, Jake Green's song, grandad. The guy you're looking at. And thanks for spoiling the buzz.

So I back off and hear him out. I like this song and I'm listening to it wondering where he got it from. All artists are thieves even if they don't know it, they're magpies, they have an impulse, a sharpened sense for the pieces that shine and sparkle that look like junk to you and me. Their art is putting all these seemingly worthless pieces together to create something that doesn't just shine but shimmers. Shine on, say you'll shine on little star. The song was really growing on me and from a mesmerising little harmonica solo he segues into a Bob Dylan number, exposing at least one of his influences but that's okay. He's a thief, he just doesn't know it. And they're all just loving it. The whole crowd. And I'm about to move off when he breaks into a John Lennon song I hadn't heard in so many years it took me by surprise. Free as a Bird. Remember that one? A funny choice. Never heard anyone play it before. It was one of those found songs, an old demo that had been rinsed and reworked. I remember it being a nice song even though Lennon's voice sounded like it had just drifted in through the bathroom window and there was only so much could be

# THE GHOST SONG

done with it. But when this guy sang it that morning, it was the first time I'd heard someone else take it on and it was like he had taken the voice that had drifted in through the bathroom window and sent in back out through the hall door shining like a new coin.

Now, there was this kid there, a young girl, seemed to be with her dad and she wasn't going anywhere until the song was over. She was even holding her dad's hand to stop him from moving away. A young girl, 15 or 16 maybe, really digging the whole thing. And I took note of that too. Because this was really music for an older generation. On paper, this guy belonged in the past. Like you picked up a magazine from the late 1970s or early 80s, you know, the ones printed out on cheap paper that smelled of piss after a few days, shook it and out fell this guy. But there he was, playing to people of all ages with this self-confident determination that, you know, in most cases, particularly for us guys, falls away like your hair unless you really believe in yourself. And he had immaculate hair too the bastard. Things should have seemed out of place but they didn't. He should have been out of place but he wasn't. Maybe that's the mystery of music. Pieces fit where they shouldn't.

And on the subject of mysteries, the next thing, I spot this bird cage, and I'm thinking, what the fuck is that? Is it symbolic? Was there a bird in there at one stage? Why is the door closed on it? What's it all about? Maybe it's just to heighten the whole Fly-in gigs idea. Maybe he goes back in there at the end of the show. Who knows? So I dismiss it as just a silly prop. Morrissey had the daffodils sticking out of his arse. You leave people with this talking point. It's a ploy. It works. So I didn't think any more of it. But I wish now I had given it more thought. A lot more thought.

Then this warden comes along and Jake takes a bow, genuflects, waves, salutes, puts his hands together in gratitude, does all this superfluous stuff and then it's over. And as people retreat from the tree he'd been playing under I thought about going up to have a quick chat with him. But then something else kicks off. This kid, the one who was with her dad, rushes up to talk to Jake. And there's a girl still standing under the tree, late twenties, very, very attractive, you can tell straight away she's with Jake. And she's watching this kid, watching the interaction with Jake. And there's something not right. I'm thinking she knows who this young girl is. She must do, because you can sense this hostility rising up. Then the father, he comes up and there's a bit of banter before Jake takes out his phone. And with that, the girl is over in a flash, moving like bloody Wonder Woman, and a row breaks out. And Jake has to step in between them and the poor dad he looks like a rabbit in the headlights.

And I decide something like this is probably the last thing to be getting involved in. But as I go to leave I make sure to catch Jake's eye. And he sees me. Wasn't sure he would recognise me it's been a while since my face was out there. But he does and I give him a little nod. That's all. That's really all I needed to do. Leave a visiting card. So he knows he's been visited. And what he would do next was either going to send out the right or the wrong signal. I would just wait. And what he did certainly surprised me.

## *Katie Ryan. Girlfriend.*

I can't decide which day matters more to me when it comes to Jake and I. There's the day we met, which plays out like a movie when I think back on it . . . or that morning in the park, Merrion Square, a beautiful oasis in the centre of Dublin. We'd always wanted to play an open space like that, somewhere tranquil, something people would remember. No matter where we played, there was always that novelty value, even if we always got moved on fairly quickly. A business owner might come out, or a security guard, even residents. Jake might only get two or three songs into a set and he'd be told to leave. But that morning in the park he was doing so well. We had made plans to try some new material, Jake was in great form and a sizeable crowd had turned up. Then after about forty minutes we see a warden coming down the path so we have to call it a day. We never want any trouble at these things. When we're asked to move on, we do it as quickly as possible because it won't do anything for your reputation to argue.

So as soon as we see the warden coming, Jake goes into his last song, which is the cover of Free as a Bird. That was always his closing number. And just as he finishes playing it, I'm not kidding, this young girl comes running up and I could tell straight away she had a purpose. She had an agenda. I could just sense it. And in situations like that, Jake needs someone to protect him from his own impulses. Because very often he can't control them. He acts from the heart. And he might do something that just makes no sense. No business sense, no artistic sense. No sense. That was Jake.

And I suspected there was something going on with this girl and I should have got Jake away before he agreed to do what he agreed to do. But, guess what? It was too late. It only took seconds and those few seconds changed everything. Everything. Not just for me, us, but for everyone involved in this story. And while we all have our views on how things developed, we all agree from that day on nothing would ever be the same. And that much was true. Nothing from that day on would ever be the same.

### *Andy Kirwan. Music writer and journalist.*

I had been meaning to catch a glimpse of what this guy Jake Green was up to because of the bit of noise he was generating on social media, that bit of heat that people were feeling out there. And I remember when I got to the park that morning he was finishing up a Bob Dylan song, My Back Pages, blasting into this harmonica on a neck rack. And it's a long time since I'd seen someone play the harmonica using a neck rack. I mean, that sort of thing just hasn't seemed cool for years. Or maybe it's been that long since someone has mastered playing the guitar and the harmonica at the same time but he just made it look cool and he made it sing, sweet as a canary. Speaking of which, now here's one for you to think about, he had a bird cage right at his feet. A bird cage. A big one. And he was perched on a bit of a rug, raising one leg after the other, stomping like a flamingo as he sang.

But it was the bird cage that baffled me. And whatever was in there was no longer in there, and unless he was planning to catch something flying in the park I haven't a notion why it was there.

And as I was trying to get my head around it he breaks into this nice flighty version of Free as a Bird. And it just takes off and hangs there, in the air, gliding up over the trees of the park and slowly finding its path through the clouds. I was hungover, maybe I was getting carried away. I'm a big Lennon fan. Big Dylan fan as well. And he was on my page this guy and these songs were a real joy to hear. The crowd just adored it. Then, just as it seems to be getting going it's all over, just like that. Along comes the warden, like some villain, to spoil all the fun and that's the end of the gig.

So I decide to make a B-line for a coffee only to notice this figure, a man in black, a creature from the black lagoon with blackened soul and black intent, lurking like a pike under a lily, watching with that malevolent gaze of his. Ooooh. Brian bloody Blake. I couldn't believe my eyes. And you can probably tell that Blakey and I go way back. And we do. So far back that the distant past is exactly where I've always managed to keep the bastard, so I didn't hang about. In fact, I had to cut across the flower beds to avoid him. I'm not in a great shape anymore. Not obese or anything. Just not the spritely self I once was. But I scarpered quite well I thought. But, there is no avoiding a guy like Blake if he wants you found, as we will see a little later.

Now, Jake and I, we also go back, maybe 20 years back or thereabouts. And being brutally honest here, the reason I wanted to catch him was through this terrible sense of guilt that still lingered after I'd spurned him when he reached out to me before, when I was a diehard journalist, mid-30s, prepared to do anything to further my career and Jake was a starry-eyed kid in his early twenties who needed someone like me to make things happen. It was a long time ago. I mean, I was a bit naïve, a bit precious, ambitious, a bit ruthless and a lot less forgiving really. I suppose I just wasn't a very nice man then. So I had come along to this park gig to see if I could put things right. And after watching him that morning, seeing how the people there reacted to him, even Blakey, I made the decision that I would try and do something for him, use what little influence I had left. Make amends. Make something good happen before the chance vanished entirely. It wasn't too late for him, the years had been kind to him and he still looked great. He still had that confidence, the way he held himself and the way people took to him. Things can always happen as long as you're alive and kicking. And he was still kicking.

# THREE

## *For the Record*

*You sang from the heart, you loved from the soul but you woke with the blues every morning. Where was your muse, did you poison her with booze, slip away when the day was just dawning. Shine on say you'll shine on, too beautiful to fail. Burn on, say you'll burn on, blaze another trail. Open up and look outside. Little star, your world is wide.*

### Paul Smith (Smithy). Jake's childhood friend.

If there was one word to describe Jake, one word, for as long as I've known him, it would be generous. And I don't really mean in monetary terms, because for as long as I've known him he's always been pretty bloody broke. I mean generous of soul, you know. He sees someone in a situation, he helps them out. That's kind of the way he's wired. And on paper, you know, giving away your best song, your flagship track, to a schoolkid made absolutely no sense. Made no sense to me at the time either, but I was well used to that sort of thing with him. He always had a reason, always.

We grew up in the 1980s, awful messed up decade so it was, I don't know how I ended up in it instead of the 1970s or the 60s 'cos that's where fellas like me and Jake really belonged, you know? We just landed badly, the two of us. Seriously. The 1980s? We just wanted it to be all over. Mods. Rockers. Punks. Teddy Boys. Rude

Boys. Nutty Boys. Metal Heads. They were all there. We'd no interest in any one of these groups. We didn't care. We were two kids, staying out of trouble in each other's gaffs listening to our records. We just wanted to hear the music. That's all there was. We didn't want anything more out of it. Just the music, nothing else. That was the buzz, that was our lifeblood, it was the pulse. And I couldn't see why you had to have this sense of loyalty when it came to music. Dress this way or that. Stick a bleedin' safety pin in your cheek to prove it. Patches on denim jackets. White socks and black loafers. Hair wax and quiffs. I mean, me and Jake, we could just as easily pull an Elvis or Buddy Holly record down from the Ma and Da's shelves and spend the evening listening to that. Or the Beach Boys. Status Quo. Perry Como. Charlie Bird. Andy Williams. Aretha Franklin. Shirley Bassey. Stones. Beatles. Who bleedin' ever. It didn't matter. We were just miners looking deeper down the hole to dig up anything we could. We were little boys in the sweet shop, hallucinating on all the coloured confection.

And speaking of shops, the big day of the week was Saturday. That was the holy day. Not Sunday. That was the only day in the week that gave us any reason to leave the house. The rest of the week was this inconvenience. All we wanted to do was to get any money we had and head into town to this record shop down the basement run by this American fella, Donnie. He was a character. Big bearded bloke, like he had come down out of the woods after killing animals with his bare hands. But he was harmless. There were all kinds of stories about Donnie. All kinds of tales. Someone told me once he was an ex-convict and had got to Ireland, via Canada, via Greenland, via, I don't know, where's next? Denmark maybe. Whatever, it wasn't true anyway. Another story had him in jail again getting guitar lessons from someone who had played with someone who had played with Johnny Cash. Whatever, that certainly wasn't true. Or if it was true it was a bad story to be spreading cos he couldn't put even two fingers together on the fretboard and that made both him and Johnny Cash look bad. So that was most definitely a silly rumour. But it was funny. The truth though, as always isn't so much fun.

Donnie actually came over here with a blues band who were on their way to England to play at a festival, and like a lot of touring bands who had never flown across the pond they decided to use an Irish crowd as guinea pigs before heading to the UK. Donnie, who was down the lowest rung on the roadie ladder — he humped gear basically — did his back in and couldn't make the boat to Wales. And he never made the boat to Wales. And the closest thing to a jail story for Donnie was the threat of a conviction for selling bootleg tapes in town out of a wooden wheelbarrow. He used a wheelbarrow because all the other bootleggers would set up a bit of a stall on tables and had no means to hide them in time when the coppers came. Donnie could just wheel himself away. Eventually, he got citizenship and was able to set up his own record store. And that was where Jake and I would go, regularly, every Saturday. Down into a basement, sticky carpet on the stairs. Posters all over the walls on the way down, all the icons, Hendrix, Dylan, Lennon, Morrison, Bowie, Joni Mitchell, Joan Baez, Nina Simone, everyone. All those people who would come to you in your dreams and sing you to sleep. The people who made the world a better place just by being alive.

Down we'd go, where the air was clammy, fogged up with cigarette smoke and the music was too loud. That was our hangout. And if we weren't buying we were looking, and if we weren't looking we were badgering Donnie for music stories. He was full of information and he liked us, for whatever reason, so he'd talk to us a lot. We spent a lot of money, all the money we had went into his till, so it did. We did odd jobs whenever we could just to buy records. We used every penny of our communion money on records. We asked Santa for records and we sold our Easter Eggs to the kids in school to get money to get more records. We didn't care about the scarves and the T-shirts, or the patches to sew onto the back of your jacket. Button badges. Mirrors with band logos. All that shite mattered not one bit. Records. That's all that mattered.

Anyway, Jake was a fairly cool cat, he didn't have to try too hard. Bit eccentric, dressed a bit off the cuff. Actually, on paper, he shouldn't have looked cool. Wore a blazer, velvet one, wine-coloured and had his hair like some sort of seventies page boy. But he was still a cool cat. And he could play like a, well, remember they used to say Muhammad Ali could float like a butterfly and sting like a bee? Well, I used to think if Jake ever made it, and I always believed he would, they'd be saying something like that about him too. I'm just not that great with those words. But we'll come on to his playing and songwriting and stuff later. Now Donnie loved Jake, so he did. He encouraged him too. Used to point to the posters on his stairs, the stairway to the stars he called it, and say, Jake my man, you got to look at those faces every time you pass them and tell yourself you're going to be among them. So he was completely bleedin' gobsmacked the day meself and Jake came into his store with boxes of records. Boxes of them. We probably had more records in the boxes than he had in his shop. We were students then, moved on a bit. And I suppose by then people were moving onto CDs anyway. But still, any self-respecting music collector did not part with his records, ever. But Jake did and I never thought I'd see the day. Thing was, he had a very good reason and one which is crucial to this story. Just like he had a very good reason to give away his best song to that kid in the park. Just remember that, as we go on, okay? Jake had a reason for every single, tiniest little thing that he did.

## *Donnie Miller. Record store owner, old friend.*

Jake had been coming to my store for years with his buddy, Smithy, two teenagers they were who just wanted to stay off the streets, I guess. They were like brothers back then. They came in almost every Saturday to hang out and if they weren't buying they were browsing and if they weren't doing either they'd be asking me all sorts of questions. They were kids, I didn't mind. I made it my business to know everything there was to know about the world of music. That's how I was able to stay open and survive when the CDs came along and wiped out the vinyl and the smaller stores were forced to close. Tough times. I even survived the online juggernaut, just about, and now vinyl is hip again so I've got a second wind. All good. I'm still here. I was almost looking at having to go back to where I came from several times but thankfully I didn't. And you can probably guess that's Stateside. I came over here thirty years ago, I was on tour with a small blues band called The Whitewall Tyres, it was a line from a Lightnin' Hopkins song, and our slogan was 'We just keep rollin'. Only they rolled on out of here without me after a good gig started to go real bad. My bad, I won't deny it. I was a roadie, never played. Hadn't a note in my head. It was only a small club we were playing at, a stopover on the way to a festival in the UK. I was given charge of the sound that evening for the first time and someone, one of the other roadies, gave me something to smoke, convinced me it sharpened the senses. Of course, it doesn't. It really doesn't. And, well, it got very ropey and I was already on a final warning and, cut a long story short and all that, they rolled on out of there without me. The Whitewall Tyres. Think they're rollin' still too.

Anyways, I remember Jakey, he had this profound fascination, not just with music but with the people behind the records. The stories. The history. The lives, all that stuff. I remember his favourite question was, so where are they now? It was like he had this notion that every recording artist was doomed in some shape or form as soon as they'd done their first record. Like a curse or something. Often wondered if he was cursed. Or maybe he believed he was and brought the misfortune down on himself. Me, I'm a positive vibes kind of guy. Always kept telling that to Jake, be positive, man. Jake kind of, I guess he thought positivity was something you were blessed with in certain amounts. Like failure was inevitable at some stage in an artist's career, that their creativity would dry up at some point and maybe it was better to be a shooting star, burn out with one big hit and leave a trail rather than strive for longevity. And if he liked a record by someone, he'd want to go and buy everything they'd ever done, the whole back catalogue. Dissect their careers like he was in some lab. He was a fascinating kid, Jake. Smart and alert and full of wonder. I liked him.

Then they grew up, the two of them and I didn't see them as much. But the day he came down the stairs to my store carrying a great big box in his arms was the day that kid I knew was really gone. Sure, he was older. Jake had moved on to college by then and he maybe only came in once a month if there was some new record he wanted to order. But growth had never really changed Jake much. His mindset, I mean. That sense of wonder I spoke of, he always had it, it was part of his charm. But I could see straight off something wasn't right. And behind him came his buddy Smithy, carrying another box. And Jake looked like he was carrying a coffin, I swear. And he placed it down on the counter and he let out this sigh, it was like a death rattle. And I knew. I knew right away what was in those boxes. So I gently lifted the flap on the top box Jake had put in front of me and I could see the spines of all these beautiful vinyl records. And he's almost too ashamed to look at me.

So he takes a quick glance at Smithy and he says to me, I'll be back in a second. And the two of them bail back up the stairs and return again with another box each. And they're big boxes. And I'm rubbing my beard and doing a guesstimate of how many records are in these boxes altogether and I reckon about 500, and I was close enough.

So Smithy goes off to the back of the store and Jake is standing there looking at me, his arms on the counter, like he has a confession to make or something. So I just say, Jake, you're not doing what I think you're doing, are you? And he just nods at me. Yep, I'm doing exactly that, Don.

Now, this would have been back in the 90s, when it was CDs or nothing. I don't even think you could buy a vinyl player then unless it was second hand. That format was finished, unless you were one of those diehard collectors. And one of the greatest diehard collectors I knew was standing right in front of me.

So I look at the boxes and shake my head and say, well, I'm going to give you another chance to think about it, Jake. And he just shrugs and says I don't need another chance, Donnie. Take them. Take them all. I know you'll give me a fair offer. Then he grins at me and says, I probably bought them all here anyway. So Smithy comes back up to the top of the store and looks at the two of us before patting Jake on the back. I'll wait outside, he says, and off he goes up the stairs, leaving the two of us with this deathly silence.

Look, I say, I'll have to go through all of these records and see what I can get for them, but they're not selling anymore, Jake. There are still the collectors out there, but, I'll have to catalogue them all and they could be sitting here for a while. You know, it's all CDs now. Is that what you're doing? Buying everything all over again?

No, he says, it's nothing like that. And Donnie, you know what kind of collection I have, you won't have a problem shifting these things. And if I could keep them . . . then he trails off and I notice something. Something in his eyes, not right. It was the same look you got from a lot of people coming in to sell their records, they usually needed the cash. You could tell. There's awkwardness there, hesitancy, they're almost weighed down with a sense of shame having to sell something they spent their youth and more building up. Like pawning the family jewels. Your records are kind of like your life's markers. Think about it? They all tell a tale, every one each of us have bought, we don't want that tale to fade away and Jake, he was standing there and I could see the pain. But whatever it was, he must have needed the cash. And I could sense too that he had something to say but that for whatever reason, he just couldn't say it. That worried me greatly. But I couldn't push him if he wasn't ready to talk.

So I just say, come back tomorrow, Jake. I'll do whatever I can do. And he just slaps my shoulder, says thanks real quick and off he runs up the stairs. And when he came back the next day, he had his guitar with him. He was off busking somewhere, though you never said the word busking, he didn't like it. And after a quick chat, he said, okay, what have you got for me? And all I could offer him was two hundred. And he just nods and says, I'll take it. So I grab the cash from the till and count it out and he's looking at it, still with that kind of hesitancy, but he's watching me count every note. Then I take a chance. I say to him, Jake, can I ask you something? And he has his fingertips on the notes I'm holding in my hand but I'm not letting go yet. And he stares at me. And I say, this cash, is it going to a bad place?

And I asked him that because I knew a lot of folks who were in trouble with narcotics. Especially around that age, late teens, early twenties. The streets were eating them alive. I just wanted to be sure because I was so fond of Jake and I wasn't going to be contributing to his lying dead with a needle stuck in his arm or slumped in the toilet of some club with his brain fried. And he didn't look too good that day. He wasn't the biggest guy physically, Jake, good lookin' but a bit thin and he had these big dark eyes that were sometimes sunk under the surface like ice cubes in a glass of bourbon and he rolls them at me and finally cracks a wide smile.

No, he says. Donnie, it's nothing like that. You sure, I ask him. Are you looking after yourself okay? I'm fine, Donnie, really. I'm the first person I look after first thing every day. And he teases the cash out of my hand and he says, Donnie, this money is going somewhere I didn't think even my worst nightmares would take me. But I need every penny that I can get for us right now. I really do.

So I say to him, Jake, here's the deal, I'm going to hold on to all these records for you. I found a Black Sabbath LP in there last night, first edition, gatefold sleeve, I'll go to Hell selling that for what I'll get for it. And he smiles at me. So Jake, I tell him, you come back in a month or two, three, four, whenever and pay me that money back and you can take your records home. How about that?

And his face, I swear, it lit up like a Christmas tree. Now, I didn't have a lot of spare cash hanging around, I gotta tell you. Didn't even have much space to spare. And I wouldn't have done that for anyone. But I didn't pry any further. I didn't want to know what kind of trouble he was in as long as it wasn't the bad kind. And he assured me it wasn't and I trusted him.

Now, people made a big deal out of the fact that he gave one of his nicest songs to a kid that day in the park. For some drama. Nah. Didn't surprise me at all. Jake, you know, he probably felt that it wasn't really his to own. His philosophy was that life is so damn short, you can't cling on to things that don't really have any tangible substance. So for him, a song is just, I don't know, an expression of a sentiment, it's like a little spiritual burp. Was never good business talk, but, I don't believe Jake ever had a business head on his shoulders. And I probably shouldn't have been surprised that he never came back to claim all those records, even when he started making some money. He just abandoned them and moved on.

But here's the thing. Later that day, it did strike me that he'd used 'us' instead of 'me' when he mentioned how much he needed the cash. At the time, you know the way you don't really hear every word in a sentence that's been put to you but then out of nowhere it comes back. Us. So I just figured it was this girl he was seeing at the time. Nice kid. Looked like Kim Wilde I remember, big blonde eighties hair and bangles jangling all over her arms. So, yeah, thought they were just poor students needing to pay the rent. But I had no Goddam idea.

## *Brian Blake. Promoter and manager.*

When David Bowie died. When Prince died. When Leonard Cohen died. George Michael. Glen Frey. Maurice White. Robert Miles. Keith Emerson. Glen Campbell. Chuck Berry. Joni Sledge. Merle Haggard. Scotty Moore. Ralph Stanley. Rick Parfitt. Chris Cornell. Lemmy, for Christ's sake. The man Rock was never supposed to kill. Tom Petty. Dolores O'Riordan. I'm getting tears in my eyes just uttering all these names. I have to stop. When all those stars fell, one after the other like nine pins, in what . . . a few short years? BANG! It was like part of the sky was torn out. It left a big gaping hole in the world of music and you looked into that hole and all it did was look back at you and growl. Who was going to fill it?

Sure, we have some fine pop artists rolling out the hits like fucking pizzas. And you've got to respect them. From Rihanna to Katy Perry or Kelly Clarkson, Britney, or the queens of the business like Beyoncé. Taylor Swift. And I've purposely put the females in there because really, over the last number of years, the big stars have been the ladies. You have the Ed Sheerans, Bieber, Sam Smith, the guys from One Direction yadda yadda yadda. But I don't think you can rate their artistry as highly as all those we've lost. But time will tell.

And in saying that, I do understand time is not on your side if you want to be a success story now. The way the industry has turned, time is on nobody's side. It's certainly not on the side of the record companies because, hey boys, hey girls, your days are numbered. And this trickles down to the kids who are under pressure to become stars overnight. Over. Night. BOOM. Without ever hitting the road. Without ever spending months in flaky hotels and in the back of vans, scratching a living from years of gigs in these anaemic venues because that's the only way they can pay the bills. They want it overnight only because they are under such pressure to deliver the goods early. So they sit in their bedrooms and make videos of themselves all day and put them up on YouTube.

Listen to me, are you ready? Boys? Girls? Here's some great advice. For free. And I'm not asking you to click a fucking link to get it. FREE. You want to make a life for yourself? In anything? Stay in your bedroom with your phone. Yeah. That's such a fucking great idea. Don't move from it, let the world come to you.

So, before I get into how Jake and I got involved together, and how he, despite the odds being stacked against him, found a niche and burrowed down into it like some gorging tick, let's look at the state of the industry for a moment. Because I think it's important to understand why Jake felt he had to do what he did and give away a song that, when I heard it, thought right away, that could have been his first hit.

I'll never forget my first compact disc. It was Pink Floyd's Dark Side of the Moon and that came out in 1984. CDs first hit Europe some time in 1983. But it was Dire Straits who really put the CD out there when they became the first band to hit a million sales. KERCHING. That was in 1985. Bowie then became the first artist to put his back catalogue onto CD. Bowie was never going to get left behind, ever. So there was competition on every front to make money out of these things. Good for the record companies, good for the fans. Or so it seemed. These little discs were revolutionary and the industry was clapping itself on the back because although they were cheaper to manufacture than the vinyl LPs, they were being sold to the public for outrageous prices. It was all about the sound. Remember? Crystal clear. But we now know the sound was shit. Plastic, just like the discs themselves. And people went and dutifully bought their favourites artists' back catalogues all over again. There were even execs making new careers out of repackaging archived work from bands and artists who had left hours of music behind them in the studios. You know, the outtakes and the bootlegs and the sessions. Most of it was inferior. Songs that were left behind for a reason. But the appetite was there and it was a huge earner for the companies who had just gotten very, very greedy.

But they forgot something, and I don't know how they didn't see it coming. Because the clue was in the cassette tapes that we used to record stuff on back in the day. You'd buy your vinyl LP and record the album on tape and give it to your pal who couldn't afford to buy the record. Or you'd make up your own tape from a pile of albums and write 'My mix' on the label. Mix tapes. But when you took the record out of the sleeve there was this big skull and crossbones plastered all over it, warning illegal recording was killing music. Piracy, they called it. But it wasn't piracy. Those mix tapes, it was never a commercial operation for anyone. At worst, it was a little cottage industry that wasn't even going to put a dent in the books of the record companies.

But the industry execs never saw it coming with CDs, which were compatible both with the CD players themselves and on people's PCs at home. So some bright spark, somewhere, realised this digitised music could be ripped from the CDs and recorded on blank discs on their PCs. But this still didn't mean people were going to sell pirate CDs by the truckload. You could go to a market in Eastern Europe and pick up Brothers in Arms with a photocopied sleeve for a quid but it wasn't enough to damage the industry. What it was though, was a warning the industry didn't heed.

Then, one day, an even brighter spark got an idea that would bring the whole house down. He discovered that he could get the songs that were ripped from the CDs and compress them into MP3s and just pass them on to the whole wide world over the internet. And that was it, that was the start of the decline in the record business. Because it was only a matter of time before the Napsters and the torrent-sharing Robin Hoods popped up and the damage really was done. Now, they faced real piracy. And the response of the industry was all wrong and they are paying for it to this day.

Think about it. Napster had over 60 million registered users. The record companies should have got together and bought it together with its millions of subscribers. A first year marketing student could tell you that. Instead, they moved to shut it down and it just spawned more and more pirate outfits. It was like Whack-a-mole. WALLOP. And another one pops his fucking head up. And everyone liked seeing the record companies squirm and, rightly or wrongly, nobody wanted to pay for their music anymore.

The only hope for the industry came years later with iTunes but that never hit the heights it needed to. Spotify doesn't make any profit, it can hardly pay the artists. So to make money, you need hits. And to get hits you need the acts that are not just some standalone artist or band who want to do what they want to do for their art. The real earners are the ones who behave like entrepreneurs. And they're team players who are happy to be assigned a production team from Sweden, a hit-making team from LA and a manager who has worked with the worst and the best of them for years and will have them on interviews on morning radio show, singing at some supermarket at lunchtime, then doing a thirty minute slot at a seaworld somewhere, only to be taken to a mobile recording studio in a car park for the night to redo a pile of vocal tracks that the manager wasn't happy with. Because the record industry who signed them up put a shit pile of money into getting that team together and you will bleed out your ears if you have to, just to get that hit.

The music world is in chaos. Most of the bigger record companies have collapsed. Call it karma if you want. They spent decades fleecing their artists and the buying customers. The more commercial releases still get the majority of airtime while everyone else has to compete with the masses online and a lot of good music rarely gets heard. So the only hand musicians have left to play is to give away their music for free. Choose a song, release it, like a dove, into the big bad world and hope it takes flight. And that's all Jake did. And I don't think it was on a whim either, though at the time, it seemed that way. And, when I first got wind of what he did, I thought it did seem a very strange thing to do. I mean, giving one of your best songs to a young girl so she could use it in a drama? In a school? Why?

## *Miles and Jenny Adams. Father and daughter.*

So it was a curious thing, remarkable in fact, to watch the change that came over Jenny after she first bumped into Jake. Everything else they tell you about girls growing up went by the book. This chapter just wasn't in the book.

Jenny was at that age, where, God, most fathers want to crawl off to die. And she had been experimenting with musical tastes for some time using channels like YouTube. She'd be on about Grime, techno, look, I'm not even going to pretend I knew what it was or who it was because I'd stopped trying to keep up after some of the magazines I loved had died horrible deaths in a barren market. I grew up devouring magazines like that and navigating music websites, or Spotify or Deezer to remain informed is way too cumbersome. But you don't want to see it slipping away, do you? The musical horizon that you spent your youth gazing upon? The unfortunate thing is, as you get older, that horizon does change. And as much as I tried to educate Jenny, my musical tastes didn't ever have much appeal. I used to sit her down and go through my collection. Try to wheedle her into making that journey into the unknown. But it's not going to happen, is it? You've had your time. That's the way it is, you have had your time.

I remember how my parents were when I was growing up. How they just didn't get the music I listened to, or the way I wanted to dress, me and the boys. And you just stared back at them and scoffed as if they were past it. And in a way, they were past it. That's how the generation game plays out. Young people are entitled to have their own movements, their own spheres of influence that the elders don't get and don't understand. It's their moment, it doesn't last long, so let them have it. And that's what stunned me about Jenny after she met Jake.

And I remember the Sunday morning after we had seen him in that park. I woke up, well I was woken up, in fact, by music. And I'll tell you what it was that woke me up. It was Oasis. And, so much of my early married years were built around Oasis and Blur, Brit pop and so on and when they say there's a soundtrack to your life, well Oasis, among others, mapped out our best days together, Sarah and I. They were just in the background all the time. You just couldn't ignore them. And when I look back on my life, I see every period, every momentous occasion as a picture, a postcard. You have the canvass, the subjects and an outline. And the music adds the colour and completes the whole. There's no picture that doesn't have music in it. Look, I'm a frightfully sentimental old bugger and nothing sets me off more than the music of my youth. If I'm being perfectly honest there are occasions where I can barely summon up the courage to delve into my own collection in case it brings me back to places I know I'll never reach again, ever. Shocking, isn't it?

But you grow a pair and it's onwards you go. From every picture you move on, they're like staging posts. And we had moved on, my wife and I. So had Oasis of course, and a lot of the other bands we had listened to. And when you have children, that really is the end of that road. So much from your past just gets shelved. You hardly ever look back. But then, occasionally, you get those moments of recollection. They drift back in every once in a while, float in on the bars of a song, that's the route they take. Creep up on you and remind you that you're still very much alive and able to enjoy it all if you so desire.

And on this morning, I woke up and I could hear an Oasis song being played downstairs. And it sparked something. Just a vivid memory of Sarah and I somewhere, not a lot happening but we were there, vibrant, youthful, our faces bright and alert and it was like looking at a Polaroid. And I turned to Sarah. And I was giving her the elbow, Sarah, did you turn that music on? And we'd been on the wine a bit on the Saturday night and she pushed me away and said nothing. But there it was. Oasis. Coming from downstairs. And it was Let there be Love, the song that really got the lazy journalists going. There's the real proof they ripped off the Beatles, that was always their line. But it was truly a wonderful, uplifting song.

So there I was on a Sunday morning, forgetting about how this song was mysteriously playing downstairs and instead lying back, back in that moment from the 90s, reliving my best days in a very condensed but very vivid way. And I let the song play out fully before I got up and crept downstairs and there she was, my little girl, lying on the rug in her pyjamas with her hands beneath her chin and she'd just gone and pressed play again on the same track. Only she heard me coming in and of course, she knocked it off. Jumped up, pretended she was rooting for something else on the shelf. Then she gives me this look and quickly tries to hide the little stack of CDs she has beside her, which she'd obviously been probing believing we were still dead to the world in our beds.

So I sit down on the floor next to her and look at the little stack. I have everything filed alphabetically, which everyone thinks is a tad over the top. But I've a couple of thousand CDs, how else am I to find anything?

What are you looking for, I ask her. So she picks up the little bundle, lets out this sigh and starts sifting through them. And she'd pulled down all kinds of artists, from Tom Waits to The Who, The Stone Roses, Mike Oldfield, Massive Attack. All kinds of stuff.

I was actually trying to find that song Jake Green was playing yesterday, she says. Then she looks up at me. So I take the CDs out of her hand and put them down on the floor. And I nod over to the left. Second shelf up, it's in there, I tell her, pointing. The Beatles. And she looks at all the albums, and just goes, Oh, right.

And over the next few days, Free as a Bird is played over and over again. I tried to get her to listen to Blackbird just to coax her away gently but no, it was always Free as a Bird. And that was how Jake flew into our lives. And, in some ways I regret I had ever encouraged her to explore my collection because it then became an expedition for her. She'd find something she liked and without even asking me about it off she'd go onto Google and read all about the band or the artist there. Dylan was next. She was determined, driven by this newfound fascination with musical history. Perhaps I should have just let her carry on listening to what she was listening to, just like my parents had done with me and never interfered. But this is what happens when you try and disturb the course of music. Music is a journey for everyone. Each generation has its own gift that the previous one has no right to meddle with. Well, I'm trying to sound profound here. I like to believe that good music is timeless one way or the other. But it's an interesting theory, isn't it? I was punished by the music gods for trying to foist my own tastes on my little girl and deprive her of her own time and place. And they sent me Jake.

So after a few days of this carry on, I finally confronted her about him. Jake. Who is he? And was it a spur of the moment, to go up to him like that in the park and seize one of his songs? Or had she being plotting all along? I hadn't a chance. That gaze, a teenager's gaze. It's like you are the rabbit and she is the headlights. But she swore it was purely fortuitous. Her drama work had been on her mind, they were missing an original song to put their own mark on this play they were doing and when she heard that song, it was like a sign. I wasn't sure if I believed her or not. But you're not going to get the truth out of a 16-year-old. Maybe someday she'll tell me, when all this has settled down. She'll tell me she had no idea what asking a chap in a park for a song, on a whim, was going to lead to. That she hadn't intended it to spiral the way it did, from a tiny little eddy, into a whorl before creating this menacing whirlpool into which all of us were consumed. It was just a school play after all, what were the chances? Well, the odds at the time may have seemed slim. But my God did it spiral.

## *Katie Ryan. Girlfriend.*

Yeah, I could never shake off the image that seemed to just cling to me after that morning in the park, like . . . I might as well have been branded with a cattle iron or something. There were loads of posts up about it afterwards. The bitch in the park, one troll called me. And that name stuck. The bitch in the park. In tweets I was shortened to BIP. So you had BIP RIP. Shit like that. I got over it quickly enough.

I try not to let that other world corrupt mine. But having a public row with a girl younger than myself was probably not a good idea. I only stepped in because I knew exactly what was going to happen. Someone needed to protect our interests because this girl, Jenny, had already been messaging Jake, asking could she take this one song, probably his most commercial song, potentially, and use it for a drama. Seriously? I'd managed to talk him out of responding but I was always wary that she would actually just turn up one day. And guess what? I was right. So when I saw this girl approach him that morning I knew it was her straight away. And Jake just caved in, right there in front of everyone, as if he was going to earn this reputation as a modern Jesus figure or something, who parts with his God-given gifts for the sake of the children.

People have always failed to realise how much work I'd been doing with Jake. I'd a whole strategy in place, a marketing plan, a business plan, branding, everything. And things were working very well until this girl came on the scene and within months it was like I'd never even been a part of it. Actually within months I was no longer a part of it. He more or less fired me but, dressed it up as being for the good of us both. Hmmm. At the time it was all rather charming and romantic and . . . I was totally gullible.

No one wants to acknowledge the work I had done, because the trail of lithel bwead cwumbs always leads back to that morning, and lithel Jenny, taking the song like it had been gift-wrapped especially for her and making up this story that it was for a school play. Come on. Jake was fooled. Everyone else seemed to be fooled. But I wasn't. Not for a minute. And because things happened so quickly after that, the story was spun, by that journalist, Andy — an old wet sock, is quite possibly the best way I can describe him — that this act of kindness just before Christmas was Jake's lucky break, the one he'd been waiting so long for. How a teenager became an ageing artist's salvation. The secret gig in the secret garden. Never too old to go back to school. Andy just trotted out these clichéd lines because he felt he was part of it all. He felt he was one of the people making it all happen.

Jake's, shall we say, success, was measured by how quickly things seemed to happen after that. And, yeah, that was understandable. It did appear to be this unlikely success story in the making. But when the dust settles we'll see it for what it was. Because it wasn't a success at all. Look at how it ended. It shouldn't have happened like that. If things had simply evolved at a slower pace, the way I wanted them to, Jake would still be around today. Anyway, deep breath . . . let me stick to the chronology here and go back to the beginning, shall we? Day one, if you like. The day I first met Jake? Here we go.

I can actually recall everything about that day. The weather, it was spitting rain, even though the sun was peeping through little chinks in the clouds. It was just after 10.30 in the morning and I was late for tutorials. And I remember I had my earphones on, listening to music while I was scrolling through the news on the phone. And I remember I paused at this heartbreaking photo of a child. And I was staring at it, wondering was it a boy or a girl? You couldn't tell because the poor thing was covered in this grey dust. It looked like a little ghost. And the reason I remember that image so well is because suddenly this piece of music came on. I had some Spotify playlist on shuffle and it was like a flood of emotion all at once. And I often wonder if these playlists are somehow synced to suit the mood of whatever you're looking at on your phone at the time. Of course, they're not . . . not yet. But this piece of music was so poignant, beautiful but so achingly sad. And I could feel myself welling up uncontrollably and the train was slowing down approaching my stop so I got up quickly and jumped off.

But once the train pulled away I realised I was one stop early. So I sat on a bench on the platform for a minute and just, like, took a few deep breaths. I could walk from there to the college so it was no big deal. There was a nice breeze on my face coming in off the bay and I'd my eyes closed so I thought with nobody around I'd sit and chill for a minute.

But suddenly I could sense someone else was there. And I opened my eyes and looked up and there was this guy, tall, thin guy who cast a long shadow standing right in front of me with a guitar case in his hand, just looking at me with these dark eyes. It was weird, but not a scary weird. And I just wanted him to move away because he was spoiling the moment, standing there. But he wasn't moving.

Then he just says, are you okay? Yeah, I'm fine, I say. Yeah. And I turn away and . . . he doesn't move. Are you sure, he says. So then I look directly at him. Yeah. And I'm purposely scowling a bit. And I repeat that I'm fine and sort of motion with my hands to, well, piss off really.

But then he points to the earphones, hanging around my neck, and asks me what it was I was listening to. Which was a bit weird, and I should have just told him, for the third time, that I was fine and would he mind moving away from the only bit of sun that he was blocking. But, you know how you sometimes bump into people for the first time and they have this warmth about them? You sense they've actually nothing to hide and so you've nothing to fear. And you think, well, with the pace of life these days and all that shit, is it really that hard to take a minute out to talk to someone?

So I humoured him. Which was unusual for me, I'm generally a bit more cagey. I tell him I actually didn't know what it was, that it was on a playlist but I suspected it was being controlled.

And he just gives me this blank look. He didn't get the joke. By whom, he says. Whoever. Whatever, I tell him. The cookies. The algos. The bots. And he laughs. Must have been powerful though, he says.

So he points to my earphones and asks if he could have a listen. So I put my hand in my pocket and take the phone out and then he leans down over my shoulder and we both put one ear piece in together and I get a closer look at him. He's not as young as I thought. And though he looks a bit dishevelled in a long, dandyish coat, he smells really clean and his hair is perfectly trimmed but no bloody beard thank God. And he's looking at me, leaning down listening to the music, then there's a smile of recognition and he stands back up and takes the ear bud out and gives it back to me. Ennio Morricone, he says.

Yeah, okay. Morricone was always someone I kind of avoided and dismissed as this cheesy stuff for cheesy couples. But the track was from Once Upon a Time in America and this guy seemed fascinated by my reaction to it. He knew it obviously and looked a bit bemused by the fact I didn't. I'd never even seen the film. So he told me I needed to see it. Needed, that's actually the word he used. At the time I thought that was weird, but later —well, later because obviously we would begin seeing each other — I learned that for Jake, the best music provokes an emotive response. You can dance to music, sing along, drift off to sleep, whatever, but the music that works best is the music that stops you in your tracks and reaches into your heart and wrings out the emotion. That's his thing.

So he hands me back the earphones. He's a master, he tells me, and probably, without that music playing in your ears, he says, you would have skipped right past that photo. That's a bit harsh, I say. I actually saw the photo first, I tell him. Yes, but you would have skipped right past it. It's no reflection on you, he says, how many images do we see every day now? Without a soundtrack, that's all they are, just fleeting images. Music puts the brakes on, that's all I'm saying.

Hmmm. So I point to his guitar. That's what you do then, I ask him. Thought he was going busking or rehearsing or something.

And he nods and says yeah, he's going to his rehearsal space. Space, that's what he called it. So I ask if he's gigging anywhere. I mean, it's all just small talk, I wasn't actually very interested. And this is what he does, I swear to God. He turns away and shields his eyes from the only bit of sun that he happened to be still blocking from me and looks out across the bay. And the tide was out a good bit and there's this woman walking her dog on the strand. And she's got one of those pathetic ball-throwing things people use when they're strolling with their mutts. So she hurls the ball out into the distance somewhere and when it lands on the sand it makes this popping sound and you can hear the echo. And this guy, he stares for a minute then he says, did you hear that? The acoustics? Maybe I should go out there. And I hadn't a clue what he was talking about. And maybe it was all the fish oils I'd been guzzling on the last few weeks for my thesis, but that was another thing that I remembered, very clearly about that day. The fact he had found the acoustics so fascinating on the beach.

Anyway, he goes to walk away but stops as if he's remembered something, puts his hand out and says, I'm Jake Green. We'll meet again soon. And off he goes. And . . . I remember just thinking, what did he mean by that? We'll meet again soon. Was it an invitation? A promise? Does he know me from somewhere? If he actually wanted to meet me again, why didn't he just ask for my phone number there and then, when I had the phone in my hand?

Now, I'm going to go in another direction for a moment so bear with me. I was at that stage in my life, for the second time actually, of having to make choices. You know, life choices. I'd already made a bad one. And the people who succeed in life, I mean really succeed and succeed early, only ever make the one choice and they make sure it's the right one. In other words, life choices should never come in the plural form. If they do, you know you've fucked them up. That's my take.

On that first occasion my ex-boyfriend had given me a present of a book. A real book with paper and a spine and a cover, not a college book either but a novel. It was really a heavy-handed piece of advice masked as a present. It was a book called Stoner, by a guy called John Williams. He said I should read it because I had mentioned thinking about a career as a lecturer, or maybe a teacher or some sort of academic, because in truth I didn't know where I was going. I was doing an Arts degree. Not really knowing where it would lead. So I'd applied for a Master's and that's when my ex presented me with that book just before we finished our final exams. Then he dumped me when they were over. Nice.

And the crux of the book is that people who go into academia do so because they know that within the walls of their colleges or schools or institution there is safety. There is safety in numbers, safety among your peers and safety in that steady progression of the seasonal academic calendar with the long breaks and the slow but steady rise through the ranks. Because unless you do something stupid and rock the boat —and the protagonist in the book kind of does this, but only kind of, as he still values his security – you are assured to have a long and secure life without, let's say, ever skirting danger in any shape or form.

And I got that. I didn't agree with it. If you can make a career out of what you love – in this case, literature – then you've found your place in the world. Who cares about risk, danger, proving things to anyone? You need to do you and do whatever it is that makes you happy. But I got why my ex had given it to me, because he only ever had plans to make money. He was a gambler and he was happy to spend a life taking risks. He actually got in touch again a few months later. Emailed me, just before Christmas, and invited me over to see him. He was working for a hedge fund and was earning six figures. Nice. And he didn't just want me to come over for old time's sake. If I went over, he was going to convince me to stay, that's the way he was. He clearly had a great lifestyle and I could very easily have fallen into it. I didn't go because I knew if I did, I would stay. It would have been an easy choice. Living in central London with a high-achieving, high-earning boyfriend, playing out this Gatsbyesque fantasy for as long as our twenties would allow. Surface some time in our thirties like a couple who had been on one long bungee jump, ticking it off when it was all over as something that just had to be experienced before settling down into a sensible marriage. That was his vision. And we did still love each other. He knew that, so ironically — and I hate using that term after Alanis Morissette bolloxed it up — for the first time, I made the tough choice and declined. But it was the right choice.

And it had been, for months, burrowing away in my subconscious like some irksome little larva of . . . doubt, threatening to complete its metamorphosis and become a great big winged creature of regret by the time my Masters was handed in. Which was only weeks away from that day I met Jake. And I'm not one of these people who sees signs when what they're really looking for are distractions. But Jake was the distraction I needed. Don't ask me how. It was like, you know when you have an earworm, some awful song you hear in a café somewhere and it only has to be a snippet but it's enough to act as bait and reel in the whole thing and it plays out the day in your head until something very contrary happens along and cancels it out. Jake did that. And, I still don't really know how. From that strange encounter at the train station, he just seemed to enter my life totally uninvited.

I just remember, that night after meeting him, being tempted to start spreading the word all over social media like some sad damsel about this guy on the train blah blah, I won't even bother with the third blah. And I could have put the word out that I needed to find this guy. Now. Not in the morning. Not later that week. But there and then, within minutes I wanted some signal – a tweet, a message, a poke, an email, anything. That's the thing about our generation, we demand instant gratification. But I resisted the urge to go online and start tweeting and pinging all over the place. I did none of that. I just went to bed and I put the phone in a dock and listened to that playlist of melancholic music and sort of, drifted off. And for the rest of that week, I went in late each morning, catching the same train at the same time hoping to find him. And I'd never had a romantic bone in my body. My last boyfriend, we loved each other but it wasn't about the romance. It was about this fast-paced, thrilling ride of excess and I think it probably would have burned itself out, even if we had tried to make a real commitment.

Maybe this was the good old-fashioned love at first sight. The painting seen through the prism of the heart, open and unblinkered. And guess what? Well, I'm sure you can guess what's coming. But a few days later, I was on the train, winding around the bay and up ahead you could see the strand, smooth as polished stone, the tide out so far the people were all over it, dog-walking, jogging, kitesurfing. And there, near the steps, sitting on a rock was this guy playing the guitar. It was him. Be still you violent heart. Because while one half of me was thinking this is fate, get off now and go to him, the other was acting as if it was faced with a predator, with the instinctive urge to stay put and not to look back until the scene had passed. Then the train stopped, the doors opened and I had about eight seconds to make up my mind. I think I spent five of those eight seconds hesitating before I heard the music. The song he was playing. It was like he was the pied piper and I a child. So I got off. And that was how we met.

And, that child in the news? Thought I'd forgotten... I did take the time later that day to find out who it was and I won't ever forget it either. It was a little boy, a five-year-old boy, who survived an airstrike and would become known just as 'the boy in the ambulance'. Why am I telling you that? Because I'm not just the bitch in the park.

## *Andy Kirwan. Music writer and journalist.*

Jake had sent me a CD of a few of his songs once upon a time, at a period in my life when, I suppose, I probably wasn't Mr Nice. Did I already mention that? Think I did. That's how much it haunts me. Like all of us, here, now, I do feel emotionally invested in this whole story which is why I've got to come clean about things. We're talking years ago, when that CD was sent in and it came with a letter, handwritten, in what can best be described as with a very fastidious hand. It was like calligraphy, you know what I mean?

At the time, reading the letter, I was thinking to myself, it would be nice to do something for this guy. First impressions, he had addressed it to me personally. That always helps. Because you wouldn't believe the amount of emails and letters that came into the office with 'Dear sir' or 'Dear music correspondent'. 'Dear Fuckface' I got once. I'm not joking. Someone didn't like a review I had done of a gig. A band who were on the way up and so they took it personally. Won't say who they were because they're still going. But I didn't take their letter personally. In fact, when their first album came out I gave it a glowing review. But they never got in touch then to say thanks.

But Jake's letter began with 'Dear Andy'. He was clearly a reader of the section in the paper I worked on and had gone to the trouble of writing to me, with a pen, amazing when you think about it, and asked me if I could listen to his songs. And those same thoughts that strike me every time an unsolicited demo comes in from an artist or band who don't have a manager or label behind them struck me then. Christ, the poor guy, does he really believe I can do anything for him? His brief bio explained he had studied history and English in college and had turned down the offer of further studies to follow his passion. When a passion burns inside you, he wrote, and I still remember this, you have to fuel it before the world extinguishes it. And for me, he added, that passion is music.

Fair enough. I knew what he meant by that and, I mean, he hit a chord there with me. And I kind of hated him for saying it like that. And he said something else that stirred me. Your dreams lose their sheen as you get older, through no fault of your own. Life just gets in the way, the world gets bigger and diminishes the dream; or, worse, that same dream gives up on you and finds a younger mind to occupy and leaves yours with its ghost. Yep. Yep, I knew what he was saying, I really did. And he finished the letter by writing, Andy, victory isn't achieved overnight. It's brought about through little wins, progress. Someone like you can help me with a little win and take me closer to the big dream. Whatever you can do is greatly appreciated.

Then I read his name. Greenbaum. Jake Greenbaum. Like the Spirit in the Sky Greenbaum, as in, Norman Greenbaum. Later, Jake just shortened it to Green. But I liked Greenbaum. I thought it kind of had a ring to it. Then there was the photo. Like somebody who would have strutted around Carnaby Street 30 years ago or so, you know what I mean? Mismatched garish colours, the long hair, a red suede jacket with something stuck in the lapel, I can't remember if it was a flower or just a twig, and I think it was just a twig. Totally mad. But it was a portrait, not just a snap, so he had considered it. And he had the innocent look of a young Donovan, these eyes that were deep and clear and I suppose, had really seen fuck all. He was a kid with a kid's ambition and a kid's dream. That was my initial sentiment, here was a guy who spoke from the heart, but another unfortunate struggler looking for a break. Do they have any idea? When will it ever stop? This factory line of desperate wind-up, musical toys.

The other thing was, I wasn't really in the business of breaking people, you know what I mean? I had a weekly section in a newspaper, where I would write about the rising stars, review the albums, bit of news and gossip, it was a general entertainment slot and if I could help an up and comer with a plug, great, I'd do it if the space was there. Slip it in past the editor, you know what I mean? But nice guy or not, a total unknown was a hard one to do anything for, especially when we didn't have the social media tools we have at our disposal today. All we had was the physical space on a page. You were limited to that.

So come Friday evening I was giving my desk the ritual clear out and I spotted Jake's CD and, you know, I have the bin pulled up beside the desk. It comes down to one of those decisions and there's no going back from them. And it is terrible to think that every Friday, before I went out with my colleagues for a few pints, I would bin a batch of CDs. It's awful. It makes an unmistakeable sound. It's like bones being broken and I would grimace every time as one rattled off the sides of the plastic container and landed on another with this gut-wrenching clatter. Jake, I remember his CD came in a cardboard sleeve, so I thought, I won't feel bad about this one. And just then, one of my colleagues was leaving and he came up behind me, clipped me on the back of the head, and said, come on Andy, bin that and we'll get going for a few pints. Then I looked at the photo of Jake, and, I mean, the bastard, he has this aura of virtue about him, and something made me believe that if I binned it there would be payback from somewhere. The universe would just turn a dial and I'd spill my pint or put my back out or something.

So I whipped off my jacket and took out my headphones and stuck the CD into the PC and gave it a listen. And I remember, to this day, every song. Little Star. Beat in Blues. The Future's Not Ours. The Day I Stayed at Home. I remember them all. I don't think there was anything quite like them out there. They weren't perfect, by any means, but they were fresh. And I was thinking, even all those years ago, does anyone play the harmonica like that anymore? The songs left that little bit of warmth in my belly, how about that for a summation?

And Jesus, it had been a while since a bunch of songs had got in under my skin that way and I thought to myself, I'll have to do something for this guy. If they hit me like that, they needed to be out there. But then, I thought, what could I do? And I genuinely had no idea what I could do, even though I knew something needed to be done. So do you want to know what I did? Do you want to know what I did for Jake back then? I got going for a few pints, that's what I did. That CD went into the drawer and was filed under that Kafkaesque category of things waiting to be filed when a suitable classification could be found to file them under.

And the next time I came across Jake, obviously many years later, it was in the park on that Saturday morning. What he had been up to, in all that time that had passed, I'd no idea. Nor was I enlightened as to why he had re-emerged to start playing in public spaces. And I was even more intrigued when he went and gave away one of those songs that I had listened to way back then, you know what I mean? To a kid, for a drama. In a school hall? Why? It made no sense. He just gave one of his songs away. For free. And once it's out there like that, it's out there. You can't take it back. And it's not like you're U2 and you can give away a whole album on iTunes because you're so established it will generate income in so many other ways. When you're a nobody, you don't give away your work, you know what I mean? It's the only decent piece of advice I have left to give young people nowadays but I always get this bloody dead fish gaze in return. Desperation has driven artists to that. Novel writers have been doing the same thing. Publish for free and be damned. Hopefully the public will like it enough that they'll buy your work the next time around. No, they won't. The mob doesn't respect loyalty, it just satisfies its cravings and when it can get something for nothing, it's even less loyal.

However, Jake, well, he was either very clever or very lucky. Maybe he was both. Nobody gives a song away because a young girl asks them to. Unless you're someone like Jake. And I believe he knew what he was doing, it wasn't an accident. Let's remember the difference between someone like Jake and the youngsters who, because their demands are met in the digital world immediately, expect things to happen quickly. Jake had been doing his time in the years since he had written that letter to me. Somewhere he was putting that time to use. Where it was all spent, I don't know. I don't think anyone really knows. But I do know that he never allowed the world to extinguish that flame that he spoke of. Somewhere he had still been making those little wins. Little star, your world is wide. Indeed.

# FOUR

# *The First Song*

### *Springhill Drama Society*

*SDS are excited to announce that this year's charity drama is a production of Tony Award-winning musical The Music Man, featuring special guest Jake Green who many of you will already know from his Fly-ins and his growing online presence. We are thrilled that he will be joining us this year with an original song to close the show so please check our page for booking details.*

👍 *3358*

### **Brian Blake. Promoter and manager.**

I picked up all kinds of signals from Jake the first time I met him face to face. Confused signals mostly. Did he want to succeed as an artist? What was his motivation? Had he a plan for success? How long was he prepared to give it? Had he a plan for failure? That last one was an important question by the way. There's a lot of nonsense these days about mindfulness. Focus. Positive thought. This pseudo fucking well-being mentality stuff, like, ooh, you have to imagine where you want to be in three, five years' time if you really want to get there. Great, that's a great fucking idea, you should tell that to the refugees. Do you know what matters? Negative thought matters. It serves a very important function, which is to force you to contemplate defeat and make a plan for it. Are you strong enough to handle it? Because there is something very particular about being a failed musician. It has its very own stigma. It's like you're branded with it. You fail in business, you're unfortunate. You're made redundant from your job, you're unlucky. You lose in sport, you're still a competitor. But you fail as a musician and you're a reject, because that's what you have to carry around with you – rejection. And that can undermine the best of them.

So I looked at Jake, with all those questions running around my head like army ants, getting in under the skin. I'm sure he was tough, he'd been around. I was sure he'd been in the back of plenty of vans and slept in plenty of rough hotels. He'd gone hungry. He'd been broke, likely still was. He knew desperation. But what I needed to know was how desperate he was. If you told him he had to go and do that interview on breakfast radio at eight am, the daytime slot on a lunchtime talk show, the late afternoon TV magazine show watched by women, phone interviews in between them all to radio hosts in Scandinavia, followed by a gig, three or four hours' work in a mobile recording studio in a hotel car park before grabbing three hours' sleep, I'm getting chest pain thinking about it, so would Jake be able to handle it? That's the kind of gruelling regime you got to adapt to these days. Tours? Tours are for making as much money as you can and getting as much sleep as you can, when you can.

I've been on tour with bands. And it can get very fucking boring. There's a lot of hanging around. Hotel lobbies and hotel rooms. Cold changing rooms. Waiting in empty venues for soundchecks. Back to the hotel for some sleep then back to the venue. You start to lose all sense of time and space. There are days where people don't want to talk to each other anymore. If they do it can turn into some petty argument. The buzz from the gig is unbeatable. You're not going to get a greater rush of adrenaline than from live performing. But that's the high, that's as good as it gets and after come the lows. You can't sleep so you drink or you pop whatever is going. And nowadays, it's all clean because there's too much at stake, financially. The margins are tighter. So you finish a show and you're eating chicken and broccoli backstage and hitting the gym first thing in the morning. And when I see those T-shirts, the ones with the list of cities on the back like someone has mapped out a route to El Dorado? They bring tears to my eyes. You won't even know what city you're in from one day to the next. Choirs, hymns, high masses and orchestras were all gifts from God. If you're blessed with a golden voice, go to a church. The fucking devil came up with touring, baby.

And while Jake had maybe cut his teeth somewhere, I had to wonder whether it was in him to go to those lengths anymore. That's what I needed to find out. Was it worth getting involved with him and why? Why? And the why is this whole story. Without the why, none of us would be telling it. So I had to meet him, even just to satisfy my curiosity. Why was he really putting in all this time and graft? Was there a goal at the end of it? All this work online which consumes all the hours in the day. Kids can do all that because they can operate different gadgets in their sleep. Jake, he was older. All these fly-in gigs. Drip-feeding song files online. What was going on? Why Jake? Why?

So I ask him over to my home one evening, just to make it a little informal. I have an office in town but people find it a bit intense. Maybe it's just me who's intense when I'm in there because it's a converted basement flat and it's where I get to shout and swear at a lot of people and a lot of inanimate things. So the home is better. I'm far more sanguine.

So he arrives and we begin talking for a while about the weather and the world and the state of things then I hit him with the question that I ask everyone. It's my opener, always has been. And it's not because I want to sound impressive, like one of these moguls. It's not like that at all. It's a genuine question. I say to him, Jake, you got talent and you got a heart bursting with passion. You've got a look, even if you're not altogether youthful. And you've got pulling power. In a nutshell, Jake, you've got all the parts but you paint the picture of the whole for me because I don't know what it is. How does it look, Jake? Describe it for me. Show me the picture.

And he looks at me, with those big eyes of his, and he thinks for a moment. Then he just grins. For a split second. And those grins,

I got to see them a lot after that. It was like a tic, like it was a grin that got there first to stop the lie. Or maybe give him pause to think one up. Who knows? But he says to me, that picture you're talking about, I sit in front of it every day and it'll be my masterpiece. And the cheeky bastard kind of leans forward and slaps me on the thigh. Nobody does that, do they? I mean, to a host. Slap them on the thigh? So I laugh. I thought he was joking. But he wasn't. Not at all. And the next thing, do you know what he says? He says, speaking of pictures, that's a fine collection you have here. And he just gazes around my living-room.

I collect art, so what? Contemporary stuff. Over the years. Investments. And he recognises some of the names and he's nodding away. Then he says, there must be a lot of money hanging on these walls. And he adds, but I suppose you've got to spend your money on something. Then quick as a flash, he asks me, what the hell do you do with so many rooms anyway? And he's shaking his head, looking around him like he's never been in a house before. But this is my house he's talking about and he's a guest, am I right? And I'm a bit stunned to hear him going on like this.

Here's the thing, you were always wondering with Jake what he was going to come out with next. But you kept listening even if you knew you might not like what you were going to hear. He could be a comedian one minute and a philosopher the next. An asset or a liability, socially. You just didn't know. But you always had to gamble on him coming out with a gem. Because his gems were priceless.

So before I've time to really digest what he's been saying, my wife comes in with a tray of coffee and he stands up and takes it from her and introduces himself. Jake Greenbaum. She was all over him then like seaweed clinging to a rock. Had to peel her away from him. She loved him. The presence that man had, she said. She told me afterwards. Said he filled the room like a thundercloud. And he was a real gentleman too. So he knew how to work the room and the women, that's all good.

So he helps himself to coffee and sits back down, talking to me over the top of the cup, in between sips. So I ask him again. Jake, give me the picture. Why now? Where were you 15, 20 years ago when I had more energy and more clout? Because let me tell you where I'm at, I say to him. I'm semi-retired, really. I act as a scout. I travel, I move around, I get tips and I pass on information. I'm a ghost. I've earned all I need to earn so if I choose a project to manage for myself, it's more for love than money. People say it's a short life, Jake, but take it from me it's not. I'm looking back at it from the other side of 60 now. I can tell you it can be a long and very shitty life with no end in sight unless you cram if full of new experiences right up to the day they're putting you into a box. I don't need money, power, the house on the hill because I've got all that. But I am always looking for something new just to stop me getting bored. So before you can amuse me, Jake, you need to tell me what direction you're hoping to go in. And don't fucking say up, because you know what that means? It means biding your time with your head between the cheeks of someone's arse while you wait for them to fuck up and fall down. Then all you'll be feeling is someone's nose up your arse while they wait for you to fuck it all up. We have to stop, all of us, thinking of success in terms of climbing ladders. There's no fucking room on ladders, for Christ's sake. Think of success as being granted free pasture on a wide open field where you can put your skills and talents to use and carve out your own space and shoot the bastards coming over the hill to take it from you. Now, tell me what direction are you going in?

 I understand, he says. And he'd been listening, I could see that. And he's giggling, fitfully, which I actually don't mind. Then he sits back and tells me a story, as he put it himself, another device he uses instead of answering the question. Parables kind of thing. Maybe he made this one up on the spot, maybe he had it prepared, who knows. So off he goes.

 A young man, he tells me, was once given a choice of two futures, and a form was put in front of him to sign once he had made his mind up and decided which option he was going to choose. His first choice is a future of pure chance, where the prospect of realising his dreams are as slim as everyone else's. In the second one, he would become a rock star, just as he always wanted. The problem is, the first life is in the real world, the second one takes place in a machine, it is all simulated, virtual reality, but the young man won't actually know that because he'd be living the experience of it all, even if the experience isn't real. So he'd really be living the lie. And so the young man stalls, he doesn't know what to do. And that's his dilemma. What does he do?

And I look at him. So that's you, Jake. Am I right, I say to him. Or maybe that was you, once. You walked away from an offer before, is that it? And he shakes his head and puts his coffee cup down on the table. No, he says, not exactly. This is more like one of those moral thought experiments, he says.

Morality? Great. So what's the answer, I ask him. And he says there is no answer, at least, no right or wrong answer. The question is, he says, would you take the offer of a bogus happy life or strive to achieve real success yourself, no matter how long it took, even if you knew failure was a real possibility.

So I think I see where he's at. I think. Not that I wanted to get all philosophical about it. But maybe he thinks now's his time, he's put in the road miles, he's earned it, deserves it, but not before. So I say to him, okay Jake, let me put the coda on that little story, given we are both talking music. Let's say you're this kid, and he's maybe, I don't know, let's say 20 years old and he's given this choice. So he thinks about it for a while and decides he'd rather live his life as a nobody than live it as a fake. And, I think we can all relate to that. So he turns down the offer and goes back out on the streets. And for the next 20 years, he fails at everything. I mean, everything he touches turns to shit. He can't get a decent job, his marriage falls apart, he loses his house and he just wanders like a homeless bum until one day this, I don't know, genie, whoever he was, pops out once more in a fucking big puff of smoke and presents him with the same choice all over again. This time, of course, the kid, only he's not a kid anymore, knows how tough things can really get and the prospect of living a lie but having a ball for the rest of his life and dying inside the machine is a hell of a lot better than croaking with a rotten liver and an empty heart under a bridge somewhere. What do you think then, I ask him.

And he says, that's a bit of a cheat, Brian, a bit like talking your conscience into doing something you know is wrong. You can still do it, but your conscience can't be fooled. It won't ever let you forget.

So fucking what, I tell him. Cheats, swindlers, liars, backstabbers, whatever. They're all out there. This is called a second chance. It happens in the real world. So, if it were you, I ask him again, would you enter the machine and be happy to enjoy the rest of your days as an imaginary star?

And so, to cut a long afternoon short he agreed to work with me. That was it. And leaving all that philosophical shit aside, we did get down to some constructive business. And that school drama was the first thing to come up. He had committed to it by then anyway, he'd had his arm twisted by that young girl in the park, however she managed to do it.

Did you see it coming, I ask him. Had she been in touch with you before, Jake? And he looks at me. And he just nods his head. Then it was my turn to lean forward and slap him on the thigh. Okay, I say, well, the best place to learn about evangelism, Jake, is by going back to school. So off you go. Let's do it. And so we did it. Sold our souls.

## *Miles and Jenny Adams. Father and daughter.*

So it wasn't Dylan in the Albert Hall in 66, or anything, was it? But you still had this sense that something unusual, something interesting was about to happen. I had no clue what it was. I'd been going to these things faithfully for the last number of years ever since Jenny had got involved and this year she had promised me something a little bit special.

Look, I know what you're thinking. You're thinking, wait a minute, are we talking about a drama in a school here? And yes, that's exactly what we're talking about, that's all it was. It was just another ordinary school musical. But something happened, something quite significant, I would say, that turned this ordinary evening into something extraordinary.

The show this year was an adaptation of a musical called The Music Man, which I'm ashamed to say I'd never heard of despite it having won five Tony Awards. Very briefly, it's about a conman who poses as a musician with the promise to take the kids off the streets by teaching them music and skip town with all the money he swindles from the people before he gets found out. But it transpires he doesn't want to leave this particular town because he has fallen in love with the local librarian. And despite his lack of, how would you put it, musical finesse, he manages to get a performance out of the makeshift band and the townspeople love him for it. And, they all live happy ever after. And I was guessing, that was where Jake was to come in with his song about stardom and so on.

As a contemporary school show, it was a fitting exploration of the burning issues kids face these days and the contemporary cures we have to try and get them through. So you had mindfulness and positive thought, redemption through music and creativity, and the idea that you don't always have to come out on top to succeed. It was the antithesis of the type of TV shows that are de rigueur now, the talent shows that leave the contestants with confidence handicaps and the teenage viewers at home rushing to social media with anxiety disorders. But this is the world we are living in. When I was growing up, I just remember getting a wooden spoon or a boot, depending on whether it was my mother or father who was on the receiving end of a sulk. Now, everything is an issue and has to be dealt with so the adults can pat themselves on the back. I'm not so sure it's the right way to go but, you go along with it because you're chastised otherwise. As for Jake, I was only privy to the fact his song had been worked into it at the end because the themes in the show were supposedly reflected in his lyrics. The myth of success and fame, the importance of self-belief and the view that if you fail at one thing, nevermind, the world is wide so off you go and do something else. I could buy that as a valuable lesson for today's youth, certainly. Jake, he wasn't young, as I've said so many times, does he have children of his own? Who knows? But I think he had other things on his mind when he wrote that song.

The one certainty that night was that, my God, the place was jammed. They were turning people away at the school gates. Actually at the school gates. And as I squeezed into my seat, near the back, I spotted none other than Andy Kirwan arriving. Andy Kirwan, the journalist. He looked rather sluggish, I regret to say, as if he was there against his will. Everyone knew Andy Kirwan. He was quite a prominent music writer, getting on a little, but he could still break an artist in one of his columns or boost someone's credibility on Twitter if he wanted to. But I couldn't help but wonder what he was doing in a school, midweek in that bleakest darkest month of November. So I watch him closely as he takes a seat two rows in front of me and tucks his head down and waits for the show to begin. And when it does he barely moves. I think he was asleep, to be honest. He looked like a fat little pigeon. And when he finally stirs it's to get up and leave for a few minutes. This he did throughout the performance, popping in and out, looking at his watch, seeming distracted and disinterested until Jake came on and only then did he rouse himself. Because, in fact, Jake never really came on at all. And this was when the ordinary became extraordinary.

During the interval, a message came up on the screen over the stage to make sure to 'Like' Jake Green on Facebook. That's all it said. It flashed up on the screen like that until the show resumed and, I'm sure, like me, everyone imagined this to be just some cheeky request from the guest star. But like many others around me, I logged on and obliged and didn't really think anything else of it.

So the second half begins, and I remember Andy Kirwan slipping out again and was gone for nearly the whole second half. Next thing, it's lights out. Total darkness, just like that. And you can just about make out the figures dashing off the stage and a few hands scrambling to get the props off. But it's totally dark until this spotlight hits the stage and a bird cage is brought on along with a stool and just left there in the centre. Nothing else happens, there's no music, there are no people on stage, there's absolutely nothing going on. And there is this very uncomfortable, pregnant lull that is causing those little creeping tendrils of consternation. You can see people shifting in their seats as their bums are getting numb. It's a long wait, I can tell you. Then suddenly, something happens. The screen overhead flashes once more and this time all it says is, watch Jake Green on Facebook/Jakegreen. And that's it, this bizarre directive twinkling like a bright star and illuminating the room with its brilliance. Then there is this bowel-chilling hush in the hall because it really, really looks like someone has messed up badly. Jake, by the looks of it. Has he got stage fright? Where is he? Is he drunk?

And then I hear it, not very clearly but I hear it. There's music coming from somewhere but I've no idea where, it's not from the PA system. Then I realise it's from somebody's phone. Then another one kicks in. And another, and another, until all around the hall people's faces are suddenly aglow with the screens on their phones. Ah, okay. Very clever, I see, I say proudly to myself. I see what's going on. So I switch my phone on furiously and log into Facebook and, it's ridiculous, it's a live video link from Jake. He's on the street somewhere, just strumming his guitar and strolling past bemused pedestrians and there are cars slowing down and people gawping from the top decks of buses and there he is, as if oblivious to it all, singing and sauntering along quite happily as as he's being filmed. And there's a lot of whispering around the hall as more and more people log on to watch all of this. Because it's not being shown on the screen, as you would have expected. Then we realise where he is, because he's coming through the school gates, into the grounds and right at that moment he starts singing, Little Star. And some people are standing and looking around them and behind them at the doors but he never arrives. Where is he? He's in the school somewhere. Where? In the building, walking along the corridors and at one point he stops and sings a whole verse, just leans up against a wall and sings. And this is all happening on our own screens.

Suddenly Kirwan is on his feet. He's up like a little Jack in the box. And he's just stood there, and it looks like he's doing his best not to get too animated. In fact, he's looking around him a lot, watching people's reaction more than anything else. Then he does something funny, I can't ever forget it, he turns around fully at one point and we make eye contact, the two of us, our faces aglow in the dark. But we make the little connection, you see, as two old chaps. And as we look at each other, I raise my eyebrows quickly and he, he just shakes his head, then gives this long shrug and mouths something to me. I think it was, what the hell is this?

And finally Jake arrives on stage joined by the whole cast to this rousing reception and he literally gets the one chorus of the song in with the harmonica solo at the end and that's it. He's done. He finishes up with one of his dramatic bows then just vanishes into the wings. He simply vanishes. Nobody saw him at all later. And, of course, he never appeared again after that opening night. Which really disappointed a lot of people. But that was Jake. He said he would do the opening night and thereafter everyone in the audience was shown the recording on the screen over the stage. And despite the standing ovation, there's no sign of Jake coming back and people eventually begin shuffling outside, staring at their phones, and a lot of them are looking a bit stupefied, to be honest. I heard one man joke, he'll never work in this town again. I'm sure quite a few of them had no Facebook accounts at all and were left feeling a bit cheated. So I see Kirwan texting on his phone while edging his way out with the crowd and I sidle up alongside him.

That was an experience, I say to him. And he glances at me and he puts the phone back into the pocket of his coat and yanks out an old beanie hat and sticks it on, positioning it with his hands. Going bald, poor bugger, I thought to myself. Did I just have to watch the end of a live show on my phone, he says, grinning at me through a poor set of teeth. I'm not a theatre buff by any stretch, he adds, but isn't the action always supposed to take place on stage, do you know what I mean?

I know precisely what you mean, I say. And did you know this singer then, I ask him. No, not really, he says, I mean, let's just say someone suggested I check him out. Always looking for something new and ground breaking and this is both, he says. Ha! I'd love to know who came up with that idea, it was totally bonkers. And he laughs heartily. So I say something to stifle it. That would be my daughter, I tell him. And he stops what he's doing suddenly. Stops everything. And he's staring at me. Then he clicks his fingers a few times. I remember you, he says. I knew I'd seen your face. You were in Merrion Square a few weeks ago. That's right, I tell him, with my daughter, Jenny. Would you like to meet her? I'd love to, he says and he finally stops walking. And Jenny is at the sound desk and I usher Kirwan back and introduce her. And Kirwan looks at her. Pleasure, he says, I thought you'd be older, he adds, laughing. And Jenny looks quickly at me. Why is that, she asks him. No, no, don't get me wrong, he says, happy out, it's great, if that guy reached out to you he must be doing something right. And Jenny looks at him, so are you writing something about it, is that why you are here. And Kirwan looks away, yes and no, he says. So which is it, Jenny asks. And Kirwan starts laughing, well it's a no then, he says. That's okay, Jenny says, it probably wouldn't make much difference anyway. But I'm glad you enjoyed the show, she says. Ouch.

And when we were driving home I said exactly that to her. Ouch. Could she not have been a bit more courteous, given who he is. Who is he, she asks me. He's a respected writer. One of the biggest papers in the country, you know who he is, I tell her. Yeah, yeah, she says. Nobody reads the papers anymore, Dad. Get over it.

### *Andy Kirwan. Music writer and journalist.*

I suppose I had it coming, didn't I? Deserved all I got after ignoring him all those years ago. So where do I end up? In a school hall, late November, the cruellest of months to have to go to anything in the middle of the bloody week, but an amateur production of a musical no one's ever heard of was kind of taking the biscuit. It was Blake who twisted my arm. And he did have to twist because there was a bit of history between us. We hadn't spoken for years, ever since this row over a band he was pushing, a girl band that I had no interest in because I didn't think our readers would have any interest in them and that's how it always worked and he knew that. The whole thing was silly when I look back on it but at the time we were both career-centred narcissists and we were at loggerheads over it. Basically, he wanted me to run a feature on these girls and I wanted some exclusive access and a whole other list of demands. In those days, and we're going back twenty years or so, I liked to think I had integrity and there were certain principles to bear in mind when some promoter or a record company got in touch to cajole you into covering their latest project. I mean, they were tough, these people. They were salespeople and they were pushing something new every other week like they were just dealing in a new product and in a sense that's what it was all about. So you always tried to push back a bit for something exclusive, just something you wouldn't see repeated in every publication up and down the country. Because once a band or an artist had an album or a single launch or a tour on the go the phone would ring and the same rigmarole would kick off. Everyone in the media, from the TV and radio stations to the newspapers and magazines, all got the same call. But there was a pecking order, you know what I mean? And you could tell that when a call from one of these people came in after midday, that they had already been on to the other papers and magazines, or at least the ones they wanted to be featured in. And the big shots, they got flown out to Wembley to watch the band with the promise of an interview and maybe a photoshoot. If you were down the bottom of the pecking order, maybe a small magazine with a low circulation, you might have been lucky to get a five-minute interview over the phone and be thrown a couple of photos that were doing the rounds. That's just the way it worked.

As a working journalist I was in the top third somewhere. The paper had a good circulation so we had a bit of clout when it came to our demands. And I agreed to a bit of space inside for Blakey, a column, half-page, page maybe, if there was an exclusive photoshoot. I needed good photos because I knew the bosses wanted good photos. The thinking was a young girl band starting off had nothing to say, so the photos had to do the talking. That's just the way it was. It was terrible. So the greedy bastard Blake wanted the cover of the entertainment weekly we ran if he was going to shell out for a photographer. Anyway, cut a long story short, off he went over my head and next thing I get a call from the boss telling me to give him the cover, no exclusive photos. So what do you do? You have to give him the cover. That kind of thing didn't happen all that often.

But there's always stuff going on in the background that you don't get to hear about. There is advertising to consider. If the staff wanted free tickets to gigs who were they going to ask? You scratch my back and all that. I always tried to stick to my principles until they just began to crumble. There's only so many times you can defend principles against this barrage until you begin to question their worth. Ask yourself why you're bothering when it's obvious nobody really gives a shit. So you become cynical and cynicism goes with the territory just like alcohol, bachelorhood and a bad back. Now, as we know, the tables have turned and it's you doing the begging because the bloggers, the YouTubers, the social media influencers on Instagram get the call first. Not the old hacks like me. And I'm just worn out.

Anyway, my relationship with Blakey soured after that. I told him at the time. I rang him later that week and said, fuck you Brian, for going over my head. And do you want to know what he said? He said, I didn't go over your head, son, I stepped on it. And I didn't get to where I am without stepping on heads. So fuck you back.

I didn't mind the fuck you bit. But he called me son. Son, imagine? I was in my thirties at the time. I said, fine, whatever, fuck you too Brian. And he said fuck you again. And we fucked each other back and forward until one of us hung up, don't know who it was. There was no point making a drama out of it. But we didn't deal directly with each other after that.

So when I got a call from him one morning I was stunned. It wasn't long after that lark in the park with Jake. We'd been corresponding on emails when we really had to. Or I'd talk to one of his reps if there was something urgent. But we hadn't actually spoken in a long, long time. And he was semi-retired by then anyway. But he calls me up one morning and starts talking to me like we were still best pals, you know what I mean?

Andy, how have you been old mucker? And I'm about to go, fuck you all over again but I restrain myself. Great, I tell him. How are you since you last stood on my head? And there was a pause and what sounded like a bit of a titter. Blake was, I mean, beneath all the swagger and so on, he could be good company, he was a funny guy at the best times. And I could visualise him on the other end of the phone, covering a laugh with his hand. And sometimes, that's just the best way to heal old wounds. Laugh and forget about it.

And he says, did I really stand on your head? Maybe you were looking at things the wrong way up, Andy. So I say, well I was able to see that girl band of yours disappear from whatever angle I was looking at, Brian. And there's a pause. Because they didn't last. They were gone in less than a year. And they were nice girls. But their first single bombed and the album was pretty bad. We didn't give it a favourable review. I don't think anybody did. And when the second single barely charted that was that. You don't get another crack at it. Not when you're a manufactured band like that. There's a budget and there's a window and that's it. And the word was Brian had put a lot of money into them himself. I didn't want to rub it in, but it was nice to get that shot at him all the same.

So there's a pause and he laughs. Okay, he says, you owe me that one. Now can we move on? And I say, yes, let's do that. So he asks me if I'd heard of a kid – everyone is a kid for Brian – a kid called Jake, Jake Greenbaum. Greenbaum like the Norman Spirit in the Sky Greenbaum, he says.

So the first thing I do is try to lie, a little. I've heard the name now you mention it, I tell him. And he laughs at me. I saw you in Merrion Square a couple of weeks back, Andy, come on. I know you're losing your magic but you've still got a job to do. What can you tell me about him?

Fair enough, Brian, I say. Would you believe it if I told you that guy sent in one of his CDs, we're talking years back, years. I didn't even know he was still around so it was encouraging to see him out there. And there's this pause from Blakey at the end of the line. Encouraging, he asks me, encouraging how? Well, encouraging seeing someone with a bit of vintage in them still out there trying, that's why. So why didn't you do something about him at the time then, he asks me. Ah, you know how it is, he just slipped through the cracks, I tell him. And he laughs. You don't let something good slip through the cracks, Andy, he says. Anyway, he has a real sense of purpose this guy and I'm getting behind him. Just wanted to let you know.

Now, after so many years of silence Blakey would not just call to let you know something. And it surprised me. It really surprised me. Because the last I heard, Blake was winding down and getting out of the business. But he goes on to tell me he'd already talked with Jake, up at his own house and I was gobsmacked. That's how fast he'd moved on him. And Blake does not invite people to his house unless he has clear intentions of following through with an offer. He has an office for everything else.

So you want me to write something on him now, Brian? Is that what this is about, I ask him. No, wait, hold off, he says. There's a bit more to it than that. He's doing this play. Don't know if you witnessed the row that morning with the young girl and Jake's girlfriend, he says. I did, I tell him. Which is why I'm even more surprised you're willing to get involved. You normally steer well clear of any conflict. This is the good kind, he says. Anyway, I've become more tolerant.

So he tells me Jake was going to do a slot in a school, which I admit I thought was just, underwhelming, you know what I mean? How was that going to boost someone's profile? But I was missing the logic behind it. It had been so long since Blake and I had had any dealings with each other I'd forgotten he was in possession of, how would you say, Machiavellian tools that had placed him at the top of his game for so many years. So he asked me to go, just to gauge the temperature, see if Jake was generating any real heat. Heat. Blake liked that term. And I knew then he had a strategy already in place.

So I agreed to go without expecting too much and used the pub around the corner as a refuge and got back just in time for Jake's entrance, which was — do you know, I still can't make up my mind about it. I sat there watching this piece of theatre on my phone and I didn't want to enjoy it all, I'm a traditionalist. But I was still captivated by the sheer audacious nature of it, pushing the audience to their limits with something like that. It was very courageous. I mean, talking about breaking the fourth wall. And I looked around, and almost everyone in the audience was fixated, staring at their phones when their attention, as we all well know, should be fixed on the stage. That's where the action should have been taking place but it wasn't. Look it was just a cheeky device that well executed and hats off. Even his exit broke the rules. He just vanished like a ghost, not a word. I was hoping to talk to him afterwards but nobody knew where he was. Problem is though, pull a stunt like that and you raise the bar. What's he going to do next? Where is he going to go next? That was going to get out there quickly and he was going to need to respond to the sudden wave of fresh interest, you know what I mean, that tricky follow up.

So on the way out who did I bump into only that girl, Jenny, with her father. Feisty little one, so she is. Don't think we saw eye to eye on the whole evening and a couple of days later I get an email from her to check Jake's YouTube channel. And there it was, the clip from that night clocking up thousands of views. And it just made me feel like an old donkey put out to pasture. It made me feel small, insignificant, past the sell-by date. However you want to put it.

I mean, here's where I'm at when it comes to technology. I still have rolls of 35mm film at home and a room full of obsolete camera gear. I have one digital camera with a fixed lens that I use for work and at a push, I'll use my phone for convenience. But whatever this girl did, it just reminded me that I had now become a victim of entropy. That irreversible process, you know what I mean, where you slip off the peak and begin that long, slow slide back down. It's just inevitable. That super motor you bought ten or fifteen years ago that fails to start most mornings. The obsolete camera gear that's no longer worth taking out and cleaning up for a day out in the hills. The things that used to take minutes that now take hours. And all those dreams you still harbour? Young girls like Jenny will come along and take them from you. It's not theft, it's not a crime. Those dreams are just not yours anymore. Which leads me back to Jake. He was so right, all those years ago, when he wrote me that letter. Those words were coming back to haunt me. 'The world gets bigger and diminishes the dream; or, worse, that same dream gives up on you and finds a younger mind to occupy and leaves yours with its ghost.' Do you know what I call this, this thing, this process if you like. I have to give it a musical sobriquet. The melancholy blues, I call it. A good man feeling bad about the things he never did.

I watched that clip from that evening in the school over and over and over again. And I admired it so much. But what I admired most was that somehow Jake had managed to keep his dreams alive instead of allowing them to become regrets. That's what I admired. And it would never matter if Jake went on to fail, because he was still an authentic individual. That's what I admired. So maybe Blake was right. He was moving with a real sense of purpose. But as an old hack, my question was, where had he been?

## *Paul Smith (Smithy). Jake's childhood friend.*

See, you have to ask yourself, why does a chef love doing what he's doing? And going back to the very basics, the answer is feeding people, right? Seeing his guests enjoy the food he's made. They get a buzz knowing they've made others happy. Jake was no different when it came to his music. That was his first rule, to get a response, emotionally, to bring joy and sadness and laughter and tears and all that. Here's another story.

One of the first songs Jake ever learned to play on the guitar, it was a weird choice, right. It really threw me at the time, so it did. But it was chosen very purposely. And it wasn't what we were all learning to play when we were teens I can tell you that much. Because there was, like, a kind of standard list of songs that you had to know if you wanted to be taken seriously as a guitar player. And most blokes growing up wanted to pick up the guitar. Some learned the piano, violin, wind instruments, whatever, but the lessons were, you know, way more structured with loads of theory and all that. You could always find a guitar teacher for a few quid to teach you the basic scales and chords and before you knew, seriously, within a couple of months, you had a few songs under your belt. The guitar was doable. And it was portable, you know. And of course it was cheap. Get a second-hand guitar, steel strings, few quid, no probs. Throw it on your back, away you go. Off to parties and jam sessions, great craic, so it was. The guitar was like, the instrument of the troubadour. It was independence, even for those few hours when you got away from the Ma and Da for the evening and turned up at a house party. And the other thing was it was just cool.

If you were a good guitar player, and I mean a good player, not just someone who could just strum through a few Beatles numbers, or Donovan, or sing a couple of verses of Mr Tambourine Man or whatever, if you had the real edge on the other players, you were the coolest dude on the street. And with that came the confidence, and the credibility, and the swagger. You know, the swagger. The bravado. Think back to those brazen bands who started all that swagger. Like the Faces, with Rod Stewart and Co giving two fingers to convention and taking fashion to a whole new level of sheer stupidity. They were just looking for ways to say, look at us, we can dress the way we like, right? But Jake, fashion wasn't his purpose. Being cool wasn't even his purpose. The bravado and swagger wasn't his purpose. Actually, I used to think he looked a bit shit a lot of the time, his taste in clothes was pretty brutal. But his real purpose was just to play, just to be heard, listened to and to write what he wanted to write and watch other people enjoy what he did. That's what he put his energy into. And maybe – and this is an argument for later on in the story – but maybe if he did actually concentrate more on pushing the swagger, the cool and the bravado further, he might have been snatched up.

Because the big lead guitar players, the Gallaghers, the Claptons, the Becks and Pages, transcended the music and became giants. Did you ever see those fellas holding back?

Anyway, when we were young fellas, on the streets, to move in the right circles, to get the invites to the parties and to be in demand, you had to know the right songs, the songs that reflected the whole ethos of what it meant to be a great guitar player. And if you went into a musical instrument shop you'd have fellas sitting there in their denims and the long hair stinking of body odour and the whole lot, playing Stairway to Heaven, Smoke on the Water, Paranoid or the riff from Don't Fear The Reaper. Eric Clapton. Layla was so easy, which was why it was so brilliant. Stuff like that. Actually, it got to the point where most of the shops started to put up ban lists on the walls.

You could come into these shops on a Saturday afternoon and pretend you were interested in buying a Fender Strat and plug in and play away for half-an-hour as loud as you like. And you'd have this drone of Smoke on the Water going on. Motorhead. Metallica. Guns N' Roses. It was gas, so it was. Bowie's big songs like The Jean Genie or Moonage Daydream. If you could play Mick Ronson's solo at the end of Moonage Daydream you were the coolest human being in two shoes. I swear to God, that solo still makes the hairs pop up on the back of me neck when I hear it. Eventually, the staff in these places started cracking up, so they did, and the ban lists just got longer and longer. And just like they started to do in the record shops, where you used to be able to go in and listen to an album before you bought it, the practice of using musical instrument shops as rehearsal rooms and record shops as listening booths came to a halt. But you always had the acoustic guitar. That could go anywhere and you could play anything you liked on it. And that was really Jake's instrument of choice.

And Jake, he would have been able to play the instrumental folk stuff that had been big across the water. And a lot of it has become cool after its time, like Nick Drake. He became a massive cult figure years after he died. Jake knew a lot of Nick Drake and he could play those open tunings and leave most guitar players scratching their heads. He was always striving to do what everyone else wasn't. Which brings me back to that song, the first song I ever heard him play to anyone. And, deadly serious now, it was Moon River. Would you believe that? But wait for this. The first person he sang it to was his Ma. God bless him. I was there.

It was a Saturday evening, right, with nothing much on and Jake and I were in the back room of his gaff, just listening to music as we did, chatting, playing darts. And I think there had been some sort of row. His Da wasn't there, he hadn't been around all day and I had the feeling something was up. So it was just his Ma in the kitchen, watching the telly by herself. His brother was gone for the night, he was always out that fella. Anyway, normally, if we were in on a Saturday night like that, and there might be a few of us hanging out, Jake's Ma would come down with a tray of tea and a few biscuits. You know, she was a real motherly type. We were all her boys if we were in her house. But there was no sign of her coming in that evening.

So Jake says to me, Smithy, I want to do something for Mum and I need you to help me. So he explained what he wanted me to do, and I thought it was a bit bloody weird. But it was Jake, nothing was ever really too weird and you just went along with him.

So he had me go into the kitchen, knocked on the door first. And his Ma was sitting there at the table, in her dressing gown, head on her hand, cup of tea, with the telly on. One of those small tellies she had in the kitchen but she wasn't really watching it. She was gazing out the window at the streetlamps outside. And I had a sweeping brush and a desk lamp in my hands and she looks over at me, and nods to the lamp and the brush. What are they for, she asks. And I tell her Jake has something to show you. So I pull out a chair from under the kitchen table and plug the light in at the counter top and switch off the main lights and turn the telly down. And a smile has broken out on her face. She knew it was one of Jake's tricks. But in he comes and just takes a little bow and sits in the chair, strums the guitar for a minute and says, I'd like to sing this song tonight, for my wonderful mum. And he sings it. Moon River. A little slower than I knew it to be. But I only knew it from the Tiffany's film, that was the only version I had heard at the time. Jake had learned the Andy Williams version.

Now I'd heard Jake singing a bit before, but never a full song. As far as I was concerned at the time, he was a guitar player, you see. He'd hum through stuff mostly whenever he was playing. But he never sang until that night. And you know that line you hear, when people say so and so has found their voice? Well, he hadn't. He wasn't a crooner like Andy Williams. It wasn't him just yet. But it was almost his type of song. Almost. Because of the simple emotion in it. He'd made the connection even if the pitching was off. And we felt it. I felt it. He was singing for his Ma because he loved her and he knew she was hurting, it was as simple as that. A young fella showing this affection for his Ma.

Now, thing is, what I didn't realise at the time was that his Da had left that morning. Ran off with another woman. Jake had never told me. And this might sound strange, but it was the only time I had ever seen that situation. We grew up on a street where that kind of thing never happened. Or it was kept well hidden. And it became huge news, it was a scandal. And Jake's Ma had to suffer all the way. And it hit Jake hard, so it did. And the reason he was playing it was because it was one of her favourite songs, you know. I thought it might have been the wrong choice for someone whose husband had just walked out. But she loved it. She just watched and listened while her boy played the song and when he finished, she hugged him and thanked him and whispered something to him. Something along the lines of, we're going to be all right. Maybe. Maybe that's what she said, I didn't hear it too well.

And later that night, Jake's Ma had gone to bed and we were outside the back having a smoke and we got talking about the song. And I put it to him that I'd never heard anyone actually play that song. At least, not anyone our age. And maybe that's the direction to go, I said. Try a different path. Everyone else is still thrashing out Led Zeppelin.

And Jake, he was always this pensive, sensitive sort of kid, always overthinking everything. And he was looking up at the stars, dragging on the cigarette, and he said to me, Smithy, you know what I love so much about music? And I said, what. And he said, it doesn't really have a direction. And he pointed up at the stars briefly. You can't plot a course through music, he said. There are no paths from A to B, you just got to set out and see where it takes you. And I was surprised to hear him say that. So what do you want to be, Jake, I asked him. The big stars don't think like that. And he looks up again at the night sky and he just says, a little star is big enough for me, Smithy. The world is wide and we'll all get a chance to shine. I never forgot those words and they were nice words. And I thought he should have looked after them better.

So, getting to the point finally, after that night in the school he came over to see me. It was early on a Saturday morning when he called and I don't think I'd ever seen Jake that early in the morning. Ever. On any day of the week. But there he was at the front door at, what was it, just after nine o'clock. The little ones were still in their pyjamas – I've two kids, boy and girl, four and three, so I was well up anyway trying to get me head together. And in he comes with his coat swinging off him like a blanket and grabs the little ones, one in each arm, he's a big fella, Jake, and starts tickling them and tossing them round the place. They love him, and they're giggling away, which sort of takes the sting out of been disturbed on a Saturday morning. My missus was still in bed, so I made a pot of coffee and brought her up a cup and stuck the cartoons on for the kids, then we sat in the kitchen and Jake was buzzing, so he was. His knees were going under the table like kango hammers and I was looking at him wondering how much coffee he'd already had.

And I knew he'd done that play in the school just two nights before but it would never have crossed my mind it would have excited him that much. You're talking about the type of thing most people run a mile from every year. And to make things worse, this year was a Broadway show from the 60s with probably no memorable song in it whatsoever, so they wanted Jake's Little Star to help them shine. Something like that, you know. Whatever. I knew that clip had been clocking up a load of hits but, so what? I was really thinking that. So what? I mean, a clip of some guy falling off a ladder can get thousands of hits a day on YouTube. I was happy for Jake but I just wasn't sold on the idea that this was progress in any way, shape or form.

So I ask him, what brings you to the house so early on a Saturday morning? Do you need a loan of a cup of milk? Our Mas used to get us to do that when we were little, go to each other's houses for milk and sugar and stuff when we ran out. It doesn't happen anymore. But it's one of our jokes. Might have been a bit cruel because I knew exactly why he was there and I hadn't seen the clip at that point but I know he's dying for me to look at it.

So he pulls out his phone and plays it for me. Clever, right? Very clever. The whole Facebook live thing going on was clever. That was Jenny now who came up with that. It must have been. Because I don't think it was Jake's idea. And maybe I should have been more excited but don't forget, I've been listening to Jake playing and singing since we were kids. Moon River. So, you know, I've seen a lot of this stuff and forgive me, but I couldn't get over animated about this one either. He nailed it, fair play to him. And at the end of the song, they just gave him this thundering applause and that did send a little shiver. Great, he nailed it. But I didn't say much to him. Still hadn't finished me coffee. Maybe it was because I was just wrecked tired with the kids up at dawn or maybe something in me finally forced me to take a tougher line and instead of clapping him on the back as I always did I just said it out straight. Jake. What the hell are you doing?

And he puts the phone down on the table and the smile is gone suddenly. What do you mean, he says. Do you not see it, he asks me. See what, I say. See how innovative that was, he says. The reaction I'm getting. Something is happening, he says. And I look at him. But you don't know what it is, do you? Mr Jones? Dylan wrote that when he was, what, not even 25, I tell him.

And he just sips his coffee and sort of shrugs a bit. So what's your point?

My point, I tell him, is that you were writing great stuff when you were 25. Now you're forty-something and you're showing me clips of yourself playing for kids and grandmothers at a school. I mean, why don't you go and get a job on a kids' programme, write songs about rainbows, create a new character, some floppy-haired old hippy who sings for the children. Whatever. Earn a living instead of fuelling this fantasy. If it were meant to happen, it would have happened by now, Jake.

I was getting annoyed and the kids' cartoons were blaring in the background. I might have got carried away but I was wasting my time. He just stares back at me. See, if you want a reaction from Jake, there are only a few buttons you can press. And to get to those buttons you got to find where they're hidden. And to find where they're hidden, you got to get through a labyrinth of shite. And to get there, you need a bloody road map that's criss-crossed with thousands of minor routes, deadly serious. It's a nightmare. There are only certain things that are going to rouse him. And me ranting was never one of them.

So he just sits there and waits until I'm done. Then he says precisely that, so are we done? Don't forget, you were the one who pulled me back into this, Smithy, he says then suddenly.

And that was sort of true. Sort of true. But again, that's for a little further down the road. And I felt a bit bad then. So I say, here, well done, Jake, you know I'm happy for you mate. You blew them away, obviously. But I worry about you sometimes, that's all.

Then he suddenly leans over and hugs me, across the kitchen table. And he says, you just worry about your kids and let me worry for myself. Which made me laugh, but when I thought about it later, it wasn't funny at all. Because he was actually believing things were falling into place. And at that point, that morning, I didn't know he had been talking to that bastard Brian Blake, or Andy Kirwan even. I didn't know. And I reckon he had come over to tell me that too but had probably backed off when he saw the mood I was in. So instead he went in and joined the kids on the couch for like, an hour, while I went about the jobs that have to get done on a Saturday morning in a busy family home. Not that Jake knew anything about that. He literally sat there, watching Thomas the Tank Engine and stuff, laughing and joking with the kids.

## *Katie Ryan. Girlfriend.*

Jake revealed himself in small doses over the months we started seeing each other . . . stories, tales, anecdotes, fleeting memories. As if they came to him in voices. And I'm sure those voices didn't talk or whisper or shout or scream they sang, because every episode he'd relate was connected in some way to music. Sometimes these stories would be dark, but more often than not they would be quite lovely. Jake didn't just deal in sound he could deal in sensitivity.

There was one night, we were in town and we passed by this bar and he just stops and cups his hands against the glass and stares in through the window like a small boy at a toy shop. He was gazing in and his reflection was looking out at me then he suddenly starts singing this song to himself very quietly. Murmuring really. The dream's not real, something like that. Sounded like a nursery rhyme. What's that you're singing, Jake, I ask him. And he turns back to look at me. That Katie, he says, pulling his hair back into an elastic and looking back in through the window once more, is a very significant song, he says. How so, I ask him. It sounds more like a nursery rhyme. I loved nursery rhymes, he said. And we look in through the window together, even though it's a busy restaurant and there are people eating, there we are, both of us with our noses pressed against the glass and it was cold that night and . . . there we are, creating little halos with our breaths.

This used to be a cracking little venue, Jake says. There was music six nights a week back in the day but it closed down when clubbing became more hip than live music. It was one of the hottest places in town, he says, with music every night except Monday, which was the day they put the bands in the diary. And my plan, one of the first plans I ever made with my mind set on music, he says, was to get my first real gig in there and once that was done, I would move on to something else. But my first challenge was to get a spot in there, any kind of a spot, whether that was opening for a band or playing the break, just something that I could tick off as done and set myself something higher for the next one.

And just as he was getting into the meat of his story a waiter comes over to the window and waves at us like we were two little wasps. We better move on, he says.

So what happened, I ask, giving the waiter a finger, did you get it. Well, he tells me, pulling me closer as we walk, I can only assume that the dream-dispensing machine was down to the last couple of coupons that night. I used to call in every Monday to see the bookings manager, he tells me, a guy called Ernie who used to have this huge black, hardback diary that he'd open up every time I came in, turn a few pages, and just shake his head. Nothing yet, son. That's all he would say. And I used to count the pages he'd turn every week and it was never more than four or five. And Ernie — he was a very influential guy, knew all the A&R men who were moving about at the time and should really have been called Big Ern but he was a diminutive figure, deepset eyes and a smoker's rasp so he was known only as Little Ern — once he'd given you his answer that was it. He'd close the book and walk away. Eventually, I came in one Monday afternoon and he grabbed his book and flicked through a few pages and as he was about to close it again I stopped him. Can you look a bit further on, I ask him. And he picks his cigarette up from the ashtray and drags on it, staring at me. That's as far as I go, sunshine, he says. And I was just a kid, and I nod politely at him. I know Ernie, but what about turning over a few more pages, I ask him. I've gone into April, he snaps back, do I look like a fuckin' time traveller? And he glances up at me and turns over a few more pages then brings his index finger down suddenly. Twenty minutes, can you do that, we've an opener free May 9, Saturday. Big band in. Big night. Big fucking opportunity sunshine, can you take the heat?

So you did it, I ask him. Well, yes and no, he says. I had planned to play five songs. Five was a very good number. A strong opener, a strong closer and three in the middle is more than enough. And I had practised those five songs so much I could play them in the dark. That's actually what I used to do, he says. In fact, that's exactly what I used to do. In the kitchen every night I'd turn off all the lights and practise the songs. The only light I ever had was from the moon or the stars or the street light outside. But they were orange, he says, and I didn't like orange. Mum came in one night, he says, asked me why I played with the lights out. So she called me my little star, my little boy, the romanticist, gazing out the window and up at the night sky.

Anyway, we start walking on and he pulls the exact date out of his head. May 9, 1987, he says, was Eurovision night. It was a big thing back then because Johnny Logan was representing Ireland for a second time. And Johnny, he was up for a second win. And as it was approaching the time for me to go up and do my slot, he says, someone asked for the TV to be turned on because the points were coming in. Even the sound guy had left his desk and gone up towards the bar to watch the voting and everything was delayed.

So I had to sit it out and wait and watch those 20 precious minutes slip away as Johnny Logan was clocking up points for Hold Me Now. Don't be afraid the dream's not real, that was the line from the song I was singing earlier, he says. So I only got to do one song, very quickly, with the main act standing next to the stage looking at their watches. And I wasn't asked back. Not on the strength of that one song. Because I picked the wrong one to play, he says. What was it, I ask him. Well, he says, I knew I had one song to play and one only.

So I panicked and chose a popular choice because the place was so lively, and knocked out a busker's favourite, Neil Young's Heart of Gold. Great song but what I should have played was the one that was really nagging at me, the one that I was already singing in my head as I climbed up onto the stage. It was one of my own songs, I should have just gambled on it. Put it out there. At least I would have shown some courage. But I bottled it and I decided after that night to always trust the first voice you hear. Even if you don't like it.

And you didn't get a second chance then, not when there were hundreds of musicians and singers and songwriters all over Dublin and beyond looking to play.

So Katie, he says, Johnny Logan won that night. His dream was real. People say success is like climbing a mountain, but sometimes success is more like cleaning toilets. You're always one brush away from hitting shit. That was my lesson that night, he tells me. Getting that gig was the hardest thing to do. Learning the songs was hard. Going in every Monday facing Ernie was the hard part. Not having a father to share my wins and losses and stories with when I came back home on a Saturday evening was hard. And the gig should have been the reward. The easy bit. But in the end, I ignored that voice. And it was a sweet voice, I still remember her singing. Her, I ask? That's right, he says. The voices to trust are always female.

And it wasn't long after that he decided to go and play in the school. Guided by a voice, no doubt. And when he went out that night I thought to myself, Jake, sorry, did you not learn from that experience? And guess what? I didn't bother going to that play at all. Does that surprise you? I didn't want him doing it so I just didn't go. There was no row, no falling out or anything like that. I just believed it was regressing, after all the progress we had been making it was the wrong thing to do. In the space of just a few months we had grown our base and had a few thousand fans on Facebook. And that was only the beginning. And it was all my work, by the way. So for Jake to go and do what he did for this girl and her drama society was like a slap in the . . . actually, no, I'm not even going to give him that. I'd take his fucking hand off. But seriously, I had put a lot of thought into choosing the places to perform in and he opts for a school hall. Coming up to Christmas? Bet you know what I'm going to say next. Jesus Christ Jake! You regale me with your allegorical tales. I'll stick to practicalities. And every chance is either a potential opportunity or a dud. And you have to learn how to spot which is which. You got your voices I got mine and mine is called reason. I know it's a school you're off to, Jake, but what are you going to learn from this calamity? But he went anyway. And I let him go.

## *Donnie Miller. Record store owner, old friend.*

Remember those records that Jake brought down to my store. Would you believe, I actually held on to all those boxes. For all those years that Jake went into retreat, I held onto them, figuring one day he'd come back. Put them out the back and waited. Eventually, when green shoots started appearing in the vinyl market again I had to start selling them off. But they'd always been Jake's records. That's how I looked at them.

I remember Smithy would be in every now and then, and I'd ask him for a heads up on Jake sometimes. How's he been? And Smithy would be like, you know, he's doing fine, I'll tell him you said hi and so on. And one day I really needed to make some space, so I said to him, listen I still got all those LPs that you and Jake brought in and he just said, hey Donnie, you go ahead and get rid of them. Jake's not going to be able to get them back now. What do you mean, able, I asked him. He's just not in a great place at the moment, Smithy said. You just get rid of them.

And I thought the worst for sure. I really thought he was in trouble. I'd thought that the day he'd come in, he looked a bit shook, and just as I'd thought then, I was just hoping it was nothing to do with narcotics or anything. But other than that, I didn't know much and it wasn't my business to ask. So I began selling off the albums a few at a time, put them on the walls and displayed them. Put a few on eBay. And I sort of forgot about the rest and put them into the store room out the back. Then, boy it was few years later, Smithy comes in, and he wasn't in to browse or anything, cos I could tell he had a purpose. I'm looking for an album, Donnie, he says, and it's a long shot. Eric Clapton's Rainbow Concert and I'm hoping you still have Jake's copy. Have you sold it yet? And he's looking at me with these hopeful eyes and I can see something is going on. I've no idea, I tell him. They're all over eBay, I say to him. You can pick one up easy.

No, no, well, if I can get the original that Jake had it will be brilliant, he says. And I start laughing. That was about twenty years ago, Smithy, I say. But, we go and rummage in the boxes, he helps me, and it's there.

How much do you want for it, he asks.

Who's it for, is it for Jake?

And he nods his head, yeah, he says, I want to bring this over to him. So how much do you want?

So I say, you go and take it. Then I finally ask him, what's going on, Smithy. And he looks at me as he takes the record out of the box. Well, now that you're asking, he says, I need one more favour. Shoot, I say. And he slides the album back in the sleeve and says, Clapton's Rainbow Concert, I'm sure you know the background to it, he says. And I say, sure, more or less, it was when Clapton had gone into hiding out of his mind on all kinds of substances and his good buddy Pete Townshend organised a concert to drag him back to the land of the living and this was the result. And Smithy smiles at me. Right, so I'm hoping when we bring this over to Jake he'll understand the, you know, the symbolism or whatever, he says. And you want me to tag along, I ask him. Right, you can play Pete Townshend on his guitar. Sure, I say, I can't play. Doesn't matter, thing is, Donnie, he says, Jake has squandered a lot of valuable time, you know, and it's running away on him fast. And Jayzis Donnie, he's my brother, you know? I just want to see him doing something that's going to make him happy. You mean playing again, I say. Yeah, exactly, Smithy says. Now, he'll see the irony in this. I'm not trying to give him anything other than a laugh and a reason to get out and start living again, do something that'll make him happy.

And I say, sure, I hear ye. You're a good guy, Smithy. I hope Jake realises that. And Smithy just shakes his head, doesn't do praise, that kind of guy. So I say, look, if I can help, I'll help. But I do ask him if it's narcotics. It's not drugs, he assures me. It was a personal tragedy, and it was very hard on him and it's taken a long time. And I think, when his Ma passed away recently it compounded everything, you know, Donnie, it's not drugs. He's fine, he's actually fine. He just needs to know there are still fellas out there who care about him.

I guess, I wasn't even sure whether I was the guy Jake needed to see. But Smithy assured me I was the guy Jake needed to see and I was cool with that.

So later that week, we go on over to Jake's house, and I'm kind of expecting the worst. I'm expecting him in squalor, damp, some run-down old place that had been neglected and Jake, looking twice his age and all out of shape. I guessed if he hadn't the money to come back in and claim his prized records for twenty years then I only imagined he wasn't looking after his life and health too good either. So, it would be true to say I approached his house, gingerly, is about the best way to phrase it.

But from the outside, it seemed all good. He had hanging baskets in the porch and the windows were clean, everything was painted, the front door and roof fascia. All looked after. Then he opens the door before we'd even knocked and I'm seeing this totally different guy to the one I'd known. His hair is tied back when it was always a mess and he's fit-looking and lean, I recall him as this scrawny sort of guy who maybe needed sleep. His skin even has a glow to it, like he's been juicing or something. And he brings us straight into his, man, it's this lair. It's like a Bedouin cave or something, with rugs and stuff on the walls, posters and trinkets and things. It's cluttered but it's clean. It even smells clean. And he has the fire lit and a couple of candles burning and I can see out through the kitchen into a yard that's abundant with greenery and it's like his own little world. And he hugs me, great to see you, Donnie. And we sit down on this sofa stacked with cushions and he's looking at what I have in my hand.

It's been a while, he says, nodding at me, studying my face which has probably aged twice as fast as his. It's been years, Jake, I say to him. I tried to hold on to most of your records, but… and he puts a hand up and shakes his head before I even had time to finish. Don't go there, he says. I needed the money then and a deal is a deal. Did you sell many of them, he asks. Most, I say. Even the Hendrix with the gatefold sleeve? First to go, I say. The Sabbath? That too. Bet you still have that Moody Blues double live album though, he asks me. I do, you can have that back, I say. And we all start chuckling. And I'm thinking, I have all these questions on the tip of my tongue but I'm holding fire, and I'm looking around the room and there isn't one photograph anywhere apart from that of Jake with who I'm sure is his Mom. So he sees me looking. That's my Mam, he says. She died a few months ago. I heard, Jake, I'm sorry for your troubles, I say. It's fine, he tells me, she went peacefully. In the hospital. Her last request was for me to go in and sing a song for her. And I did, in the ward with three other people lying in their beds and a nurse sitting on a chair near the door. It was weird. Moon River she wanted to hear. It was the first time I'd played a song to anyone in years. And they all started singing, even the nurse was humming the tune.

How did that feel, I ask him suddenly. And he looks at me, grinning. Come on, Donnie, you Americans. How did it feel? Do you want me to lie down on the couch?

No, I say, to him, I'm being serious. How did it make you feel, to bring those couple of minutes' joy and peace into a hospital ward? It's the first I ever heard of anyone playing in a hospital ward. And I turn to Smithy. Have you ever heard of anyone playing in a hospital ward, Smithy?

And Smithy, he's sitting back on a lounger and he's opened a bottle of beer. No, he says, but Johnny Cash played in prisons. Maybe you could make a couple of hospital albums, Jake? Hospital Ward Blues. I hear my trolley coming, rolling around the bend, Smithy starts singing. But Jake shoots him a look and it was like it had been fired from the mouth of a Magnum in the hands of Clint Eastwood. And Smithy recoils and sits his ass back down and I was glad, cos as much as I would have wanted to see the lighter side of all this, well, there wasn't really one that I could find. So I continue. But, really Jake, I say. Did it not feel good to be playing for someone after all that time? I know your Mom was dying and it wasn't a place for mirth but surely you saw the magic you brought into the room. It's a magic, Jake. No matter how big or how small it's still a gift. Not many people can do it. So, come on, you got to get out there and start doing it again.

And he winces a bit and looks over at Smithy, knowing it was him who had wheedled me into coming over. Donnie, he says, it's good to see you again, really. And I'm happy you've come over and I understand why you're here. But I'm not going to try and go out there and compete with the youngsters who are doing what they are doing now. With pitch perfect voices, all the technology and tools I don't understand even if I wanted to, not to mention the ruthlessness that's required nowadays. They're like kids from Silicon Valley some of them. I mean, where has the fun gone? That's not me. I'm not built to go up against that. Besides, Donnie, I'm staring my forties in the face now. My time has been and gone.

And I laughed then. It was my turn for laughter. Jake, I didn't come here to flatter you. Coax you out of retirement like some old wrestler. Nobody's talking about having to compete with anyone. You bring the fun back, have all the fun you want. You can start in my store. And Jake throws me this look. Why not, I say to him. If I could play, I'd be out playing to the goddam trees in the forest. But I can't. And, by the way, I'm in my sixties Jake and I haven't discounted doing that someday. And it's not cos I'm some old hippy either who wants to serenade the trees, it's because I never impose any limitations on myself until I'm, well, on my dying bed in a hospital ward. And I might just call on you to come in and sing me a last lullaby. If you've gotten up off your lazy ass, that is. Won't be Moon River though. Jake, you come to my store next Saturday afternoon. Do an hour, forty-five minutes, half an hour even and I'll give you the rest of your albums back, whatever is left, I say. Deal?

And he looks away for a minute, over at Smithy who is swigging his beer, and he just gives him this shrug. So I take the album out of the bag, Eric Clapton's Rainbow Concert, and right away he picks up the signals from it, and he's smiling and shaking his head at Smithy. That's your copy, I say to him. And he takes it and gives a bit of a chuckle. But actually he seems a bit overwhelmed. Then Smithy pipes up. When we were kids, Jakey, do you remember how we became mates. Do you remember Jakey?

I remember, Jake says. Swapping records in school, we hardly even spoke to each other much, just swapped records every Friday. Think this was originally yours, Smithy, he says. It was, you kept it, Smithy answers. And he's staring at the album in his hands and I'm suddenly seeing how emotional he has got. So I hug him, a big hug, a tree hug if you will but Jake is a thin guy so I ease off and just stare him in the eyes. Hey, I say, come on, buddy. What do you say?

# FIVE

## The Puppet Master

***All the world's his stage by Andy Kirwan***
***(published in his weekly column, Planet Rock)***

*We know not the hour nor the place; we know not the time he will spend among us; but we do know he will come. Thus I found myself reflecting a little more than 30 days out from the eve of Christmas, not on bended knee before a crib but in a hall, a school hall in suburbia awaiting the arrival of one Jake Green, a musical muse steeped in the values of the troubadour and given to unannounced appearances in locations not normally disturbed by the sound of music. And we are talking hill tops and ground floors, of record stores and cafes and vintage clothes shops selling leather jackets with jangling key chains and button badges and cheeky skirts that have hugged a lifetime of voluptuous flesh. Lord, do forgive me. Jake Green is not your common-or-garden busker, but he may appear in a garden near you at any time, so take note. On this night, the night before the night, before the night, before the night (count to 30 if you will) before Christmas, there I was on hard chair seated, a joyous spectator of the first performance ever on these shores (I'm quite sure, please Google if you wish) of The Music Man, a little known but apt setting for Jake Green who arrived not to the beat of an angel's wings nor even on a mule because, in fact, he never arrived at all. Can I stop with the liturgical linguistics now? Good.*

*For those regular readers who normally find me in the arenas and concert halls, particularly at this time of year, cosying up to the PR reps to be sure of the hottest tickets for the new year, it might seem a tad shocking that I went to see an act in a school hall. But then, those of you who are already familiar with the mature and sophisticated songs of Jake Green (and the numbers are rising as I write) you are probably seething that this was a missed opportunity to see him in – yet again – very unusual surroundings. But, this was no stage entrance that I had ever witnessed before. Are you ready? On this occasion Jake proved that he is out to do his damndest to compete with the youngsters by surpassing himself in the novelty factor and broadcasting a live feed of himself as he trod the path, singing and playing, up to and into the venue, appearing only at the last moment to play himself out beautifully with a celestial harmonica solo that would have silenced the birds. And speaking of . . . fans are still bemused by Jake's bird cage which bedecks his every setting. And no, I don't know what it means either but one day, I hope, Jake Green will indeed fly. The question is how high, because there is just too much stacked against someone who is, at this stage in his life, trying to get a foot in a door that is being beaten down by artists half his age, and in the crowded singer/songwriter genre, I fear a real bruising. My other concern for Green is the amount of ground that has to be covered before you are even considered these days by record labels, radio plays, shows etc. And I'm not just talking physical ground here, the pavements and highways and bars and clubs where one's stripes as a live performer are earned; I'm also referring to the virtual ground, this vast, bottomless otherworld, that must mirror one's endeavours in the real world but be an even better reflection of one's true self. I wish him well, but, I do worry that Jake's hour has been and gone. Oh dear Lord (I know I said I'd quit the liturgical linguistics but one last time).*

*To check out Jake Green's latest clip, visit his YouTube Channel.*

## *Andy Kirwan. Music writer and journalist.*

Before I go any further, it's probably right and proper that I lob my own cards on the table. Because if I don't, people are going to accuse of me of all kinds of terrible things. Bitterness mostly. So, here it is.

I'm what you might call a failed musician. There, I said it. It hurt actually to say that, because I've never said it before. I've never spat it out, just like that, do you know what I mean? Out loud. But, because of all this, all the events and occurrences and, him, basically, Jake, and how involved I became I just felt inclined to get it all out there.

And I now find myself lost somewhere in that wasteland of post-middle age. And it's an awful place to find yourself if you're dragging the weight of failure behind you. You don't have to. I mean, you can always cut it loose. But that's easier said than done. So it's a different place for different people, depending on what your life has been like in the years leading up to it. Some people are washed out and as good as gone by the time they reach it. Others have long achieved their ambitions and are just happy to be alive, living it out to the max and looking forward to winding down as they head towards the next big decade.

Then there are the eternal optimists, the ones who say 50 is the new 40, the ones who try to reinvent themselves and, fair enough, many do. They find a new niche that suits them. And you get the odd straggler, who through pure perseverance, finally manages to achieve a lifelong ambition at this late stage. They have just never given up.

Then there are people like me, who realise that, whatever it was they really wanted to do, whatever dream it was that kept them awake at night as a child, it's not going to happen. I mean, you hit fifty and life is tough enough, even physically. Strange things happen to a man's body at that age. I was always thin, now I'm thin and fat at the same time. I'm a borderline alcoholic, as in, I've got to the border and just haven't crossed over. Yet. I'm not fit and I probably never will be. So you're struggling to row down this river, against a heavy current, in bad weather and with tired bones. And you think, well, I've got to jettison something. So you look over your shoulder and there seated right behind you is that other you, that dream you. And he doesn't look too happy either because he's still in the back seat, you know what I mean? He should be in the front, up there leading the way with a big grin on his face sailing off into the sunset. So what do you do? Here's what. Don't mind all your mindfulness and coping mechanisms they teach you at these overpriced well-being classes. It's very easy.

You go home, you stick on some music, pick a favourite, whatever it is, in my case it was Miles Davis's Kind of Blue. And I chose that one because there is no other album, ever made, that penetrates the dark recesses of the human soul like that masterpiece. I know it gets an airing at every nouveau riche dinner party every weekend. It's almost like the token jazz album everyone has in an otherwise sprawling collection of mediocrity. It's left conveniently on the coffee table for guests to take note of. But somewhere, right now, out there, those opening piano chords to Flamenco Sketches are being played in someone's home. Somewhere in the world. Those simple, percussive notes on the bass. They're out there right now. And they're doing what they do to everyone. They're providing the human condition with a melody. It's like he was the supreme puppet master when he recorded that. It's a universal piece of music that will force you to probe every crevasse in your psyche and question its worth, you know what I mean? Try it, if you don't believe me.

And that's what I did one night, not so long ago after I had met up with Brian for a chat about Jake. We had a very frank discussion. One of those frank discussions that you want to tear yourself away from but you know you need to stay because it's doing you good while making you feel bad at the same time. That's the melancholy blues. You feel bad but you know it's doing you good. And I got home afterwards, with a knot, in the stomach. I could feel it. Because I knew that if I got in any deeper, into this whole Jake thing, I'd be helping him realise his dreams while mine remained submerged under the weight of my years. I knew that, but Blake, he talked some sense into me, not that he was charming at all about it. He was like someone coming into your room early in the morning and very roughly pulling back the curtains and pushing the window open so you're blinded by sheets of light and chilled by the fresh air and although it's not pleasant at first, eventually you're just thankful for it, otherwise you would have slept on in the dark.

So Brian and I, we had a meal in a steak house in town and got down to business with a couple of Scotches – you need a drink when you're doing business with Blakey. It's like two guys in a saloon with one hand on their guns and another on the bottle. You hammer things out with a threat of near violence hanging in the air. I would work with him on the right terms. And I believe I got them. But my salvation was going to be at the expense of finally facing my demons. If Jake hadn't come along, I might have just lived out the rest of my days without ever confronting them again. Write a couple of books. Do a bit of radio. There were options. I had a small pension. I wasn't going to finish up on the streets. But I took Blake's offer to go freelance and work with him on the PR side of things. That was it. Deal with the devil done.

When I get home, I, I blindly lurch for cold vodka, the frozen tears of a goddess which upon consumption glazes the eyes with a beautiful frost and the consciousness with a fog which, far from inducing blind panic, brings instead an air of comfort. A curtain descends on the future and its blank canvass is such a relief. Feel free to draw as you wish. Me, I'm on a river, rowing hard against a current. I'm not alone. Behind me sits my dream me and after all these years his voice is fading, it's down to a whisper. But he's still there. And he taps my shoulder softly. Andy, he says. Andy, is it going to happen? When. I ignore him and he raises his voice. Loser. Loser. Keep on rowing, loser. He's whispering into my ear, tapping me on the shoulder, when's it going to happen? Is it ever going to happen?

It was well dark outside, no stars, no moon. I use the phone to light the hall and catch my ghost in the mirror, pale, retreating. Then I finally did what I had to do, what I needed to do for some time. I turned around and tipped him overboard, into the water. And you're probably wondering, how did I do that? Some mindfulness technique or something? No. I broke the mirror. With the butt of the bottle, into hundreds of pieces, and as it shattered and fell to the floor I looked down and saw my reflection in fragments. A hand there, a limb here, an ear and so on.

I didn't cry or anything like that. In fact, I had this surge of sobriety. And I found my eye on the floor and frowned at myself first then I smiled. Because it was just me. My dream was gone. No more torment. No more nights of splintered sleep. And I know this all sounds insane, but there has to come a time in your life when, if the dream hasn't happened, you've got to let go of it. Jettison the broken dream. Push it overboard. Otherwise, it will tear you apart slowly. And the land of broken dreams is a lonely, terrible place to live out the rest of your days. And once that act is carried out, you've got the weight off the shoulders. And it'll hurt. But that pain subsides, you know what I mean? The hurt of a broken dream though, that's a long hurt. But there is nothing wrong with a bit of reinvention. Jake taught me all that. He's been teaching me for years, ever since he wrote me that letter. You know how you give that other you a voice? That voice, for me, was Jake. And would you believe I told this story to Jake some time later. I told him because I was convinced he would relate to it in some way. I never planned to tell him. And maybe I should never have. We just got talking one evening and it felt like a good time. What was I looking for in return? Maybe a bit of empathy?

But it was very foolish of me. I told him everything, the whole thing with the metaphor of the river and me on the boat, my dream haunting me and goading me in the back until I threw him overboard. Miles Davis. The vodka. The whole thing. And Jake, he sort of looked at me and nodded slowly and the response was a long time coming, and he said, well, would it not have just been easier to swap places?

And at first I thought it was a joke, one of his dark jokes that comes with that grin of his. But he was kind of frowning at me and waiting for an answer. I think he was genuinely expecting an answer. There was no badness in it, there was no badness in Jake full stop. But there was certainly, at times, no tact. Or, some kind of ineptitude when it came to being on a level with other people's emotions. And for someone whose music claims to be so in touch with sensitivity, the response floored me. I just thought, what a heartless bastard.

And when he sat there, gazing at me, I thought – you know the way you can have hundreds of thoughts condensed into a moment in a conversation – I thought, so what are you up to, Jake? Why haven't you done what I did? That's what I was thinking. I had the courage. He didn't have that many years left before he found himself in shit creek with the fog coming down, just like me. But of course, he'd no intention of ending the dream. He'd only begun dreaming all over again. And he was lucky that life was giving him this second chance. And, I mean, as much as I hated to admit it, I now needed his dream to work out too. We all did. So I smiled back at him. Good one, Jake. Why didn't I just swap places? Good one, Jakey.

## *Brian Blake. Promoter and manager.*

BOOM! That's the sound it makes. BOOM! That's a hit. A hit song is explosive. Is that what I wanted from Jake? Is that what I was hoping to get from Jake when I signed him up? What did I want from Jake? Did I want a hit? One of those huge songs that takes over the airwaves? Well, it didn't matter. I was never going to get that because those songs, they're put together in the type of room that a kid like Jake wouldn't last an hour in.

Here's the thing, Jake is your old-school, melody and lyrics, meat and veg songwriter. Nowadays, a single song can be the work of so many different people, it's like an assembly line. You got a producer with a whole library of beats and chord progressions. And he's sifting through material from songwriters who have to sign up on some website and pay just to submit their work and get it heard. Anything from five up to fifty dollars a time. It's criminal. The producer might fancy a song. He might just fancy part of a song, a mere segment. So he sends it over to a hook writer to work on the melody, someone else might drop in a bridge and someone else provides a chorus. It's a collaborative process and you can hear the difference between a song that was put together with a hit in mind and something that was created by an artist or a band for themselves, something more cohesive and organic. But I wasn't going to get that kind of explosive hit out of Jake. With Jake, I wanted to build something. Create something very different. It was going to be like building a brand. I was excited about it, I really was.

So I sat Andy down one evening to discuss where we might start with him. I needed a team of people on board and Andy would prove very useful. He was a good writer, bit self-indulgent at times but writers are like that. Can't help themselves. He still had the contacts and he knew a lot about the industry. Problem was, he'd been doing the same thing for years. And so had I. We both needed our eyes opened to how much the landscape had changed.

Here we were, two veterans of our respective industries, with all the experience between us amounting to a whole lifetime. But when you're doing something the same way for so long you're like a big old rock, stuck in the bed of a fast-moving stream. You're safe and secure there and nothing is going to shift you, and that's exactly the problem. Things just pass you by. You're not moving, you're sat still while the waters rush by all around you.

And we both know that what we're really trying to do with Jake is put an old dog into a school of new tricks and make him fit without forcing him to learn too much. All he has to do is bark the way we tell him to. So we needed a team of trainers, like ourselves, but we also needed some youth on our side. Someone who knew exactly what the new tricks were. We needed someone young and able enough, someone with the nous to wag the old bastard's tail. And I had someone in mind.

So I'm sitting there with Andy and we're teasing things out. And eventually I say it, Andy, do you think with the two of us, being at the stage we are, we're missing a vital ingredient. And he looks at me, frowns. Like what, he says?

That clip, from the school drama that went up, I say to him. It did really well. That kid, Jenny, that was all her doing, you know that? I wouldn't have thought about that, Andy. I worry I wouldn't have had the wherewithal to do something like that. All that stuff, it's a whole other world. And he laughs at me. There's really not a lot to it, he says, it's more time consuming than anything else but it's not rocket science. No, no, I tell him, that's where you're wrong. It might as well be rocket science because you're never going to really understand it. Neither am I for that matter, so don't go getting upset, I say. I mean, you write your copy and it's published and away it goes, same time, same day, like clockwork. The people who buy it know it will be there, it's like your pet dog approaching the bowl at feeding time. But that cycle has changed. That clip of Jake, it was genius and somewhere out there, right now, while we sit here contemplating, people are watching it. I read about a new artist the other day, well, she was new to me, had over one billion views on YouTube and she's only 22. We need someone on board with us who can give us reach, 24/7. We need those kinds of numbers, Andy.

So Andy suddenly leans forward. I met that girl the other night, he tells me. Which girl, I ask him. Jenny, he says. The one who orchestrated that whole scene with Jake. You should have been there, it was special, Brian, he says. Totally bonkers, took everyone by surprise but it was just brilliant. We could do worse than pick her brains, he says.

CLINK. The penny, as we used to say, dropped. Andy, we need to do more than pick them, I say. Suddenly, he sits back, looking very uncomfortable. I don't know, he says to me. She's only a child, a young teenager, it would make me a bit uneasy.

We want her brains not her body, Andy, I say to him. Come on, she's a little seer, you and I we're like blinkered old workhorses on the way to the knacker's yard.

So he says nothing for a moment. Poor Andy, he doesn't have that instinct. And he sits forward and rubs his eyes like he's seen the fucking light then he sighs loudly and reaches for his drink but he doesn't pick it up. He just twists the glass on the table and creates this little wave inside it. And he stares at it for a moment, single malt, probably the third or fourth that afternoon, and it's lapping the sides of the glass all thick and viscous like honey. What's the matter, I say to him. You look like I've told you someone just died.

And he gives me this look. Have you ever been rejected, he asks me suddenly. And I sort of shrug and say, yeah, rejection is part of the process. It goes over your shoulder like shit in the wind. And he nods his head. Sure, after you get the first break, then it's all behind you, like shit in the wind. But until you get the break, you stink, isn't that right?

And I don't know if this is a question, an observation, a lament or fucking what. More or less, I tell him. I mean, you take nothing for granted, I say. Rejection can always visit you again. Thankfully, for me it didn't. But I've had failure too, and it's not the same thing, I don't even know which is worse, I tell him. Where is all this coming from, Andy? Are you really uncomfortable about all of this? Is it the money? Spit it out if it is, give me your price, I say. And he's shaking his head at me. No, no, it's not that, he says. What's up then, I ask him. Talk to me, Andy. You're worried about pulling this girl into the circle. Don't. We'll make it worth her while, I'm not in the business of exploiting people. Then he just says, I won't take failure well at this point in my life. Do you understand?

And I'm like, fuck me, what's all this about? Does he need a couch to lie down on and spill his guts out. Something stinks here. Some deep wound that suddenly got opened up. What are you telling me this for, I ask him. What's this got to do with Jake?

I'm just telling you, Brian, you know your business and I know mine, he says. If we press ahead and try and put Jake out there and it all goes wrong, you'll probably get away with it. You've always been in the business of taking risks, that's what you've done. But me, I'm an old hack who has spent his life criticising artists, I'd be hung out to dry if it bombs. And I've nothing else to fall back on. Ah, I see, I say to him. There's a name for what ails you, Andy, and it's called regret, baby!

And I start laughing, very loud. And there came that little glow of schadenfreude and it warmed my insides better than the brandy I was drinking. Because these bastards, journalists, you know, they can cause so much damage to a person's career in a few short paragraphs and it's even worse now that it's moved into a 24/7 cycle. Now you can wake up in the morning and your whole world has been torn apart overnight with just one tweet. Of course, it's not just the journos. It's bloggers and vloggers and influencers and Christ, I can't keep up. But the journos are a dying breed now and they know it, and they're all starting to look back at what they've done and how shallow their lives have been so regret hangs over all their heads, every one of them. They're reeking of fear. And I give a little chuckle at Andy. How ironic, I say. And he nods at me and returns a little grin. Thanks Brian, is all he says.

But I wasn't there to nurse someone through regret. Andy still had clout. And he was a master with words and a master at getting things out of people. He could be grilling someone and they would forget they were ever being interviewed. He had sunk a band I had tried to get going some years before. A girl band. Andy's mastery of words did untold damage to my prospects at a time when I needed his purple prose instead of these bitter snipes. But that's water under the bridge. I wasn't coaxing him in to make him finally eat those words, not at all. I was just forging a chain made of strong links. Andy was one. I needed Jenny for another. But I needed Andy to be the one to ask. My reputation, well, let's say I wouldn't like my daughter to be approached by a man like me.

Andy, I say, you're either with me or you're not. And I want you on board, I do. But if you are coming along, I don't want fucking baggage, I tell him. Leave it at home. I don't care about how bad you feel either for yourself or for anyone else. There's still plenty of future left in front of you so I want you to go home and dump that regret, whatever it is. It'll drown you otherwise.

So he throws back the single malt in one shot, and I don't know which is worse, dealing with a bleeding heart or someone who throws back a scotch that was twenty quid a pop. Then he apologises and lets out this little chuckle. Well, if the worst comes to the worst, I can always go busking myself, he says.

Ah, I say to him. Is this envy rearing its ugly face too, Andy? No, he says, laughing. You sure it's not, I say. As if a music journalist ever had designs on becoming a rock star. That would be as absurd as saying a literary critic harbours dreams of writing a book. And don't ever say busking in front of Jake, by the way. He doesn't like it. And Andy looks at me. Precious is he, he asks. He is now, I tell him.

## *Miles and Jenny Adams. Father and daughter.*

So out of the blue one day Andy Kirwan called me up, which was a bit of a surprise, to be honest. I knew he and Jenny had been in touch. He'd written a short piece about Jake and got her input on it.

And it was the first piece about Jake ever in a mainstream paper or magazine and I think he needed that. All the noise he was getting on social media, look, it was great but there is something about the approval of an expert. It still trumps a thousand hits on social media as far as I'm concerned. It's not just being liked, it's being endorsed.

'All the world's his stage'. That was the headline. He went on to describe the gigs Jake had been doing and how he had been slowly building up a following. There was a very ghostly shot of Jake on stage with the caption, The Music Man, and the piece described how his song had come to feature in a school drama. There was a photo of Jenny too, as the girl who helped him find a new army of followers on YouTube, which made me proud, until I realised why he'd probably included it.

Miles, he says, I have a bit of a favour to ask. I need to catch up with your daughter again. We need to pick her brains on something. We, I say. Who's the we? Then he suddenly changes his mind. Sorry, I meant I. Me, myself and I, Miles. Don't worry about it. Listen, he says, I'll explain everything to you when we meet up. It will be an entirely confidential meeting and it's nothing to do with my work at the paper, I promise you that.

So I'm intrigued. A journalist always wields a certain power, don't they? At the end of the day you generally trust them. If you think about how people have always been willing to hand over photos of their loved ones who have died in accidents or worse, met some terrible, violent death, there is this assumption that, no matter what the context is, journalists are on the good side. And I'm not going to lie, there's also this little buzz of excitement that you're going to be involved in something. Something bigger than yourself. Yippee! I might get to be part of a story in the making! Seriously, I was intrigued. So of course I wanted to meet him. But, looking back now, if there was ever a line I crossed, that was probably it. I was proud. And you're never more vulnerable than when you're proud. I should have just said, Andy, whatever it is you're up to, you're not dragging my child into it. And left it at that. And it's entirely plausible that none of what came after would ever have happened. But I didn't. He lit the beacon and in we went.

So we met him later that week, on a Friday afternoon, in a café in town. And he sat opposite Jenny at the table. I'd warned Jenny that I'd be doing the talking and any requests would be approved by me and she was to just sit tight and smile politely. That was all fine until Andy popped the question about where she thought Jake might fit on the, how did he put it, fleeting and unforgiving terrain of today's musical landscape, and she was off. God, the two of them went off on this rant while I just ordered another Americano. And I could see Andy was trying to tease information out of her about the listening habits of young kids and how the future was going to look and so on, I suppose, he's a journalist, so he had her singing like a canary. But he had still to make it clear why he'd wanted to meet her.

So eventually I stop him and ask him, look, Andy, this discourse here, it's really interesting, but are you writing an article or what? And he shakes his head. Miles, he says, this is confidential at the moment and it concerns Jake and another interested party who might be in the position to help him, he says.

Help him how, Jenny asks him before I'd even had a chance to ask him what any of it has to do with us. And Andy gazes at us. And he's got one of those vaping things stuck to his mouth and it's like a leech he's sucking on. Go on, Jenny says. Will you tell us? So he leans forward and says Jake had a meeting with a big promoter and things were looking very positive.

And Jenny, she just rolls her eyes and shakes her head. He doesn't need that, she tells him. What do you mean, he asks her, sitting back and finally removing the vaper from his mouth. And before Jenny has a chance to answer he's off again. He quite patronisingly, in my opinion, starts explaining to Jenny about marketability. He really didn't need to do that. But she listens anyway. How the music business is still a business, and how Jake wouldn't stand a chance without someone with the right know-how and experience behind him. Things may have changed but music is still music and Jake, he says, is something of an oddity. There's too much going against him. However, there are a lot of things going for him that could be teased out with the right people behind him.

Then he looks at Jenny and gives a little shrug. He shouldn't have any appeal to you, for example, he says, or most of the youngsters in that hall a couple of weeks ago, you know what I mean? On the street he should just be getting a few coins thrown at him but people stop and listen. He takes them in. He took me in. He took you in, Miles, he says, looking at me. I went to argue but he closed me down. Is it the voice? Is it the look? The sound? These were all rhetorical questions you understand, because so far he had been seeking no input from me. He's not young, he says then, turning back to Jenny. His time should have been and gone but that doesn't really matter. What mattered to you Jenny, was that song. Fair enough. He has got nice songs to complete this package, you know what I mean? But if you think about it, there's a lot of unknowns there too. He could be carrying a lot of baggage. He could be a difficult person to work with. We don't know a lot about him.

And Jenny looks at me first then back at Andy and says, he's real though, and a lot of people are starting to want that now. And Andy just nods at her. Let me tell you something, Jenny, he says. Back in the nineties, I was running out of space in the flat. I mean, I had vinyl LPs stacked on the shelves. I had them on the floor in rows leaning against the skirting boards, you know what I mean? I had them, Christ, in my bedroom even, and apart from not being able to find anything when I wanted to, I just felt like one of those hoarders, you know? They're on Discovery Channel, nutters who are afraid to throw anything out, to the point where they can't even invite their friends over because there's no space to host them. I was almost on that level.

Then one day, something arrived that I thought was finally the answer to all my troubles. You know what that was? And he looks at Jenny, and she replies, quite brilliantly, a bigger flat? No, he says and points to me. Miles, you know what I'm talking about. The compact disc, I answer. But I'm still grinning at Jenny's answer which I should have just repeated to put a halt to his gallop for a moment. But he just nods, nods away smugly and returns to Jenny.

I just thought, he says to her, how much space could I recover with these things. So one day, I get a load of boxes and just pack up all my vinyl, everything, and there was a lot of rubbish in there, really. Stuff that had come into the office for review, bands that had never lasted more than six months or a year, but I was keeping it all thinking, maybe in years to come these things will be worth something, you know what I mean? Some guy gets a break and his back catalogue is discovered and guess what, I'm sitting on a gold mine. So then the CDs flooded in and over the years that collection grew and I eventually started throwing them out too. Now, most of my collection is stored not on the shelves or floors or bedrooms but on a great big server in Sweden somewhere. My point is, we don't own music anymore, we don't collect it, we don't even want to buy it. We share it.

And Jenny looks at him. So what's the moral of the story then, she asks. And he kind of cackles a bit and pulls on his vaper and says, well, the moral of the story is, consequently we don't know how valuable an artist is anymore, you know what I mean? If you think about it, we don't know how valuable their work is anymore. And if we're giving it away for free, sharing it, passing it around, then maybe it's got to the point where we don't value it at all. Maybe, just maybe music has now become worthless. Tell me, what price tag would you put on someone like Jake? At best, a record company, even if they were to take a punt on him, might throw a few grand at him to get some proper recording done. And they'd want it all back. Possibly it was all way overvalued anyway and finally we're realising that it's just a form of light entertainment and we can be easily as pleased by birdsong in the garden, and that's always been free. The dawn chorus, the most beautiful piece of music in the world, timeless and free for everyone to hear, you know what I mean? But I don't want to think that. I refuse to think that because, I suppose, I've devoted my life to something that has both an intrinsic and extrinsic value. So, when you say Jake is real, you've really landed on the fundamental thing for me here. Authenticity. He's authentic. And that's what we got to sell.

Your generation, Jenny, he says, accepts the digital world as the norm. You were born into it. You don't know any different. I'm too old to enjoy the party. Then he looks at me and nods his head. Your dad is probably the same. So someone like Jake comes along, and he's trying to bridge this gap, trying to appeal to both worlds. But he won't manage on his own. He needs people on both sides of the divide to help him out. Then he looks at me again and pauses, deliberately, to take a couple of long pulls on his vaper. And suddenly I realise why we were there. Oh yes, I know why it is we are here. And I'm looking at Jenny and she's not saying anything. And Andy gives her a moment then he puts it out there.

Jenny, someone like you would be great to have on board. And Jenny glances quickly at me. But I desist. I desist and, to be honest, maybe I shouldn't have. Maybe I should have advised her, as her father, to move on, that she might regret getting involved. But then I thought back to when I was a young boy, and the number of opportunities that came along were so few. I had always just listened to my parents and did what I was told. As far as I was concerned, and as far as they were concerned, they knew better, they'd been around a lot longer and knew how to make it and how to fail in this world.

But, I suppose, it's like what I've touched on before about the world of music and how the new things that come along aren't meant to be for us, the older generation. So we don't have the right to tell our children how to think about things we really don't understand. And Jenny, she had such a zeal for music. Her senses were tuned to rhythm and melody from the time she was able to sit up by herself and tap the spoon on the high chair, crawl and walk and dance like a Duracel bunny. And God, she was a tech wizard, she had a passion for the new world where I had barely a functional interest in it, saw it as something that had devalued journalism, music, literature and put news down to what we fed each other in bitesize spoonfuls on our Facebook pages. So I look at her, and she's teetering, waiting for me to either steer her away or tell her to go for it. So I just look at her. And I nod my head. Go for it, sweetheart. If it's what you want to do, go for it. And she jumped. And that was indeed that.

## *Paul Smith (Smithy). Jake's childhood friend.*

I had my reservations about Jake ever getting involved with that cute hoor Blake. I really did. See, Blake was one of the old school types and I don't think he fully understood how much things had changed when it came to contemporary music, the dynamics sort of thing. Or maybe he did, which was why he was semi-retired. So, why didn't he just bloody well go ahead and retire altogether and leave Jake alone? But apart from anything else, as I got to see and hear more of him, spouting on the way he did. I just didn't like him as a person. And that's enough for me. Blake the snake. Blake the snake.

And as for that sidekick of his, Andy Kirwan. Come on, I'm not even sure how much credibility he had left anymore that fella. I suppose I admired him for one thing, he wasn't giving up. He was resilient, so he was. But do you want to know something about Andy? Maybe I shouldn't be saying this, but I looked at him and I saw regret plastered all over his face. See, and this is God's honest truth now, Andy was, at heart, a musician and a writer of music. He'd tried his hand at various things over the years, from scores for movies to the Eurovision entries. He was in a band at one stage back in the eighties, played one or two gigs and it was a disaster. But that's not what made him a bad fit for Jake. I didn't care about any of that. And I liked his writing. He knew his stuff, so he did, and he saw something in Jake, obviously, which was all good. But privately, see, he resented him. And that's bad. That was going to be a problem.

As if that wasn't all enough to be getting on with, right, into the mix comes little Jenny. I mean, why? Well, I know why in the bigger picture. It was Blake's conniving there, wanted someone who knew how to push the whole thing out there, into the brave new world or whatever. But she had no business taking up Jake's cause. Because that's what she thought she was doing. Granted, in hindsight, getting that song out of Jake wasn't the worst thing to happen. But she wasn't happy to leave it at that once she got a buzz out of it, because that's what young people get their buzz from. The vanity metrics. The likes, and the shares and the smiley bloody faces all over the place. It's their currency.

She should have left it alone instead of pretending to champion Jake like he was a charity case. Jenny, ah, I hate to have to point the finger at a young girl, but once she put that clip up on YouTube like that, it was like she took Jake by the hand and led him into the chocolate factory or something. She conjured up this sort of illusion. And Jake got this notion that he might actually have a real shot. He didn't need a shot, take it from me. What he needed was a bloody job, a proper job and a career, something to give him a wage and some focus. He could still play. Nobody was going to ever stop him doing that.

And while I'm on a roll here, let's talk about Katie. Katie, at least only ever had Jake's interests at heart, right? And she would have been good at promoting him and maybe even scratching a living for him on his own terms. But even she was placing this big dream in front of him. Selling him a fantasy and getting his hopes up an' all — the point is, they all wanted something out of Jake but none of them really knew anything about him. And there was one question, in particular, which none of them could answer. Right? One question. Why had it taken him so long to start putting his music out there? Where had he been? What had he been up to for so long? Why now?

So, as I've been doing all along, I'm going to go back. But this one is the real shocker. Do you remember, the story I told you earlier, about Jake selling his records, right. You probably thought, so what. But like I said there was a reason, a reason for everything in this story. So let's go back to that point. Jake had been putting his music 'out there', as they say. He'd always been putting his music out there. Jake was probably born singing. Jake used to keep the family awake at night rocking in his cot. Clattering his head on the end of it to the rhythm of whatever tune was banging away in there in his head. He was just obsessed with music. But I think I've already made that clear, with those little stories of myself and him back when we were young fellas. And when we both moved on he took his music with him. On the streets and in the pubs at night, earning a bit of a living, writing his songs, recording them and sending them out and doing the waiting game or whatever.

His songs though, if you listen to them now, they weren't a fit for what labels were looking for then. It wasn't his time. And I think it frustrated him because he knew, as a musician, time is not really a luxury you have. An actor or a painter or a writer can mature into their roles, a popular musician, in general, really needs to be discovered early, right? In general. But the A&R scouts, the fellas who spent their nights in pubs and clubs bloody desperate to bring a band back to their labels were only looking for just that. The next big band. The next U2. It's like everyone wants the next Ed Sheeran now. The shit just goes in cycles the whole time. So you had Jake, a singer songwriter who was an odd part of the whole puzzle. He wasn't going to fit. And, like I said, I think he knew that. But he persevered. He kept writing and playing when he could until something happened that just, it just caused his whole life to implode, so it did.

Jake at the time was only, I think he was just gone twenty when it happened. He was finishing up in college and he was seeing this girl who he'd met on the campus. She was a nice girl, I liked her. What was her name again . . . ? Yeah, I remember now, it was Kim and she looked like that singer, Kim Wilde. That's how I remember, we used to slag Jake about it the whole bleedin" time. Anyway, she was doing a degree in science and Jake was doing his BA. He sailed through it with good honours but he called a halt after he graduated. They were all pushing him to stay on and do a masters, even a PhD, but he hated the whole college life idea and a career in academia. He just wanted his music and that was it. If you'd offered him a six-figure salary and a suit he would have turned it down, swear to God. He was moulded for music and the only way that mould was going to break was if something hit it hard. And I really thought this was going to be it, something that would just change everything because himself and Kim only went and had a little girl together.

I mean, it happened in those days, right? You didn't have the same access to contraception and all that, it was just, it happened and that was that. I thought at the time, Jayzis, Jake, I mean the pair of them had nothing. But, when his daughter arrived, Jake was besotted, so he was. That's what happens. People change, biologically, when they have kids, it's a fact. You become a better human being. And a daughter will change the toughest bastard out there. Jake was always this sensitive sort of fella anyway but if you saw him with his little girl he was enchanted. But they'd had her when they were actually still in college, studying, so it was hard on the pair of them. They weren't even living together at the time but they wanted to do the right thing as we used to say. So they graduated then moved into a one-bed flat in the suburbs. It was grand, safe, warm, a good location, all that. She wanted to do her masters so Jake stayed at home to mind the baby, and he just became this fixated father.

He lived in a bubble. But it wasn't practical and financially it was a bloody struggle. Evangeline was her name, by the way. He called her Evie. They had some support from social welfare and he focused on getting a night job. And he tried. He did try now. He tried, whatever, all kinds of stuff for minimum pay. You know, making pizzas, security, he had a shift in a factory at one stage and it was messy because he couldn't get any sleep during the day and the shift didn't clock off until five in the morning. He was like a zombie. So he gave bar work a shot. And there was loads of live music in pubs in those days and one night, he just asked the manager in the bar he worked in if he could do a slot. So the manager, a decent bloke, gave him half-an-hour before the main act one evening and he loved it.

And you see, when it came to performing in bars Jake wasn't ever mad on the idea. He had tried before, got a slot in this famous pub in town but it backfired because he happened to play the same night the Eurovision was on and he got humiliated. It was a funny story actually, I thought. But he never saw the funny side of it and preferred to play on the streets and stuff. But pubs then were the places to go to make money and his circumstances had changed. He had to do it. Because it was all he could do. The only thing that hadn't been really tested was his stage persona. He was no front man for a band but the band scene was saturated and he was a break from the bloody noise in these places five or six nights a week.

So after he did the opener one evening, they gave him a shot on his own and he did that. And that blew them away, it was a midweek when it wasn't too mad so it was perfect for what Jake was doing. And he never looked back. He was offered more gigs and the rate was better than what he was getting for a shift behind the bar, right? So you didn't need to be a genius to work out that three or four gigs a week could easily keep the fridge full and mean more hours at home with little Evie. So that's how he really started in this whole business. Simply because he had two mouths to feed. Full stop. It wasn't about stardom, making it, talent shows, deals or any of that stuff. It was about putting bread on the table. And once you got into that scene you realised there were a lot of people doing the same circuit, journeymen with young families and, maybe they all had the dream or whatever, but their everyday lives were pushing that dream a little further down the road. There was always a chance though, back then, you know? That one night the right person would just be there and Jake might get talking to them, give him a name, give him a tip, something to go on, a lead. And I used to ask him. Has anyone ever come up to you? Asked you to do some recordings? Come in for an audition? Give you a business card? Nah. He'd just shrug it off. They're all looking for the next U2, he'd say.

And, see, he never hung around after gigs, Jake. He just took the money and went back to his little girl. He wasn't a big boozer or anything. Didn't dabble in drugs. He had a lot of control that way. It was too easy after a gig to hang back and drink but Jake never did. He wouldn't have done anything that would have put his little girl in jeopardy, put her in harm's way, except, really for his own stupidity. Maybe stupidity is too strong a word but, I can't think of another word, even after all this time. I swear, I can't think of other words.

Anyway, a couple of years went by and I think Jake was starting to think a bit more seriously about how he could forge a proper career in the music business. That's when he started taking his recording more seriously. Put down a lot of stuff. Worked his arse off at it, I remember, recording reams of tape. And it was all looking good. Then Evie got sick. They couldn't get to the bottom of it and it all happened pretty quickly. She was in the doctor's a few times and there was nothing glaring, nothing obvious. She was given antibiotics, the usual stuff. And they were on their own, really, when it came to having support. His girlfriend's parents had helped when they were both in college but had moved away down the country to a smaller house. Jake's Ma was great, she'd come over when she could and look after Evie but she was getting steadily worse.

I remember being in the flat one afternoon and Jake was there on his own and I'd never seen him so helpless. He was sat on the couch and Evie was asleep on his lap. She was a ghost of the little girl that I knew, it was scary, so it was. I hadn't seen her in a few weeks now, and she was frail, she'd lost all this weight, she was pale. She looked like a little porcelain doll. And Jake, he was holding her like she was about to crack and fall apart right there in front of him. And he said to me, Smithy mate, I don't know what to do. She was dead within a couple of months.

It was a form of cancer, neuroblastoma or something, she was obviously in the high-risk end of it because, so I believe anyway, the survival rate can be good if it is discovered and treated. But it wasn't discovered and it wasn't treated. Now, here's the real clincher. The place was a bit of a mess, this flat they lived in, a one-bedroom flat, right? And when I say a mess what I mean is it was untidy. Anytime I was in there Jake was looking for something. He was a disaster when it came to organisation. His mind was as ordered as a library. He could remember dates, music, lyrics, you could take a book down off a shelf and read a few lines and he could tell you what the book was. But the home was a bleedin' mess.

And after Evie died they did this big clearout, Jake and his girlfriend. They couldn't bear to live with all the toys, the clothes, the books, eating utensils, everything. They just wanted to hang on to a few photos and nothing else. And while they were doing a clearout they found a letter. Jake found it actually, one afternoon. Under a pile of lyrics or something, a pile of paper anyway that had been thrown on a table and found its way into the clutter that lay about all over the gaff. Now, the letter was months old, dead serious, and it was from the hospital, right? A test had been done which had raised alarms and further tests were needed. As far as I know, you did needed several tests to nail this thing early. They had done only one but were called back to do further tests. But they had never read this letter. Jake had obviously opened it one morning but, now, I'm only guessing here, probably got distracted and tossed it on the table. I don't know. It doesn't seem possible, does it? That you'd miss something like that. With Jake, though, anything is possible. Stuff can sail over his head like a kite. I mean, it's tragic and it's baffling. Totally inexcusable even. But that letter was never read. And remember, emailing wasn't around then. Mobiles were barely around. I think there was only the landline in the flat. All business was still done by letter. And they had just missed it.

Now you can ask, why were there no follow-ups from the hospital? But we don't know. Maybe they did try and call. Maybe they did send another letter that ended up in the hall downstairs with all the junk mail and post that had piled up belonging to tenants who had left and so on. We don't know. Should Jake and Kim not have just, maybe called around to the hospital or something? Yeah, maybe, but if you hear nothing you just keep going on, don't you? No news is, whatever, but it was a catastrophe. They split up very quickly, they both blamed each other and who am I to say whose fault it was, right? It doesn't matter. But Jake had what you would call now quite simply a breakdown. They didn't call it anything back then. Just grief. But it was a breakdown. And I'm talking about a guy who was physically tough and mentally strong. Now you have supports in place. People to talk to. Mindfulness and all that craic. Someone like Jake would be put forward for counselling. That was never offered. He just had to deal with it and he moved in with his Ma and they had each other. That's what they had.

And his response was to bury himself more in his music. He just pushed open the doors and went inside and didn't come out for a long time. I know that sounds mad. But for me, I understood, I got him. Music had always been his, how would you put it, his refuge, right? And for years he was off the bloody chart. When his Ma died he got to keep the house. He had one brother who was married and lived abroad. The house was paid for years earlier by his old man who had ran off abroad with the woman he had met. And Jake became something of a recluse. I say something of, because he would come out every once in a while to catch a gig in a local venue or in one of the bigger venues even. I'd be with him a lot. He was on these meds, it was gas. I don't know what they were but he kept them in this pillbox in the top pocket of his blazer and he'd be doling them out at the gigs like Smarties. He ditched them after his Ma died, said he realised they were slowing him down, putting a fog between him and his craft. I think, personally, he discovered he was now really on his own. He'd nobody. And if he didn't do something, make some sort of peace with himself, he was heading for a total disaster. So he finally pulled himself out of the shite, fair play to him. But it was nearly twenty years. And those twenty years are the makings of a person, if you think about it. It's when you establish yourself, carve out your career, get your head down out of the clouds, whatever. He missed out on the most important years of his life. And the only person he had, and I don't mind saying this, was me.

So not long after he buried his Ma, I was over for a visit and he gave me an envelope, unsealed, and in it was a cassette tape and a sheet of paper, folded over in half. And I thought a cassette tape? Now, Jake used to have a four-track recorder back in the day when he was living with his girlfriend and little Evie. Those machines, they were all over the place years ago and everyone used them, way before pro-tools and all that came along. They were probably the easiest means of recording songs yourself at home and saving them onto your regular cassettes. But, you know, apart from the collectors nowadays, cassettes are not a format that people would be using at all.

So I look at the sheet of paper he's given me, and I'm stunned. And I remember thinking, Jayzis, he's not better at all, he's actually gone over the edge now, because you're not going to believe what he'd handed me. There were lyrics on it, this piece of paper, right, which was fine. But it was the other side that stunned me. You know, I was shocked, so I was. It was the letter, from the hospital. He'd kept it, after all those years. He had kept it.

So I say, Jake, what's this? Thought he'd had some sort of relapse or something. Take it, he says. I got to get rid of it. And I pull the cassette out and he just nods at it. It's a song I put down, about Evie, he says. The way I used to record, on the four-track. And they're the lyrics on that letter there. So just do me a favour, take it away, I don't ever want to hear it again. I'm serious, Smithy, just do this for me, will you?

And I'm staring at him. I thought that letter would have been the first thing to have gone into the bin when they were clearing out the last house. And he just gives me this smile, Smithy, he says, you're my dearest, dearest friend. It felt good to record that song at the time, to write it down like that, on that letter, and I kept it. It was like a piece of her spirit, on there. But I can't keep it any longer, you understand. I need you to take it, keep it and just, never let it out. Can you do that? Do it for me, this is my way of finally dealing with it. Can you do that?

And I'm flabbergasted, but, I'd do anything for the guy and he's been through a rough time and if this is the final stage of his, whatever, healing, then of course I was going to do it for him. Sure, Jakey, I say. It's safe with me, I promise. And it was safe with me. Until the day came when I had to make a very tough choice. It killed me to make. It really killed me to make it. But, you know, we've talked about reasons for everything and all that. And, I believed at the time, I had the best reason in the world to do what I did.

## *Katie Ryan. Girlfriend.*

I've often been asked, why did I stick with Jake after he, in a sense, betrayed me. Is there a better way to put it? Would you believe it if I said I only discovered he had actually agreed to work with Brian Blake and Andy Kirwan after seeing an email from Blake one morning? And I confronted Jake about it. And he said, yes, he'd been to see him and had signed an agreement for him to act as manager and promoter. Of course, when I quizzed him further about what he'd signed, he was clueless. He hadn't looked at terms, publishing rights, nothing. All he did was show me a cheque, folded in the inside pocket of his jacket, for ten thousand.

Yeah, fine, ten thousand was nice to get but what was it for? An advance, he told me. But Jake didn't even understand the nature of an advance, I'm convinced. An advance on what, I asked him.

Do you not understand, Jake, I said, hello, an advance has to come off future earnings. You now owe him. Do you get that? What did you promise to deliver? And he just shrugged, I'm not promising to deliver him anything, he said. I'm already here. Signed, sealed and, if you like, delivered.

And I was speechless. Actually, I was enraged. I could see clumps of his lovely long locks in my hands. And for someone who could be so astute and . . . wise, to make this impulsive decision without consulting anyone, it was insane.

Jesus, Jake, don't you see, I said to him. Don't you see what you've done? You've just gone and sold your soul. Then, yeah, then he takes notice. He stares at me. This intense stare. It was like I'd just insulted him. Don't say that, Katie, he said, pointing his finger at me. I know what I'm doing. And before I had time to say anything else, he just comes out with, by the way, Katie, that girl Jenny is coming on board to help too. And that was the real kick. I felt that one.

So where does that leave me, I ask him. And he says nothing for a moment. And then he . . . he just comes over to me and he hugs me. And he says, Katie, it leaves you out, that's where it leaves you. Then he takes my hand, and I could see in his eyes that he was about to share one of his little anecdotes. And he looks at me. Take all the people you know in your life, he says. Where do you put them all? They can't all belong in the one space. You got to have different rooms with different signs on the door. Friendship. Business. Pleasure. You can break them all down. Friends who make you laugh. Friends who help. Friends to go out with for a drink. To travel with. People to borrow money from. People to give advice. You're never going to want to meet all these people at the same time. You could even go through long periods where you never see some of them at all. Then something comes up and you go and knock on one of the doors. But there's one room with just the one person in it with whom you want the share the space all the time. And the sign on that room just says love. Do you see what I'm saying? That person can't belong anywhere else.

Sure, okay. And I laughed. I laughed at the simplicity of it all. But it was so sweet too . . . he was always so good at grasping the difficult situations and reducing them to something more manageable. Even just in terms of perspective and how we look at things. He could have just said, Katie, I love you and I don't want this to jeopardise our relationship. But that would have been too straightforward for him.

Come on, he says, let them look after it. Don't worry, they'll do okay out of it. Blake, he's been around, he knows what he's doing. Andy Kirwan is on board and Jenny, she devours all that new media stuff. I couldn't keep up with her. I wouldn't want to. And I just don't want you doing it anymore, he says. And I've been around too, so you don't have to worry about me either.

Hmmm. Well, guess what? I did worry, because Jake, he didn't know who he was getting into bed with. I knew Blake. And I had dirt on him, dirt that he believed was well buried. But I knew where to dig it up, that was the thing. Blake had no idea that he and I had, to use Jake's analogy, people we knew in the same building. He'd been involved with a friend of mine in the past. He came knocking on the door to one of my rooms and took away someone who was very close to me and she never came back. But for the time being I was going to say nothing because it would have torpedoed the deal with Jake, even if I didn't agree with it. It was what he wanted. So I kept my mouth shut. And from that day on, Jake just took it all out of my hands. I no longer had access to the emails, the Facebook page, Soundcloud, Twitter, YouTube, everything. That was all handed over to Jenny and he never mentioned that end of things again.

And for a while, things got better. For us I mean. And I started believing that allegory about his rooms. He was right to sever that tie. Because seriously? When it all started to go totally insane I was so glad I wasn't involved anymore. And Jake was going to need someone valuable next to him, someone who wasn't trying to take a piece out of him. And I was happy to be that person for that time.

And when I finally moved in, because that was the best thing to come out of that episode, moving into Jake's home, I realised all that talk of people living in different spaces was exactly how Jake lived out his life. He had all the people in his life boxed off into different compartments. It was like he had an index in his head, files on everyone, but there were so few who really mattered.

The first thing that struck me in Jake's house was there were no photographs of anyone, anywhere, apart from the one of his mother on the mantelpiece. An old photograph with Jake beside her, with a guitar, probably taken about fifteen, twenty years previously. There were no other pictures. None of his father, though I knew he had left when he was much younger. None of his brother. None of his past girlfriends, old friends, you would have expected something somewhere, surely? But there was nothing.

There were plenty of posters, boards with ticket stubs from concerts he'd been to years before. He had, like, an amazing sound system of course. Souvenirs, memorabilia, and CDs, cassette tapes and vinyl everywhere. I mean everywhere. Although he told me he'd sold most of his vinyl albums years before and had only begun the painstaking task of retracing it all and getting his most loved albums back. So I can only imagine what the house would have been like then. There were books everywhere too. But it was safe and warm, cosy, a bit untidy, physically, cluttered let's say, disorganised maybe. But it was just, how best to put it, all him. It was his crib. I felt like an intruder.

And the first thing I did when I moved in was to take a photo I had of the two of us, down on the strand near where we'd met, just a selfie but it was one of the first moments we shared together and I got a printout and a cheap frame and put it on the mantelpiece. He didn't object, but he didn't add to it either.

## *Donnie Miller. Record store owner, old friend.*

Jerry Garcia once said, choosing the lesser of two evils is still choosing evil. And I don't often like to disagree with someone like Jerry Garcia but do we take it that there are times you shouldn't choose at all? Where does that leave you? It's like that conundrum that kept you awake as a kid. What if there was nothing? And what would that nothing look like? Would it be black or would it be white? Does nothing even have a colour? And if there is nothing, how come I'm lying here thinking about? And on and on it went. I used to ask my

Pa sometimes. Pa, what if there is just all nothing. And he'd say, yeah, wouldn't that be great? My brain used to hurt getting around that one and the same pain results from the question, what if you just do nothing? Well, I'll tell you what happens. Nothing happens, dude, that's what happens, not a Goddam thing happens.

Now, this guy Blake, he was a shrewd operator, take it from me. Before I opened this store, I used to sell what were called in the trade bootleg tapes. The bulk of these things, they were just badly produced concert audio, recorded on a Walkman portable cassette player or even a Dictaphone. I mean, they were bad. You had these recorders under your armpit or down your trouser leg and you'd hear people coughing and shouting, they were just plain bad. But it didn't matter. I could be at a show on a Friday night and be back on the streets by midday Saturday with a couple of hundred cassettes, badly photocopied artwork in the sleeves, and I'd shift them all and be at the bar with a fistful of cash by sundown, no problem. But there was a guy worked for a spell at the, whatever it was called, I dunno, anti-piracy something or other, and this guy thought he was the John Wayne of the music business. At the time, they reckoned the music industry here was losing about three million a year because of the pirates and this guy was out to round us all up. I just thought he was an asshole. And when we came face to face one day that's exactly what I told him. And while he was quietly confiscating all of my products he gives me this very impassioned, rousing speech about music being a precious art form that has to be protected and I give him an impassioned, rousing speech back about music belonging to the people or some bullshit, even though I was facing a hefty fine and — stroke or — a spell in jail. And I remember saying to him, look man, you know, you got to give me a break here. And he stares hard at me, genuinely wanting to know why the hell I should be getting a break. And I tell him it's because I was planning on opening a record store. And he just thinks it's the most hilarious thing ever to hit his ears because, once the bootleggers were cleared off the streets they just opened record stores and sold bootlegs there, and by that point in time we're talking quality stuff on CDs which they could order from catalogues they had under the counters. So it was more damaging to the record companies than selling the crap tapes on the streets.

And I assure him that, look, I am one hundred per cent dead set on going 'legit'. And after he stops laughing he asks me where I got the accent from, and I say Stateside. And I add that I was waiting for a Visa to come through and an offence like this would sure as hell see me back on the plane home. And when he asks me how come I ended up here in the first place I tell him about my missing the boat and getting fired from the band I was touring with. So you're a musician, you fucking hypocrite, he says. And I say, no, I'm actually more of a tech guy. And he looks at the tapes and I can see he's thinking, this poor bastard hasn't had much luck, so am I going to bury him or let him off the hook. Then he says to me, okay, fuck this, I'm moving on to better places soon. Then he snaps his fingers at me. How much money did you rake in today? And, I'm like, what? How much, he says, from your nasty criminal activities, how much did you take? And I pull out a wad of cash, there was two hundred in there easily and he just snaps it out my hand, throws the boxes into my wheelbarrow and struts off with the whole kit and kaboodle. And I never saw him again on the streets. But that guy was Brian Blake, and he moved up pretty quickly after that.

Now, when Jake was looking for some advice about him, I told him that same story, and he kind of thought it was funny. So what you're saying is, Donnie, he's an honourable thief. And I say, yeah, maybe, but you're no thief, Jake. Period. So just remember when he's giving you something, he'll be taking something else. Probably something you don't expect and when you least expect it. And Jake, he just shrugs and goes, I'll know what to expect Donnie, don't you worry.

# SIX

## *When the Deal Goes Down*

**Brian Blake. Promoter and manager.**

I was never investing my money in Jake. I was investing in the idea of him. The concept. The way he was doing things. Not him. Jake prised apart a little niche that I believed could be cracked right open. It was a business opportunity. But he wasn't the only opportunity. He could be part of it but I never planned for him to be at the centre of it. When opportunity knocks, you always look through the spyhole before you open the door. Jake didn't care to look. What I really wanted was to find more Jakes. They were out there. We've all seen them. We probably know one or two of them. The guy who's been playing the local pub for years who is so good it's an injustice. The girl who raises lumps in people's throats at a party. All those years she's been working quietly behind her desk in the office, who would have thought she had the voice of an angel. That gutsy old blues player outside the post office with calluses like candlewax on his fingers from years playing heavy gauge steel strings so he can be heard above the traffic. Bring him indoors and he's got a sound that would take the scalp off the first fifty people to turn his way. The band that has never left the basement but has made the best album that no one's ever heard.

And I wasn't thinking about an X Factor or a Got Talent show or some staple like that. This would be people discovering people. And it would all be done online because that's where everyone is nowadays. You get the website up, the app, the social media channels to go with it and you get the people to start sending in their discoveries and we all get to vote. There's a timeframe. There's promotion, elimination and the final, well, you put on a big fucking final. Of course, you do. And you put up a big prize. A big, big prize. A wow prize. WOW. A prize that gets the dogs on the street talking. So what's the prize? The actual prize? I hadn't a clue. It didn't matter. I'd think of something. Because it wasn't about the prize it was about the dream. Give them the dream, and they will come. The prize never matters. And Jakey, well, he was the first discovery. Bait, people said. You used Jake as bait. Click bait, which, I don't know. Is that worse? Click bait? Than being dangled on the end of a hook? I didn't need emotional weight when I was trying to work on the business side of things. I keep my pain away. And I know that's not how things are done anymore. Now it's all tea and sympathy. Nobody is allowed to get hurt. Well baby, people do get hurt.

## *Katie Ryan. Girlfriend.*

Yeah, well, I did try to warn him. But it was still a shock when it came. I thought the advance he got was paltry. But it wasn't even an advance, was it? It was really just a loan. We got over all that, put it to one side and chose the bright side to look at. He now had an experienced manager who was going to help him with his career. We had someone with years in the traditional media who could help with communications and someone else who was plugged in to the new media to work on a strategy. We had a team. I even came around to the whole idea, got over being left out of the picture. When we looked at it, logically, it seemed to be the best way forward. He could finally get to work with a producer, a creative director, a manager and a booking agent, I mean these were all the steps that Jake was willing to take. But we didn't see what was coming. How could we have? And it happened, and I really mean this, overnight.

Smithy actually phoned Jake early one morning, we were asleep, and Jake grabs his mobile and there was this long, long pause. And he just gets up, real slow, and goes out to his PC and switches it on and after a minute I hear him, what in the name of God is this? What's this all about? And he's going on like that, seeming to ask the same question over and over. What is this? So I sit up and look out into the living room and he has the phone squeezed to his ear with his shoulder and one hand on the mouse and the other is just clutching the back of his head like he's been belted with something. Then he just says, okay, well, thanks, Smithy, I'll talk to you later.

And he comes back into the bedroom and lobs the phone on the bed and sits down on the edge of it. And he turns and looks at me, and he has this grin going from ear to ear, but at the same time he's frowning so deeply his eyebrows are touching. I don't think I believe what I've just seen, he says to me. Then he shakes his head for a minute, closes his eyes and opens them again. No, he can't be doing that, he whispers.

What is it, I ask him. And he points back out, back into the living-room, jabs his finger a few times, Blake, he says, well, I assume it's Blake, is after going and setting up some sort of show. A talent show or something along those lines.

And at this point, all sorts of possibilities are cascading down before me, it's like standing in front of a one-armed bandit and pulling the lever, and I finally settle on the idea that, so what, Blake's gone into TV, this will be great for Jake. And I sit up, say it out loud before I've really thought it through. So, it could be good for you, Jake, if he's getting involved in TV. And he cuts me off. No, he says, it's not TV. It's online.

I'm confused, Jake, I say. So was I, he says, until Smithy enlightened me. I'll have to go and have a closer look myself, but, I've been screwed, he says. Then he starts laughing, shaking his head at the same time. And he sits forward and begins tapping his fingers under his chin. Jake doesn't do anger, really. He just does this simmering rage with physical tics he uses to control it. I've learned to recognise them when they're there. Tapping his fingers, like he was doing, beneath his chin. Tapping a pen off a table. Tapping his phone in his hand. It's all rhythm really. So I wait for a minute and he lets out this large sigh. Then he repeats what he'd just said. I've been screwed, Katie. I never claimed to have super powers, he says, but a blind man would have seen this coming and I didn't.

You mean the advance, Jake, are you worried about the money? No, no, it's not the money, he says. And he turns to look at me. He has me now, he says. He has just gone and stolen my whole identity, everything I've worked for to be . . . me. Who I am. Remember you said to me, I've sold my soul, how I reacted. Well it's worse. He's just gone and taken it.

Jake, Jake, calm down, I say. Exactly what has he done, I ask him. What he has done, he says, is use me as the promo for this thing, whatever it is. Go and look for yourself, there's a video of me, a montage from all kinds of places I didn't even know there was footage or photos of at all. But there's a slide show with one of my songs, and it's to promote this new venture Blake is launching. I didn't even look at the whole thing, Katie, he says. What song was it, I ask him. Little Star, he says.

That makes sense, I say. Little bitch. Jenny. I knew it. And Jake looks at me. I'm not going to say I told you, Jake, I say to him. But I told you. What do you mean, he says. Jenny, I tell him. I mean, you gave permission for her to act as moderator for all your social media channels, the website, the lot. Access to your files, pix, video footage, everything. And he just looks away. Christ, he says. So she's been a busy little bee. I didn't even recognise half those shots on there. Then he starts laughing, which again, is no surprise. Keep calm and carry on and if that doesn't work just laugh. That's his sort of way.

What are we going to do, I ask him. Find a way out, he says. Out, I ask him. Of what, the contract? You haven't even shown me a copy of the contract Jake, I'm sure he's covered every escape route. No, not out of the contract, he says. Out of where he has me, this place, this gilded cage.

## *Miles and Jenny Adams. Father and daughter.*

So you think you know someone and then, and then. And this was my own daughter. You'd like to think your little girl isn't capable of being so ruthless. Or, to put it another way, you find it hard to believe your little girl is capable of being so ruthless. It might be just semantics to everyone else but to me there was a huge difference. As her guardian I felt responsible. I agreed to let her work with Blake and Andy. As a kid over the age of 14 she was allowed to do a number of hours' work outside her school per week anyway. So, it was all above board. I'm sure Blake and Andy both had been aware of that when they made their approach. At least, when Andy made the approach. I'd never met this chap Blake at all. And Jenny only met him much later on, when the show was actually in full swing. Initially Andy was the main point of contact. She had been liaising with him all the time, on the phone, Skype, messenger, whatever. It was a total nuisance, to be honest. There was always some gadget in the house ringing and pinging. The first couple of weeks after that meeting, she was spending a few hours in the evening on the PC at home. But then it went totally over the top.

In the beginning I was curious about what she was up to. She was pulling stuff together, photos of Jake, music files, video clips, everything. Then I got bored looking over her shoulder and let her at it. To be perfectly honest, I didn't want to be involved at that point. Jake was, look, I loved what he was doing and I wanted him to succeed and so I trusted them all. Especially Andy, thought he was sincere. He'd sat there that day telling me everything was in the right hands. So when I discovered what was going on, I was shocked. And I didn't want to hear the usual, it was just business. Business has tainted everything. There is no area of life that hasn't become a business because everything now has to have an internet presence. And once you have an internet presence you're a business, whatever way you look at it. But I still like to think we have morals, that there still exists some code of ethics and that we can't just trot out the same line when somebody is wronged. Well, it was just business. And I don't think Jenny really knew what she was doing, how she was ruining this poor man's life, not just his livelihood. She didn't grasp the enormity of it because, I suppose, she never had to make any contact with him in person. Everything was on a phone, a laptop, a gadget. So when they said it wasn't personal, they were so right.

She'd called me over one evening to show me the video she'd created. And it was great. Yes, nice, there's Jake, in the park. On the beach, on the thing, doing his stuff. There he is in the school, great shot, lovely song, la de da de da. I was Jaked out of it by then to be honest. But it was well done and I said that to her. Nice work, Jen. Leaned down, gave her a hug, then I noticed some copy that was rolling alongside the video. What's that, I asked her.

Oh, I haven't placed that yet. I've got to work on that, it's just rough, she says. But I get a squint of what it was about. Snatches of it. This is Jake Green. A street artist through and through. Jake would play anywhere, anytime for anyone and that's exactly what he was doing . . . until we found him. That sort of thing. And I could see Jenny, she's glancing at me in the reflection of the screen and I know she knows that I know there is something not quite right about it. And I say it to her, this is not for him at all, is it? What's it for? And she glances at my reflection again then she turns around to face me.

No, it's not Dad, she says. We are working on something that potentially is much bigger than Jake, she says. We, I say. So it's we now. So where does Jake fit into it all then, I ask her. This bigger picture. And she shrugs, well, he's going to have to fight to fit in. And I'm stunned. My little girl has become a little monster. Does he know what's going on, I ask her. And I get another shrug. He will, very soon, she says.

### *Paul Smith (Smithy). Jake's childhood friend.*

I saw it first on Facebook. Not on Jake's page either but my own. It came up on my feed as a targeted post. They'd paid for it all, obviously. And they had taken the line from Jake's song, and used that as the bloody slogan. 'Little star, your world is wide.' That was the slogan. That would have been a total kick in the nuts to Jake. I mean, had they even bothered to read the lyrics? Out like a flame, smouldering in fame, you seemed so secure, what happened? They probably didn't give a toss either way, but the song is about the trappings of fame. The dream that was always going to be fantasy. And Jake had in mind, writing that thing, all those talent shows and the shit that people have to go through for the purpose of entertainment. The irony wasn't lost on him, I mean, I could hear it in his voice that morning when I rang him. I told him. I told him straight out. Jake, mate, you've been shafted. They're using you as a poster boy for this never give up on your dreams shite, whatever it is. And I said to him, listen, don't you despair now. Use it to your advantage, we'll find a way to turn this thing around.

He still had to actually talk to Blake anyway about what was going on, it was possible that we were all wrong. But it didn't look like it that morning. It didn't look good at all. And I could only imagine what was going through Jake's head. Only a couple of weeks before, he was the happiest I'd seen him for so many years, even though I wasn't happy about the direction he'd been taking. But, you know, he had some money. He had plans for recording. And he wasn't going to just hide away in a studio for months and come out with an album, throw it out there and see what happens sort of thing. He had been working on a plan, he said, and he knew he was going to be fighting a system that just wanted the instant gratification, you know, and the system was probably always going to resist. And it did. I remember looking at the whole thing and just thinking to myself, here, this is it now. They've robbed him blind, there's no way out of this. I didn't say that to Jake. I tried to encourage him, tell him we'd find a way out of it. But I didn't think he had a chance.

### *Andy Kirwan. Music writer and journalist.*

I'm going to hold my hands up and say that I genuinely did not know this was in the offing. I knew there was a show in mind, Blake's mind that is, and I was to be involved. But I had no idea, when I was sent to reel Jenny in, that Blake was plotting something as ambitious as this and that Jake was to be used so appallingly. At first glance the idea looked disastrous anyway, you know what I mean? If you looked at it on paper, you'd think, that's never going to fly. But it was Jake, simple as that. That's what decided it for him. It was what Jake stood for. It was simple and it was a message that was as old as the hills but it was something that, you know what I mean, that can always be sold if you just repackage it a bit. Never give up on your dreams. That was it. Never give up on your dreams. People love all that shit. They never tire of it but it probably has more relevance now than ever before because — and this isn't my line by the way, I borrowed it from Jake — people have become afraid to dream.

Think about it like this, right. Jake was all about tenacity and perseverance. He was about self-belief. Single-minded determination. His music was just an embodiment of all these qualities that are dying out as we rely less on those traits that make us human and more on those that drive us more towards the artificial, you know what I mean? And Blake saw an opportunity to use Jake to get a simple message out there and it would prove to be a winner. Never give up on your dreams. And he was dead right. People, I'll say it again, love all that shit. And they related to it. They saw this video, this storyboard thing going on, of Jake, a guy who was no longer that young but had never strayed from the path that he chose for himself when he was old enough to start dreaming. And nothing, not even rejection and defeat, was going to deter him. And there he is. Still. Out there doing it. Little star, your world is wide. Look at him. He's now on the road to fulfilling those dreams and you can march alongside him. People love all that shit. So here's how it was going to work.

The concern was that we'd have to go down the unforgiving route of using an independent production company, doing a pilot and hoping it would be commissioned for terrestrial TV. But one person changed our minds very quickly. Jenny. The little schemer, thank God we got her on board. Christ, it was genius. Who needs TV? That's what she said at the first meeting we had, the three of us. Who needs TV?

And I remember Blake looking at her. Well, darling, he says, I have news for you. To have a TV show, it needs to be on TV. And she starts laughing. I don't even watch TV, she says. So what do you watch, Blake asks her. And she gives one of her cheeky shrugs. Maybe Netflix, but mostly it's online. YouTube, podcasts, vlogs, whatever. Then she says, do you really think I want to wait around for the weekend to see the programmes I like to watch? I don't want to wait all week. People have their phones with them all day every day. They have their tablets, their desktops at home. They have WiFi at home. They have WiFi on the trains and buses getting them home. They want to watch what they want to watch when they want to watch it. You really think I'm going to look up the TV listings and sit around and wait for stuff to start? So what do you suggest, Blake asks her. And he was a bit lost for words for the first time that I've ever seen. Do it online, she says. And let the people vote themselves, whenever they want. Let them watch the entries whenever they want. Because that is what they want.

And Blake looks at me and I just start laughing. It was genius. You set up the website, open the competition, Never Give Up On Your Dreams, we call it. The promo video is Jake and the copy comes up telling you what the show was about and how to enter it. There would be ten elimination rounds to whittle all the entries down to ten finalists. And it would be a case of the public voting who should go through to the next round. And we got the site up and used every channel available to get the word out. And very quickly, the entries flooded in. And there was one rule. No professionals. You couldn't use footage of a performance in an actual venue. No pubs, clubs, festivals, theatres, whatever. Which is why Jake's story was perfect. The Fly-in gigs, the unusual places, the parks, the diners, barber shops, all that. It was perfect. And other contestants started doing the same thing and sending in the footage. It got bonkers. Actually when the entries started coming in, it looked, in fact, as if we were just going to get reams of rubbish. Seriously. I was worried. And I saw fail written all over it. You know, it was like entries for that Uploaded programme on TV, people singing in showers or out of their minds on the backs of buses. We had buskers, we had babies, we had old men in choirs, we had everything. But everything was given a chance. We put them all up. You had the people who were actually too good. Young girls, young guys, lookers, songwriters, all with faultless voices and looks. Some already had their channels on YouTube with thousands of followers.

We were flooded. And once the public voting started I noticed something that surprised and dismayed me equally. Because so many of the contestants with the obvious talent didn't all get through. What was happening there? What did that say? About us? And when I thought about it, I realised it said a lot about us, actually, meaning all of us. That we believe some people deserve their dreams and others don't. That's what it said. And if you're too perfect, then you've got enough already. Piss off. Let someone more deserving have a shot. Is that charity or is it envy? I don't know. But it gave me a remarkable insight into modern society, I can tell you. But it says something, when a guy in his late fifties singing Sinatra, in a bus shelter, in the rain, in a very bad suit, is not eliminated and a girl with depressingly good looks and the voice of an angel gets a handful of votes. But that's what was happening.

Anyway, once it got traction, more of the quality stuff started to come in. We left a window of almost a month for people to send footage in before the competition proper started. Then we began to get some really good material, exactly what we were looking for, in keeping with the spirit of that sort of found would-be stars. The ones that would never even get in the door of a club if you, out there, hadn't discovered them. We kept throwing that kind of line out there. This is about you and who you want to see.

Then, the idea was, once the first batch was weeded out the stakes were going to get higher and the quality scale was to be pushed up a notch. And, you know, over those couple of weeks we had got thousands of entries which were whittled down to a hundred. From there, there would be elimination rounds leading to the final ten. So ten would go every week. Voted out by the public. And because there were no judges, there would be no mentors. There would be no criticism, good or bad, to sway the public vote. There was nobody to influence how anyone would be eliminated. It was completely faceless. And the added beauty of the whole thing was, like everything nowadays, when someone registered to vote we had their details, their emails and so on, and we were able to collate all their profiles for advertisers and make a tidy sum out of the whole thing. That, in a nutshell, was how it went. And it was a terrific buzz.

Where was Jake going to fit, in all of this? Listen to me, I would go home at night wrestling with my conscience over that one, seriously. And because it all happened very quickly it took us by surprise. In the space of about two weeks or thereabouts it just took off. And we had to put everything up that was sent in. We had to, legally. We had to recruit staff to manage the sheer volume. It was that bloody busy. And eventually I got to have a word with Blake, about Jake. And he just started going on about contracts and legally binding this and that, but basically, Jake would have to enter the very competition he inspired. I'm not kidding. But that was the only way to do it. And so we had to stick an entry in for Jake. Now, recognise this guy? Should he go into the next round. Well, you decide sort of thing. And he was in, whether he liked it or not.

## *Donnie Miller. Record store owner, old friend.*

From what I could see, and I don't know much about contracts, all this guy Blake did was cover his own ass in the eventuality fortune would finally smile on Jake. So what looked like management turned out to be proprietorship, own him basically, meaning that whatever happened, nobody else would have him. It was like a simple insurance contract. Jake was an asset of sorts. That's all it was. And Jake never saw what was coming. He got a lump of cash to go into a studio and put down some tracks, that was the ruse. And, yeah, maybe it might work and then Blake could take a slice and throw some more money at him, keep his toe in.

What really bothered Jake, it was the theft. The deception. They were the words he used. Theft of my soul in a grand deception, was what he said to me. And I think his gut feeling was to just get out of it, walk away from his involvement in this bullshit online show, whatever the hell it was. I thought it was bullshit from start to finish. And I had every sympathy with Jake in that regard. It was just peddling more of that talent show trash because the folks who run the business couldn't be bothered getting up and going out to the clubs and pubs and on the streets to find new talent themselves. The whole industry had just gotten so dam lazy. Never give up on your dreams. Come on, man. No matter how you dressed it up, music from the streets, music of the people, songs from the back room, never give up the dream, all those slogans they rolled out, I didn't buy any of it. And using Jake's line, little star, your world is wide. Bastards. They just rubbed his nose in it.

But when the fog lifted, when the shit storm cleared a bit, Jake, he was able to put his thinking cap on, realised that he was in a real bind and that it was up to him to outsmart the bastards. Contractually he couldn't walk away. He had to stay in the game. This is the insurance contract that I was talking about. He was obliged to enter the competition. Of course, he could have got knocked out. Hell, he could have blown it himself, but, realistically he couldn't. It was his hopes and dreams on the line too, he wasn't going to take a fall like some old boxer. And ironically, for the first couple of rounds at least, the odds were stacked in his favour, given he was the flag carrier right from the start. And that was probably a bit dubious in itself. A bit unethical, but, does anyone really give a shit about ethics anymore?

I remember I said to him, Jake, how did you think this was all going to end? When we came and got you back writing and singing again, how did you see it ending? And he just said Donnie, I didn't envisage the end, just the process, the act of music, the art, the creativity, the energy, whatever you want to call it. There are new beginnings and new ends every day, every moment, every song, every lyric is an end in itself. Every performance, big or small. But this, he said. What did I get myself into?

It was killing him that he was no longer the master of his own destiny. That was killing him. He'd never had to say yes sir, no sir. Ever. It was killing him. But he'd signed, taken someone's money so he had to go and fight for what he shouldn't have had to fight for. So I said that to him. Jake, my man, you have got to envisage that end now. It was your dream, dude, so you have to come up with a really good exit. You got to find a way out on your terms. And, in the end, the real end, that's what he went and did.

# SEVEN

## *That's Entertainment*

***Paul Smith (Smithy). Jake's childhood friend.***

So when did it start to go wrong for Jake? Or let's just call a spade a spade here. Once they'd created this monster, I always knew things were going to take a turn for the worse. Because, as much as I hated that show — even the title made me sick, Never Give Up On Your Dreams, come on will ye? — within a couple of weeks it had the momentum of a runaway train. It became this juggernaut, so it did. So I have to put my hands up and applaud them for putting it together. It had everything going for it — the novelty value, the entertainment value, the vanity value and the bonus of being accessible 24/7. I still couldn't take it seriously as a platform for artists or anything though. It was like the floodgates burst and along with the cream from the top came all the dark shite from the bottom. And there was no gatekeeper, see. No host at all. You just went online, or used the app or whatever, watched all these clips and swiped them through — or not — as if you were on Tinder or something. And it was all logged and counted. It was a very simple process, all you had to do was swipe. Does this act get your vote? Yes or no. That was it. Done.

So quite quickly, thanks be to Jesus, the dross began to just sink back down. It all settled. And as someone who bemoans mindless entertainment, well, there I was taking part myself. And it says a lot about where we're at right now, society, you know, that our minds look to be entertained at all times of the day. All times of the day. And the technology we have at our disposal, the phones in particular, can deliver instant hits at any time. That's why the idea to leave it off the TV altogether was brilliant. This enterprise was all about delivering the dopamine hit. And dopamine is the new drug. Young people don't drink the way our generation do, or did, still do, whatever. They get their buzz from text messages, little hearts on Instagram and all that. Each one gives a little release of dopamine, that little hit. And what better way to give users a hit than to give them the power to make or break people's dreams? It's in your hands, get the bastard out of here! Yey hey! I heard Kirwan say it brazenly so many times. People just love that shit. And he was right. People just love that shit. They should have used that as their slogan instead of robbing Jake's line, Little star your world is wide. People, we just love this shit, that would have been more bleedin' honest.

    I was among the biggest critics, but I still found myself on the train home in the evening, on the app, swiping through all these people, hundreds of them, loving the good ones, laughing at the bad ones. Feeling good about passing through some kid singing her heart out, then binning some clown who thought he was the next big thing. Bin for you matey. That'll teach him. Yeah, it was a great kick. People sitting beside me were getting the same buzz. And like anything, these days, it didn't need millions behind it to work. Nobody heard about Facebook through advertising, they heard about it from their mates. So this was a very people-led success story, and it had the advantage of being able to lock onto social media as well. So, fair enough, I hated it but I found it impossible to stay away from.

    Then, within a few weeks, Jake began to drift. That promo video they needed to launch the campaign, they were able to dispense with that very quickly once they got the eyeballs. And once the elimination rounds started the numbers were culled dramatically. So you had to be on the ball. And very quickly the pressure was on. There was no TV show to come on and sing your heart out and stay in the game. No judges to sing your praises either. No mentors. You were on your own. People had to be creative. Jake, sure, he was as driven as everyone else. And for those first few weeks, he put his heart and soul into everything he did. He was thriving on it. He was working with a producer and recording material using tools that had never been available to him before and he was doing the video shoots. He stuck more or less to his trusted format and continued to shoot outside in all sorts of locations, recording a different song each week. And he did a couple of great shoots. He did one in Donnie's basement one afternoon that was right up his street. Everything went right that day, the crowd, the song, the atmosphere which resulted in this grainy, hand-held video clip that worked a charm. So he survived the first few elimination rounds. But then Blake started putting the squeeze on him. He was bankrolling him after all. He still had a stake in him and Jake was feeling the stress, so he was. He wasn't used to working like that. He never had to work like that, to produce a new song and video every week. He had a backlog of material, plenty of songs, but so much of it didn't come together when he tried to put it down in the studio. And he wasn't able to cope with these constraints of time so he made some bad choices.

And so Blake was on his tail. I remember being in the studio a couple of evenings, Jake would ask me to come over and have a listen back to what he was doing. Then Blake would pop in unannounced, with a sweaty handshake just about for me and a cheesy smile like he always had, howya, I'm just here to listen in, sort of thing. Next thing his jacket is off and he's sitting beside the sound engineer, squinting at the screen, shaking his head, rearranging stuff, tossing stuff out. Suddenly a flying visit would turn into a late-night session and effectively, Blake would take over the role of a producer. He just couldn't help himself.

Then the rows would start and you didn't even need to be there to imagine what they were saying to each other. Blake screaming, if you don't make it to the final week, what's it going to do for you and your career, all that. He would get abusive, threatening, probably fuelled by Jake's feedback or lack thereof. I mean, Jake would be as likely to go off on one of his mindfulness sessions in the middle of all that than engage with it. He just never rose to those challenges. And I think, the message came one evening, loud and clear, get some new songs together or you'll be eliminated. And, one way or the other, you're finished. He was really up against it, and I could see how badly it was hurting him.

Now, you're probably wondering, at that stage, why didn't Jake just get out. And that might seem an obvious one. Walk away. But, as anyone who is stuck in a shite job they don't like knows, it's impossible to walk away. You can't just stand up and walk out. Of anything. It involves an exit strategy and it involves having other options. If you walk, you walk alone. The only thing to follow you is your reputation, like a bad smell. Then you're just damaged goods.

I'm sure the idea of bailing out had come up in Jake's mind. But, like all the other contestants nobody was going to quit. Nobody was going to go and ring that bell. Could you imagine the label you'd be stuck with if you walked away? Jake valued what he was doing too much. He would never quit until he'd proven himself. Anyway, while they were chalk and cheese, Blake was getting good things out of Jake. I think it was good for Jake to have that catalyst, somebody goading him a bit. He never had that because he was always his own man. He needed that bit of tension to produce something different and I, personally, had every confidence that he would make it to the final show, which was going to be live by the way.

Then, I swear to God, all of a sudden, Katie stepped in. She was out of it, right? She was out of the whole thing, but she decides to step back in. Like Blake, she just couldn't help herself. And, to finally answer that question, how did it all go so badly wrong, well, that was probably the turning point. Katie — who, in fairness, was far from the Yoko Ono I feared she would become — did something that, Jayzus, really had to make you wonder whose interests she was trying to protect. She went and confronted Blake, head on.

### *Katie Ryan. Girlfriend.*

Yes, that is true, I did go to Blake. I went to visit him one morning and I had a clear purpose. I didn't just wake up, splash water on my face and storm out with steam coming out of my ears. I had a plan. Maybe I just didn't have the right means to execute it. Which is probably a bad idea, when I look back now, because you don't go knocking on the door of someone like Blake unless you have a clear idea of what you want to say. He'll just eat you alive. But I did go knocking on his door one morning ready to take him on.

I knew he had a small basement office and the morning I called his PA wasn't there. So I just tapped on the window. It had bars on it, which was, yeah, fitting. And he's in there sitting on a sofa reading something and he looks up quickly, frowns like a caged bear and marches to the door and snaps it open.

Can I help you, is all he says. But I can see by the way he's looking at me that there's a glimmer of recognition there. Mr Blake, I say, I'm Katie, and I stick a hand out. And as he takes it he nods his head, Katie, Jake's girlfriend. That's right, I say, we've never actually met and I was just in town and wanted to see if you had a moment free. Sure, he says, and he stands back to hold the door open for me. And I step in, and it's a really cosy little office, more like an apartment. There's a little kitchen out the back, the area he's in has a fireplace and a couple of leather sofas, TV, sound system and there's one other room, the door is ajar, looks like an office. And he motions for me to sit and he goes back to the kitchen and I can hear a coffee grinder going.

Coffee, he asks, peering out. Sure, I say, and I'm looking around the room and there's framed discs on the walls, lots of paintings, photos of him with bands and artists. Had trouble recognising them so I half-stood to try and get a squint at who they were in case he asked me. And of course, as soon he comes back with the coffee he's nodding at the frames.

The good old days, I say, realising straight away how dumb that was. And he looks at me for a moment then laughs not very convincingly. Well, it depends on how well you were doing, he says. They were good days but they weren't always easy and, lamentably, there's been a lot of casualties.

So is it any easier now, I ask him. Again, it's a bit dumb but as an icebreaker who gives a shit? And he puts the coffee down on the table in front of the sofa and rubs his eyes and sort of moans at the same time. I swore I was out of it all, he says. But then I got sucked back in. Your boyfriend, I blame him. And he starts laughing. When I first saw him playing, he was like the guys I would have worked with years ago and he seemed to me totally anachronistic, as if he had been cryogenically frozen for fifteen or twenty years and suddenly bounced back one day without ever raising his head to see what was going on. Like he just went right ahead and did what he'd always done. Great. Fair dues. And it was that determination that attracted me. He was really fucking focused. And he had nice songs. I could see people reacted to them in that, emotive way, they just triggered that response. And he had a plan, he says looking at me. He had a plan, he says again.

And at the point I couldn't hold myself back. That's right, he had a plan, Brian, I say to him. We had a plan. A good plan.

And he reaches for his coffee and looks away, over at his wall of fame. A plan is nothing without proper execution, Katie, he says, then he sits back and the politeness is swiftly gone like he has just torn off a mask or something.

Is this why you came here, he asks, staring at me intensely. Did I miss something when you were tapping on my window? Because you never actually stated your reason for being here. And he continues staring at me. And it's pretty daunting. Let me explain, he says, sitting forward again, mashing his fingers together.

Your Jake was a bit like a rudderless boat. Like a compass without a needle. Like a snail without, what do you call those fucking things — and he sticks his fingers on his head and starts waving them. Antennae, I say. Right. Antennae. Guys like Jake, who don't have those things, walk off fucking cliffs all the time if they don't have someone to instil a sense of direction. You say he had a plan — sorry, didn't you say, we? Maybe you, plural, thought you had a dream. You didn't. I'll tell you what you had, you had a fantasy. Which is even worse than a dream, this thing we're pushing now, and very successfully by the way. You barely even had a picture, because I asked him, the day he came up to my house, I said to him, give me the picture, Jake. And he couldn't do that. So I think, Katie, it was you, singular, who had the plan, he says, and he jabs a finger at me and he's not too far away. You. But, like I said, it lacked the execution.

And he gives me this intense look again. He reeks of power this guy. And he's there, staring at me over his coffee mug and I'm frantically trying to think of a response. Throw my coffee over the bastard. It was still steaming away in my hand. Bring one of his framed discs down on his grey head. But when the response came, it took even me by surprise.

I knew one of the girls in that band you tried to get going years ago, I say, calmly, what were they called, Girls Night Out, or something truly awful. And he puts his mug down and he's stunned. The girl I knew, I say, had a torrid time. And you've probably twigged that I'm talking about her in the past tense. And he sits forward, he gets real close, and folds his hands, one over the other. And the fear I had moments earlier was gone. I've never been afraid of anything. And I was able to outstare him, because he stands up then, begins pacing the little room, past his discs and photos, shaking his head in disbelief.

I don't know what the fuck you are talking about, he says. But let me say this, I have never, ever, in all my years in this industry, harmed a hair on one person's head. And he bears down on me and he's pinching his thumb and forefinger together. Any harm that befell anyone, they invited it in. They brought on themselves. Now, I'm going to let this one slide. Just because, well, fuck it, you're Jake's girl and I still have a little bit of faith in the guy. A little. But just like the gambler at the racecourse with a roll of cash in his jacket pocket, he knows faith is not the same as belief. You start out with an inner sense of belief, then when things start to wobble, the belief wanes and you call on that outer force of faith, and when that fails, all you have left is chance. So you toss your money on that. And your Jake, lady, is down to that, as far as I can tell. I've been looking at the figures, those reports that little Jenny has been doing. It's amazing all the tools that are out there now to analyse things, you can drill right down. Not just the figures, but where the votes have been coming from, who they are. Male, female, even where they live. It's amazing, I didn't have that information at my disposal when I was launching that girls' band. But I wish I did. So I have more than enough to know where all this is going. And it's not going too well for him. And it'll kill him if he's eliminated now. It'll kill him. Because that fucking dream is still floating over his head, after all these years, he walks around with it, it's like a speech bubble, anyone can read it. Now, let me ask you again, is there something specific that you came here for? Or is that what you wanted to hear?

And he stops pacing the floor and leans back against the mantelpiece and folds his arms, gawping at me. And I think I'd heard enough. I suppose I went to see Blake because I was looking for something . . . reassurance? Advice? Empathy. Christ, I don't really know. Jake had been wired since this thing began, he was hyper, working non-stop, like some prospector who had found this seam of gold in the rock and was determined to mine every ounce out of it until he fell over. He had become obsessed. He was consumed by it and it sort of surprised me because he had always spurned this industry ethos, the idea that your music had to be treated as a product, and you had to develop a ruthless, competitive streak to succeed. It's what he always railed against and when I met him, we both set out to prove all that wrong. I never thought of him as selling out, I'd never thought that. I suppose he'd no choice. There was the irony, the sad irony really, that you can't prove it was all wrong because . . . it was just an irrefutable fact. So I just let him have his time and that time was all good until whatever was eating him became voracious. It was changing him as a person. And when his ratings started to slip he stopped enjoying it. The change was like, almost overnight. So that was really why I went to Blake. To just reach out, to see if he could offer me something, some advice that could help Jake out.

So I stood up to leave. Blake just stayed where he was, leaning against the mantelpiece, standing there, gloating, with his arms folded, staring at me. I wasn't even going to bother saying goodbye, thanks for your time, any of that crap. I just went for the door. And as I was about to open it, he stops me.

Katie, he says. And he's toned down the bombast all of a sudden. So I turn and look at him. Sorry, okay? Listen, about Jake, you know, time might have just caught up with him. Maybe that's all he has in the tank. But we've a few weeks yet to run. If he gets a new song together, something simple, something different? Maybe if he can find something to move them, they won't be able to ignore it. A story. Give them a story. That's what's missing here. That's what they're all missing, all of these contestants. A back story. They're all running down the same road, focusing on this dream without looking over their shoulders and letting the public know where they've come from. What makes them who they are? What makes them human? You know what works every time? Give the people something to cry about and it'll make them so fucking happy. We're living in an age where people are so stupefied by technology the only thing that will get through and have any kind of lasting effect is something with an emotionally high impact, he says. Then he slaps himself on the chest. BANG. Hit them right there. Give them something to cry about. As Andy says to me, people just love that shit.

And, for those few moments, with those few words, I thought maybe Blake was actually human. Or maybe he just had so much experience with the dark, ugly side he was better able to see the light in things when it appeared. But he had just given me the key. After rousing him, making him lose his cool, lose his head and lose his temper, he finally let his guard down and decided to dish out some practical advice instead.

Sure, I say. And as I got to open the door, he raises his hand quickly, steps forward a little and stops and he's pulling at his bottom lip like he really doesn't want to say whatever he's about to say. That girl you mentioned, he says, I'd no idea, I lost touch with them but I didn't know.

She's not dead, if that's what you mean, I tell him. But the best part of her died. We lived together for a while in a place that, well, I'm not going to say too much about it, but in a place that wasn't very good for either of us. I managed to get out, she didn't.

And he winces, just a little. Can you tell me which one it was, he asks. And I open the door and I look straight at him. Maybe you should have stayed in touch with them, Blake, I tell him. And that was it, I left him there with his regrets, if he was capable of them.

And I think I left with something I could use. At least I knew what I had to do.

## Brian Blake. Promoter and manager.

I'd like to take a pause at this stage. End of side one, for those who use your vinyl. WHOOSH. And I'll repeat what I said already, this was not all about Jake. It might have started out that way. He might have been the seed. But it grew bigger than him and bloomed into an opportunity for me. It was an organic process that yielded something I wasn't expecting. That was all that happened. But, it wasn't all bad for him, I was still on his side and he was still very much in the game. I told him that several times. I was helping the guy for Christ's sake. And you think back to the afternoon when he made that smug appearance at my home and shook my hand and said he was ready to go out there and be a fucking rock star. He'd used some parable about a kid in some time machine or something. But when he found himself in the real world he discovered it was tougher than hell. Nothing imaginary about it at all.

It's like the guy in Columbia Records said to Leonard Cohen. Leonard, we know you're great, we just don't know if you're any good. But of course he proved him wrong. I was waiting for Jake to prove me wrong. And you're on your own out there, baby. Only you can dig deep, call on the muse, beg her, whatever it takes to produce something. You can ask for more money. You can ask for advice. You can ask for a shoulder to cry on. And you might get all of those things. But the one thing you can't get is this big thing we were selling, the dream. Because, surprise, surprise, baby! It doesn't exist. It's just a grand illusion. It's this unattainable entity, because nobody can ever define what it is. You chase it, you think you're getting closer to it then suddenly, POOF! It's out of your grasp. Because at what stage in anyone's life are they seriously able to sit back and say, this is it, I've done enough. Now I have everything. I'm LIVING the fucking dream. This dream, it's made up of all these moving parts that keep on moving, like marbles whizzing across the floor. And there's never enough time to catch them all and gather them up and say, this is it. I've done it. So you just keep on going. Keep on crawling on your hands and knees going after this dream without ever being able to define what it is. Is it success? Fame? Wealth? I don't know. Maybe it's just happiness. Maybe that's all we want, that's the dream. To just be happy. But you show me one person who has truly found it.

Now here's the funny thing. I still didn't know what kind of prize I was going to come up with at the end of this process and we were over half-way through. Seriously. I was so taken aback by the response. And I had to put my hands deep into my pockets to get a team together to run the operation and work hard on pulling something out of the bag at the end of it all. It scared me, the way it just took off. And I think it scared Jake. And, I could give him more money, advice, even my shoulder to cry on if he wanted it, but I couldn't predict the future and give him his dream because he — HE — didn't know what it was either. Nobody fucking did. But do you know what? Everyone wanted it.

So when Katie came knocking on my door — actually, she came banging. Banging on my window, not my door, at my office. It's not even an office it's my little retreat, a place I go to just get away and gather my thoughts. I didn't think she knew where I was but, I mean, fuck, you can't hide anywhere now, can you? And I was very busy that day and I was very worried. Because I'd been on the phone all morning to record companies, production companies, promoters, tour agencies, friends, acquaintances, old flames and even old enemies. Everyone I knew, trying to work on this dream prize. I'm not kidding. I had to come up with something substantial even if it was something predictable. A record deal and a tour. That's usually enough to make them feel they've clinched it.

So she comes banging on my window and I recognise her. We had never met though, which I always thought was odd. She was never out with him. Jake. They were never out together in other company at all. I'd even said it one day to Jake. Where's that pretty girlfriend of yours got to? And he threw me a look. She's no longer involved in the music end of things, Brian, he said. And he was so serious. So I never asked him again. And when I saw her at my window I thought at first there was something wrong, with Jake. He'd had a meltdown or something. So we chatted casually for a couple of minutes and she suddenly brings up this thing about one of the girls in a band I used to manage. They didn't work out, it was well documented at the time, and I'm going back about twenty years or more, but the dissolution, as far as I can recall, was all amicable. When it was done, it was done. I'm a fair guy, I put the capital in, I took the hit, not them, and it didn't work out. We moved on, all of us.

But Katie, she said she knew one of them and the way she was looking at me, her body language, everything, it was just fucking nasty. And I'm suddenly reminded of all this Weinstein stuff, the scandals. And I'm really thrown off guard. For starters, my basement has bars on the windows. And a door with a double dead lock or something, and she's sitting there alone with me. All she has to do is scream. This lecher, the guy who doublecrossed my boyfriend on some power trip, trapped me in his den and so on. Next thing she'll be doing all that fucking hashtag METOO stuff. Ooohhhh.

But I also saw it as a threat. That she was there to blackmail me. But for what? I couldn't do anymore, or give anymore, other than the money, the advice and the shoulder to cry on. So naturally I lose my temper a bit. Can't remember exactly what I said. But I stemmed the flow pretty quickly before I said something that she could really use against me. Gave her some advice for Jake which was so simple. Maybe I got emotional thinking about one of those girls getting hurt. I wouldn't have done anything to hurt one of those girls, I swear. And I said sorry. You learn how to do that. Apologies become the easiest things to do when you don't really mean them. But they always have the desired effect. Whoever you apologise to will just go away. So she went away.

I'm not even sure she knew any of those girls personally. I started to doubt it. She was a bit too young to have been one of their peers, in the same school or college or anything like that. Maybe she had a sister who knew one of them. But later that day, I was thinking about it. I was almost tempted to dig up those girls and see exactly what it was I might have done. But I resisted the urge to do that. Let the past stay in the past, leave it alone. I never caused any harm to those girls, never. All I've ever done, is exactly what I did with Jake, and just brought them to the door they thought they wanted. There you go, there it is. If you want to step on through, go ahead, I can even help you. But if you don't like the spot you're standing on, if you can't stand the glare, don't look back and point at me. So I don't look back either.

## *Andy Kirwan. Music writer and journalist.*

I began to suspect a few things about Jake the evening we sat down for a bit of an old chat. I said it was a chat, it was really an interview that by chance turned into a bit of a grilling, that's just how these things develop, you know what I mean?

The more I probed, the more I realised there were a lot of holes in Jake's story that needed a bit of filling in. Blake had set it up, asked me to go and talk to him and get something I could put out there for the show's blog and the column in the paper which I was still writing. In fairness, I had been meeting some of the other contestants who had been climbing the ranks over the last few weeks, so it wasn't as if interviewing Jake was biased or anything like that. In fact, Jake had been refusing the offer of an interview and hadn't even filled out the simple Q&A form that went up with the other contestants. That was a bad idea. Joe public wanted to get to know the contestants after a while, you know what I mean? It had gone from a turkey shoot to something a bit more intimate, people had their favourites, wanted to know their stories. But Jake had preferred to stay in the shadows and it was going to become a problem for him as the show progressed and it became as much about the personality than the music.

So one evening we got together and we had a few drinks and I could tell he was starting to feel the strain a bit. Only weeks earlier, I had met him and he was on a roll, just shot one of his Fly-in gigs and he had been high as a kite. He was cocky, confident and full of zest for the whole competition, despite only weeks before feeling shook to the core after he had been used as the poster boy for the show. And I didn't blame him. You know, it was probably unscrupulous, a bit shameless. Okay, it was ruthless, now I think of it but, God, it's the most ruthless business in the world. But Jake was a finisher, you know. And he bounced back with a real sense of purpose and it was all water under the bridge very quickly. And I think it was week four or five the last time we'd talked and he had stormed up the rankings after his entry for that week. And this one had been a bit different. Rather than just record him at one location, he had a camera follow him around the streets of Dublin. Something like Phil Lynott did with Old Town, or Richard Ashcroft did with Bittersweet Symphony, but without the attitude. And it was a clever piece of footage. He used his song, called Beat in Blues, which is about two people, older people, losing their home after being in it for so many years and they're on the streets, reminiscing, trying to remain stoic, facing the fact they are in deep trouble and yes, we've lost everything but they can't take our love for each other sort of thing. It's a love song, I suppose. *The streets are all ours and they're calling, follow me down through the years. The night's getting older, lean on my shoulder, there's a place where we used to go, right around here. You and I, we're born to lose, cos hearts like ours, beat in blues.* That's how it goes.

So I began by asking him about that. How do you feel now compared with, say, three weeks ago, on the streets, singing those lines. And he grins at me. Jake will grin facing the firing squad, so I didn't read much into that. Then he just shrugs, hits, highs and lows, he says, which is a line from the same song. Then he starts singing it to me. *On our way surely, on our way surely, didn't we get close to it all?* I don't know, Andy, he says then. I'm not used to this level of competition.

I don't think any of the contestants are, Jake, I say. What will happen if you get eliminated in the next round? Will you just go back to doing what you were doing or has this spell in the limelight made that too dark a place to return to now?

And he grins again. Is this for your blog, he asks me. And I nod. Thought it might help, I tell him. And he looks at me for a moment then he does something I wasn't expecting. He touches my hand lightly, in this unusual show of affection which I wasn't sure I deserved. Thanks, he says then, putting his hand back on his beer glass, which was a better place to be than my hand I got to say.

Yeah, well, it's not that it'll be too dark, Andy, he says. It's just that it won't be there anymore. An object in motion wants to keep going, that's a simple fact, and I've been flying for a while. You don't want it to stop. You don't want to turn back.

So you can't turn back because you'll be viewed as having failed, is that the fear, I ask him.

It's not about failure, Andy, he says. I'm not afraid of failure. I'm more afraid of all the bullshit that goes with it. You know, the usual tropes that people tell kids nowadays because we're afraid to hurt them, afraid of their sensitivities. We hear them all the time. Not winning doesn't make you a failure, not trying makes you a failure. You don't have to win to succeed. All that stuff. The fear, as you put it, Andy, is having to go back to what I was doing before all of this and failing at that. Because then I'd be left with nothing.

So your options, Jake, I say, are limited should you get eliminated. And it could happen this weekend, you do realise that. You could wake up on Monday morning and be out of the game and, you don't need me to tell you, Jake, people forget — well, we won't use the term loser because you don't like it — but people will forget very quickly about those who got knocked out, even though getting to week four or five is a respectable achievement. But it's still losing, Jake, in anyone's book. It's not achieving the goal. It's not reaching the summit. The only chance you have is to get through to the last week, the last ten contestants, am I right? Otherwise, you'll have to go back to doing what you were doing before, on the streets, which is treading over old ground that might not now be very sure underfoot. That's what you're getting at.

Yeah, yeah, you're right Andy, you're right in all that, he says. You've got it all figured out. And if you're pressing me for a plan B, a failsafe, a little gem of an idea that I can dig up then the answer is – well, let me put it this way. People are afraid of losing because they don't see the potential in loss. You can be a good winner, but you can be a great fucking loser, Andy.

And I laugh at that one but Jake's not laughing, he's just giving me that look with those eyes that cut through ice on a cold night. Right, I say, that's a good line Jake, but seriously – seriously he says quickly as he cuts me off. So you want seriously? Okay, so I don't have a plan B. This all landed on me very abruptly, this wasn't ever part of the plan, any plan. But I'll get to the last 20, the penultimate week, I will. I guarantee that and you can stick that in your blog. Then, like everyone else, I'll have to pull some surprise out of the hat to reach the final. And I will. You wait for it, Andy. I will. Because this competition, it's not like anything anyone has ever seen before. Ever. And it has succeeded because it has given the public another little pill in the box that they can reach for to get that short-lived high. That tiny, passing buzz they get when they open their Facebook page and see they have ten or fifteen notifications. That little tick on their WhatsApp when they know their message has been read, the anticipation, the rush from it. But this goes one further, Andy, this show, if you insist on calling it a show. It goes one further because this gives people out there actual power, in their hands. Commuters, on the buses and trains every evening. The office workers facing into monotony every day. The people in the waiting rooms. The folks sitting in Starbucks. All these people, they're all at it. On their mobiles, looking for a distraction, any distraction, they can now just log in and flush someone's dream down the toilet.

Or get them closer to it, I say.

True, well, your glass is more half-full today, Andy, he replies, at which point he orders another drink and we're in this bar where the music is, well, Jake just points up over his head, do you hear that, that song that's playing, he says. And I listen for a second. Do you even know who that is, he asks me. And I don't, I've no idea. Because they do, he says, pointing at a group of girls at the bar who are singing along. And they do. And he points to some other group at a table. And them, and them, and them… then he starts laughing.

You worry about being relevant, Jake? Is that it? You're probably the oldest person on the show. That bothers you, clearly. But don't forget, you probably kick started the whole idea with that live feed at that school drama. That was your idea, am I right? Once word got out it was all over the place. Maybe it was you planted the seed for this whole thing from the very outset. Maybe, you, Jake Green, have been leading us all in the direction you want us to go in.

And he grins at me again.

Was that a question, Andy? Listen, why do people like us do what we do? Choose to do something where the odds are it will end in failure and all of its cousins — shame, ignominy, self-loathing, inadequacy and probably poverty too if there are no back-ups. Why? Writers. Painters. Poets. Musicians. All of us poor souls who predominantly use the right side of the brain. And why does someone like me, at my age, as you say, continue to pursue this thing, even as the odds grow slimmer? Why do we insist that all we are doing is following our passion?

I don't know, Jake. Are you going to tell me? And he laughs again. Over one million years ago, he says, our ancestors learned how to craft a hand tool. It was made out of rock, that's all. But with that tool, they were able to do things they could never do before, like strip the flesh off their prey, crack open the bones, get to the marrow which would transform the development of their brains. Around the same time, others began to paint pictures on walls. Then eventually, the people who made the tools, found a way to sell the pictures the others were painting. I'm one of the latter, and for hundreds of thousands of years people like me haven't done anything differently. We've accepted this is the way things have always been. But technology has changed a lot of things. Now, it's not just the toolmakers who are in possession of the tools. We all have them. Even the painters, who, like I said also have the power of that right side of the brain.

All right, Jake, that's a nice story, I say, so you'll keep doing what you're doing because that's how you and all the others are wired, that's fine. But you mentioned failure, and all its cousins, including poverty. There's more at stake isn't there, at this stage. What about your partner, what does she think of all this?

And he looks hard at me for a moment. Well, Andy, Katie has nothing do with this anymore, he says. But she must have some input,

I say, you guys must talk about the future and what will happen at the end of this, one way or the other.

And Jake looks away for a moment. We talk, of course we talk, he says quietly, but not about the future. Not yet. At present, it's just too unknown.

Ha. Nice one, Jake. Okay, so where did you meet, you and Katie? She's younger than you, right? I'm trying to build up a picture of you, Jake. I get thousands of people reading the blog every day now. And we have profiles of everyone, interviews, just like I'm doing with you here. People want to know. This is the world we live in. We live among people who take their phones out whenever they want and demand answers. You have to give them the answers, Jake. Otherwise, they swipe you off their screens and in a flash, the dream is gone.

I know, I know, he says, nodding at me. Well I'll give you a story, a nice romantic one. One day, a girl gets off the train at the wrong station because she had got upset at something she had been reading in the news. So she sits on the bench to compose herself and wait for the next train to come in and this guy walks past and he sees this girl, and she's beautiful, really beautiful. And he stops to ask her if she is okay, maybe she needs help, and they talk briefly, about music mostly. And she asks him about his guitar and whether he was playing somewhere. The truth was he hadn't played anywhere for years. The truth was that he had abandoned the idea of playing anywhere ever again, a long time ago. And he hated himself for it but he fought, daily against that thing called hope. And to remind him of that daily struggle he would take his guitar with him, sling it over his shoulder like he was engaged in a daily act of penance. But this girl, this beautiful girl, she asks him where he's playing again. And the guy looks around, and for a joke points down onto the strand, where the tide was out and there was a nice shimmer on the landscape, all that going on. You can do the purple prose, Andy, you're the writer.

And he says to her, as a parting line, we'll meet again. But he really wanted to say and what he thought he had said was, we should meet again. And when he saw the look on the girl's face, he did walk away. Because she looked totally bewildered. And he kicked himself later, for making such a mess of things. But he understood that being so overwhelmed in the presence of such beauty, the omission of just one simple word, should, a basic auxiliary verb, was so understandable but so costly. So he decided, each morning, he would go to that strand, as long as the tide was out, and most mornings he got that right. But not every morning, it's quite technical. It's to do with the moon, Andy. But most mornings he would go down to the strand and sit on the steps and play his guitar. And although he had been out playing for quite a while, he was struck by the amount of people who would stop and listen then want to give him money. And this was a public beach. In fact, one day, he managed to attract quite an audience which pleased him greatly. But he refused to take money, fearing he would anger the gods, because the real prize was of course the beautiful girl with the flaming red hair. And one morning, she appeared. And they embraced and never looked back. So there's your story, do you like it, Andy, he asks me.

So the idea to go on and do these Fly-in gigs as you called them, was born there, I ask him. More or less, he says. I was back on the streets playing for some time, but the idea struck me that there were really no limits to where you could play and the more novel the better. We worked on that together then, Katie and I. It was just a way of getting traction, getting the metrics. And it worked.

So the term, I ask him, this Fly-in gig thing. What's that all about? And the bird cage? Is there a theme going on with all of this stuff, Jake? And he laughs at me. Then suddenly he stops. It's a concept, Andy. It will all come together, don't worry about.

So again, he's not revealing all his cards. That's fine, I have had enough anyway. Okay, well, it's a nice story, Jake, I say to him. Not sure I believe it, but it's a nice story. And he grins back at me, I told you it was.

Fine, I say, let's wrap it up. But as Columbo used to say, one last thing. You say you were back playing again. So where had you been and what enticed you back? And I get another stare from him before the grin kicks in again. Well, I never really went away, Andy, he says. I was just waiting for my time. Waiting for the right tools to come along.

And, at that point, I stop recording because I'm not sure I can believe another word that comes out of his mouth. So I put the phone away and I ask him, off the record, because I'd been witnessing how much pressure these contestants, all of them, had been under to produce the goods each week, had he written any new material lately with four weeks left to run. Nope, not of late, he says. I've been too busy working with what I already have. So what will you do, Jake, if you get to that last 10 and you've to come up with a real humdinger of a song to take you through?

It'll need a miracle, Andy, because, if you want the truth, I'm fatigued, tired and just, trying to write something new is going to be a very big ask. But, let me say this, whoever decided to call this thing Never Give Up On Your Dream, knew what they were doing, he says. My essence is at stake, Andy. You go through your life and you become defined by what you do. We spoke about winners and losers and achievers, it's not about all that, it's about how successfully you do what you have chosen to do. Because that's who you are and how you will be perceived by others. Without my music I have nothing, therefore, I am essentially nothing. That's what keeps me awake at night, Andy. If you woke up one morning and could no longer write, what kind of person would you be?

And I laugh at him. It was my turn to laugh. I've made peace with myself, Jake. I don't feel I owe myself anything anymore. I told you, a few weeks back, remember. That dark night of the soul I had at home, drinking, smashing the mirror? And he nods at me. That story about the boat and the river and you looking back at your other self and all that, I remember, he says. I remember all that. Then he adds what I can only call classic Jake. But you're forgetting Andy, I don't have another self.

# EIGHT

## *The Ghost is Real*

*In your light I'm ready to burn / In your dark I wait the return/ In your passing forever's a day, now your memory's as cold as the clay / Your ghost, your ghost is real, real as the moment you were born in / Your ghost, your ghost, real as the day you left our home*

### *Paul Smith (Smithy). Jake's childhood friend.*

Katie calls me one morning in a state of, you know, grave bleedin' distress. And by this stage, my involvement in all of this had waned to the point where I had only voted for Jake in the last round out of a sense of duty or something. Loyalty. You know? I was that tired of it all. Tired of it all being about Jake. That was probably the nub of it. I'd done so much for the guy and, I hate saying this, but, when did he ever do anything for me? I had my own problems. I really did. And Katie, she rings me one morning and I could tell right away by the tone of her voice that something had hit the fan, and so she tells me that she'd gone to see Blake. Gone to see Blake. As if he hadn't enough on his plate too.

So she starts telling me how it had gone, this little meeting, and how scared she had got when she mentioned having known one of the girls Blake had worked with. Went off on a mad tangent by the sounds of it and I'm listening to her and I'm thinking, what in the name of God did you expect to achieve with that. Were you lying, I ask her. Did you make that shite up, all that stuff? But you couldn't make that shite up.

And I do believe this Blake guy is an incendiary character. He inflames people. I can only imagine she had gone there to have a heart to heart but when that wasn't going well pulled out the only weapon she had in her arsenal. So she told me she had lived for a time with one of the girls who had worked with Blake and when things didn't work out she was left with nothing, only to realise there is still a lot left to lose even when you have nothing. Because she spiralled into all sorts of shite. Abuse, drugs and alcohol, you know, and finished up in a very bad place. So when I asked Katie for more information on this bad place, where she had actually met this girl, was it an institution or something, she didn't want to disclose it. And I'm not saying Katie was lying but she wasn't making it easy for me to believe her.     And it seemed to me that this girl, whoever she was, was a fragile sort of person to begin with and just because Blake didn't deliver the sun, moon and stars didn't mean he hadn't tried. I'm not defending Blake, but he had put all his own money into that project. The same way as he had put money into Jake. And, you know, I said to Katie that, sometimes things just don't happen. They don't work out. And there is no one to blame, it's just life.

Listen, Smithy, I know guys like Blake, she says straight away. This girl and I, we shared the same space once, not a nice space either. That's all I'm going to say about it. And I saw all I needed to see of Blake that morning in his office. And think about this, she says, the last thing he needs on his hands is another failure. The show is a success but everyone knows he championed Jake. We need to get Jake a new song, something with a story, a proper story, not like the nonsense that bastard Kirwan wrote for his blog. That piece was dripping with resentment, she says. Jake is a ghost if we don't come up with something for him, Smithy.

And she was right about that blog. I don't think he did Jake many favours with that interview. He seemed to have an agenda anyway, but he basically painted Jake as this broody, reticent, tight-lipped, tortured artist sort of guy which would not go down well with the public. Nobody likes a diva but that's pretty much how he was portrayed. And there's nothing worse than a diva who hasn't earned it. The only redeeming feature was the story of how Jake and Katie met. First I heard of it. He probably made it up. But then again, when I thought about it, I'd never really pressed Jake on his relationship. Presumed he'd met in a bar or something, he never told me. But it was a nice story. The unlikely love match, you know. People like a soppy story. Katie obviously didn't like it. So she started banging on about a new one, a new story, something else, something that would show the more sensitive side, the human side. And, fine, maybe she was right. But what was I supposed do? I mean, I'm not a bloody songwriter.

So I say to her, look, Katie, he's got to go and write something new, just turn a page. New won't cut it, she says. I was onto Jenny too, she tells me. And I'm going, who else have you been talking to Katie? Have you not even considered all this skulking around is wrong. Fuck wrong, she says. The whole thing was rotten from the start, Smithy, she says. The only things telling the truth now in all of this are the stats and it's not looking good. Jake barely got through the last round, she says. He just needs to get to the last ten, he doesn't even care about winning, Smithy, you know that as well as I do. But it will kill him if that doesn't happen. He'll become a ghost. All over again.

Yeah, you said that already Katie, I say to her. Then it hits me. Just for a second it hits me. The way the thoughts of doing something wrong hit you and your conscience very quickly takes over and strikes it out. When she said that. Ghost, he'll be a ghost. Because I'm thinking, now there's a story. His daughter. Christ, there is a story and a song all ready to go. But then I just say to myself, no. No way am I letting that out of the bottle. That would be such a betrayal. I mean, his daughter's death? Using his daughter's death for a bloody TV – not even a TV show, an internet show. He would rip his own heart out rather than do that.

Smithy, Katie says then, you know him better than anyone. Have you got any ideas? That pause, why did you pause like that? So I say to her, Katie, I'll call you back. Please, she says again. Smithy, call me back with something, will you? And the poor girl is clearly desperate. So I go away and I think things over. I mean, really think things over. And it's not something I can take to my wife and ask her what she thinks. Because she wouldn't understand the nature of the betrayal. Male friendship, you know, a lot of men have relationships with guys that go back longer and continue longer than the love they have for their own bloody wives. It's not a gay thing or anything like that. And most men will never even admit such a real, you know, depth of friendship can exist. But there will come a point where it's tested and they would almost lose their own wives than their best friends. I say almost. But I had to recognise that if I let the whole episode out of the bag, I would jeopardise our relationship. Actually, let's not mince words, he just wouldn't speak to me again. But boy wouldn't it save him? I had listened to that song on occasion, on the cassette, and it made me bloody cry every time. I suppose I knew the circumstances, but, and here's what I started thinking. Andy writes up the story in advance of the penultimate round and Jake shoots the song. He performs the song. The lyrics roll over the video. I mean, show me the hard-hearted bastard who won't vote him through on that?

## *Katie Ryan. Girlfriend.*

I had a hunch Smithy would come up something. But when he called me back, about an hour after we talked, what he had to tell me was pretty heavy. It explained a lot, about Jake, let me say that. Jake was always very slow to reveal his past and the dearth of photos in his home always suggested to me he was hiding something. I never suspected it was anything sinister, but, when it came to digging a bit deeper, the shutters came down.

So when Smithy called me back, the first thing he said was, Katie, I'm very likely never to count Jake as a friend again after this. Can you get that? I'm on the path to perdition now, okay? Seriously. But I've thought it through and for various reasons, I think, the time has come for this to be let out. It's been buried way too long. So, while this will be something of a sledgehammer, I think it's for the best, he said.

Now I didn't know Smithy that well. We had met socially on occasion but not very often, and this was the first time we had spoken like this, privately. I always saw him as a rational, stable, prudent, practical sort of guy and it's why I went to him. I knew, if he had an idea and it would be of help to Jake, he would share it. And when he did, my God I felt this sudden weight bearing down on my shoulders, like he had now burdened me with it, this shocking secret they had been concealing for so long. That's why secrets are so hard to keep, aren't they? You only want to share them to lessen the load. And, God, he was such a loyal friend he hadn't told a soul, just as he had promised, all these years. I was stunned. I was speechless. But Smithy, he didn't wait to get to the nuts and bolts of how this needed to pan out. He was going to give me the cassette with the lyrics on the back of the headed paper and I was to go to Blake with it. He just spat that out like a confession. Once it was in Blake's hands, he would realise the value of it and he would confront Jake. He wasn't going to let him bury it a second time, it was too good not to use.

And, as he was saying this, I was getting palpitations listening to him, and I said it, I said, Smithy, I'm shaking here, this could really be detrimental in so many ways. And he just stops me. Stops me dead. He says, Katie, I've been carrying this around, actually, no, do you know what? I've had this thing, in my possession for bloody twenty years. I haven't even told my wife about it. And I've never kept anything from my wife, ever. This tape, with those lyrics, even came with me when we last moved home, that was about five years ago. The box is in the bleedin' attic now, as we speak, and at times I can feel the weight of it up there, you know? It's been bearing down on me all this time, I want rid of it. It's not my hurt. It's not my pain. It's Jake's. Sometimes he asks me about it. Do you still have my ghost song? That's what he calls it. The ghost song. And I say, yes, I still have it, Jake. It's in a good place. And it's in my attic, you know? And Jayzis, I love him, Katie, but he has to take this now and with you calling me like that, I realised now is the time. Now is the moment. Let's set this free and, do you know something else? This will clinch it for him. I just know it will. This will get him through, just like he wanted, and he'll have his little girl to thank for it. He'll be doing it for his little angel. It's a blessing, so it is.

And that was that. We arranged to meet and he gave me this box with the envelope and as resolute as I was about moving forward with this I really was in two minds about it. And he hugs me. Smithy, giving me a hug I never thought I'd experience that. But he hugs me and just says, be brave. Be brave, because you might have a lot to lose too when Jake finds out it was you whipped all this up. And he was right. Was I prepared for that? No. But I was going to prepare for it. I was going to script every word for that moment when Jake would arrive home and confront me. And I would tell him, just like Smithy had told me. He needed to set the spirit free and let it do what it was meant to do.

## *Brian Blake. Promoter and manager.*

Of all the people I didn't expect to see, ever again, at my window, it was young Katie. But, you know, when she did come tapping with her little ringed fingers again, I was quietly relieved. She had left a bad taste, you know. I had felt bad. I'm getting old. It happens. Remorse comes just before rigor mortis, it's probably a Catholic thing. But when I opened the door and saw her face, I knew she hadn't come to kiss and make up.

So I invite her in, and she just steps about two feet inside and without saying a word, puts her hand into her bag and pulls out this battered old brown envelope, the type with the bubble wrap. What's this, I ask her, glancing inside. And still she says nothing. So I pull out this letter which is wrapped around a cassette tape, a really old cassette tape. And I see the letter is dated November 1998. And it's from a children's hospital and it begins Dear Mr Greenbaum. And I don't go any further because right away, I'm not liking the weight of it. I just want to drop it. I give it back to her and ask her to come inside and sit down because it's clear as day that she has come to me with something very significant about Jake. And we sit. And she tells me. Tells me the whole thing. And I'm swallowing this ball in my throat and, eventually I just stop her.

Katie, I say, does Jake know you're here? He doesn't, does he? She shakes her head. And I'm looking at this letter on the table with the tape sitting on top of it and I say, look, I know after the last time you were here, I told you to come back with a story, but I didn't mean something like this. Where the fuck did you dig this up? This, this is going to damage that guy. Do you really think this is a good idea?

And she stares at me. And I'm quite surprised actually, at how ruthless she suddenly becomes. Brian, he needs this. Don't start getting soft all of a sudden and just think about what this will do. It's a great fucking story. They'll love it. It's what's been missing, it's getting boring. The whole thing is getting boring and I know you're getting worried. It needs an injection of something real, something to have them crying into their phones and Jenny, think about what Jenny will be able to do with something like this, she says. Then she looks around the room. Play it, she says. Have you got a cassette deck? And I had, of course, I had. Had a gramophone too.

So I put it in the deck and I play it. And we look at each other as he's singing, Jake. Those lines. He could be singing about anybody, but Christ, once you know the story, it takes you by the heartstrings and just pulls. You can feel the pain in those lines. *In your light I'm ready to burn, in your dark we wait your return, in your passing forever is a day now your memory is as cold as the clay.* Fucking hell. And, I just don't know. *Your ghost, as real as the day you left our home.*

Katie, I say, we can't do this. For me, this is just going a bit too far. And Katie sits back and rubs her eyes and sighs, then she just gazes at me and the mascara is smudged and she looks like she's been up all night. Maybe she has, chewing this over. And she just says, Brian, you owe this to him. You owe it to him. If this was the first tragedy in his life, you were the second.

And I say, take it easy now lady, that's a step too far. And she's just shaking her head at me. No, Brian, it's true. It's true. You weren't in the room the morning we discovered what you'd done. You weren't there to see what it did to him. It tore him apart. Now you owe it to him to go and talk to him.

And I stand up, I've got to stand up. Katie, I say, to begin with, I took Jake on, I gave him a down payment on future earnings. I've been mentoring the guy, I got him an excellent producer paid for out of my own pocket and what you're all missing is the fact that this, this competition, has actually been the perfect showcase for him.

And Katie stands too and she's getting agitated. But he's not going to win, she says. Look at some of the other contestants at this point. He's not even going to get into the next round and do you know why, he hasn't even got a song ready and it's only days before the clips have to go out. He's got nothing, Brian. He's sitting at home, sleeping with his guitar, hoping it will play him a tune in the middle of the night. His muse will sing it out to him in his sleep. He even took it to the bathroom this morning. But he's got nothing, she says.

And maybe she was right about that. He'd spent all his silver bullets and some of the older songs we had looked at weren't going to cut it. I mean, I was forced to spend less time with him because I was too busy, too involved with the business end of the show. I'd even brought him songs from other writers, there are thousands of good songwriters out there, but no. He wouldn't hear of it, had to be his song. So I couldn't give him anymore of my time. Fuck it, the word was out that Jake was on my books, that didn't really matter, I had two other contestants on my books in earlier rounds who didn't make it. I was a music manager. But I'd put my trust in the producer I'd hired for Jake and so far, he had delivered. Now it looked like Jake was running on fumes. It was tough, I understood. But was the way forward for me, a guy he doesn't really like, to come to him and say, hey, that song about your dead daughter, the one you entrusted to your best pal? Well, he's gone and given it to your girlfriend who came to me with it. I mean, even just picturing that scenario made me physically sick.

All right, Katie, I say. I'll do it. But look, there is going to be a lot of injured parties when this wheel stops spinning, do you get me? We've got to lessen the impact and at least try and keep the head count low.

What do you mean, she says. I mean, I'm taking you out of the picture, that's what I mean. I got this from his pal, that Smithy guy, okay? You were never part of this. You never came to see me, ever. And she turns away for a moment, she's upset. I can't say that to Smithy, she says. He doesn't have to know, I say. He won't find out. Jake's probably not going to talk to him again, so he won't even suspect you were involved. Okay? Trust me, Katie, I'm great at containing explosive shit like this and the less people involved the better.

Why are you doing this, she asks me. You're not a nice guy Blake, so don't say that to me. And, the truth was, like I said, she had left me with a bad ache on her last visit, regret maybe. I didn't need another damaged girl on my conscience.

Jake needs you, I say to her. He's going to need you to lean on even more once I go to him with this. Don't worry, I know what to say. Believe it or not, I've been in worse situations. And she looks at me, and I know she wanted to say, I'm sure you have, Blakey, but she doesn't. She just nods her head, says thanks, quietly. I just hope it works, she says. Then she leaves. And I look at this package, sitting there on the table. And it's like it has heat, you know. Like it has suddenly become this hot potato nobody wanted to hold. And it was in my hands.

## *Donnie Miller. Record store owner, old friend.*

I'd never seen Jake look so wretched, so cut up. Boy he was distraught. He was almost a broken man. I had to take him out of the shop, close up early and go to a quiet bar a few doors down and he spills it all out, his daughter, the hospital, the lost years, the whole thing.

I'm stunned man. Stunned. Part of me, I dunno, part of me felt let down cos I'd been left out of so much when I thought I'd been his buddy. But, hey, I guess friendships works on lots of levels and we can't all meet each other on the same one or life would just be uneventful.

And besides, he's sitting there and I can see he's wrestling badly with all kinds of demons and for a while we don't even speak. Then he just looks up at me, Donnie, I don't really know what to do, he says quietly. And normally, when I'm like that, I just do the first thing that comes into my head. I just act on it. But now, what's in my head is just bad.

You know, I had a ton of questions I wanted to ask him. The whole story was just off the scale. Why didn't you do this, why didn't you do that? How did you miss the signs and why weren't you more careful with all the documents from the hospital, all this stuff. But what would have been the point of any of that then? Besides, he wasn't opening up to seek any comfort about that whole tragedy, that was done, that was over. He was more concerned about Smithy's betrayal. That's how he put it, betrayal.

Now Smithy seemed to me to be about the most loyal guy you could meet. So I found the use of the word betrayal a bit tough on the guy. And I say that to him. I say, Jake, man, you and Smithy go way back. You're like two brothers. Remember where you were a year ago? You were lost. You were a total outcast, doing nothing with your life. And Smithy, he coaxes me into coming over to help you get some fire back in your belly. You remember that? Twenty years you did nothing and Smithy was there all that time to look after you, man. Do you not think he would have really thought this through? He did it for a reason and you got to take a step back and see why.

That still doesn't make it the right thing to have done, Donnie, he says. All he had to do was say it to me himself. Instead of going straight to Blake. Well that might have been a bit out of character, Jake, I agree. And what did Blake say, I ask him, how did he put it?

And Jake grins at me. How does Blake ever put it, he says. I was in the studio, and, Donnie, the last couple of weeks have been a bit dry. The pace of this thing has been relentless. When I look at the stuff some of those kids have been producing, maybe I'm just too old to keep up. I've been mentally and physically fatigued, feeling the pressure of it all. And Blake had been on my case, if I didn't get into the final ten, then it was as good as over. But I knew that myself and nobody puts more pressure on me than me. But Blake came into the studio the other night, and he's carrying something, under his arm, a little package. And I look at it for a second and there's this flash of recognition. I think I know that package. And he just nods his head and calls me out, there's a little kitchen in there and we go in and sit at the table. And he says nothing, just slides the box over and then I do recognise it but I'm just refusing to believe it is what it is. And I open it, and the padded envelope is there and inside is the tape and the sheet. And I'm just stunned. And Blake still hasn't said a word. And I'm speechless too. And, I'm not joking, we sit there like that for almost a full minute. Not a word passes between us.

Then finally he breaks the silence by saying, I'm sorry, Jake. And that's about as good as it gets from him. Not that he had to be contrite at all, but at least he acknowledged he was capable of emotion, empathy. So I just say, where did you get this? And he doesn't flinch. Smithy, he says. Came over to my office and gave it to me. And he says, Jake, I've put this on the table, literally. I'm not here to provide support, comfort, solace, any of that. I'm just not. I'm not even here to try and convince you about what to do next. I'm just going to say one thing. This song, this story, is your ticket into the last round. Further even. Then he just stands up, pats me on the shoulder and says, Jake, we've two days before you got to put something up. You can give this tape to Robbie – Robbie is my producer – and he can do something with it. Clean it up a bit. You don't even have to ever sing it again if you don't want to. I understand that. Jenny can put a video together and you don't even have to put yourself in it. It's all there. Like that Lennon song you used to sing. And if you do this, Jake, you'll have them eating out of your hands. Like little fucking birdies.

I was near speechless, I have to tell you. Christ Jake, I say, how the hell did you even get into all this? All you wanted to do, from the time you were a little boy, you just wanted to sing and play. You played for your Ma when your Pa walked out, I remember that story. In the hospital. In the school. Jesus, you played in the parks, out on the beach when you met Katie. Free and easy. You just got to wonder, why does something as simple as that have to be this goddam hard? Then I look him in the eye, you know, in the eye. And I just say to him, Jake, this isn't you, have you got me? This isn't you. And sometimes, you got to find a way out to find another way back in.

And he chuckles at me, finally, that humour is back, and he says, come on, Donnie, I don't need riddles now, seriously.

Jake, I say, I know you do your own thing anyway and that's cool. But here's my thinking. Let them use that song. It's your song, Jake. It was meant to be out there, not stuck in a shoe box. And when you're through to the last round of this bullshit thing, and you will get through, then we can find a way out.

## *Miles and Jenny Adams. Father and daughter.*

So Jenny had become this, how best to describe it, you know one of the crew on the Star Trek bridge. I devoured that in my youth. I loved the way they all looked so focused. So on edge. Constantly reaching out for this button, that control, eyes darting from one screen to the next. Something was always imminent. Something big and dark and forbidding. Jenny was like that. She had laptops, tablets, the desktop and of course the phone, on the go, whenever she wasn't asleep, I swear to God. The heat in the house, it was like the whole place was melting. I couldn't help wondering if there was some black hole looming out there that would eventually suck us all in. At the same time, I was rather enjoying it, this competition. And as the weeks went by, you picked your favourites, leaving Jake aside. There were some great artists in there and apart from one woman, who was late thirties maybe, Jake was one of the oldest, definitely. And you could hear that, in his songs, the production. The videos too, were just different. They had a different pace about them to those put out there by the younger kids. And they were kids, most of them. Some of the girls in particular were light years ahead, vocally, like the candidates you see in the final rounds of the X Factor. You mightn't like the show, you mightn't like the contestants, but do you remember how some of them could sing?

But, look, this was a different set-up and it was a totally mixed bag. There was another troubadour, a blues player, a dazzling blues player, Seasick Steve type but he got booted off just when I was beginning to really get into him. Gone, just like that, like he'd just died. And there were no hosts, no explanations, nothing. Just a Monday morning and . . . then there were thirty, or whatever. There was a girl from Scandinavia somewhere, who was off the radar batshit crazy, reminded my wife of Bjork. Her videos were stunning. Yes. And there was this other girl, God she wasn't much older than Jenny and she played a guitar that looked like it took two men to strap it over her shoulder, way too big for her. Had this Dolly Parton voice which bewildered for a second until she got into her song and you just thought, now that is a proper star. But, it was about making dreams, not stars, and it was impossible to predict. Jenny though, had her finger on the pulse. She was in that Star Trek engine room. And obviously she was able to use the analytic tools to segment the votes and get a full picture of all the user interaction. And it was into the final three weeks of the show when she realised Jake wasn't going to make the last ten.

I remember she called me into the bridge one evening. Dad, look at this. I didn't know what I was looking at. I might have a very tender grasp of Google analytics but she had all kinds of stuff on the go and she just said to me, Jake is not going to make it. Well, that's a pity, I said. And it was a pity. I liked Jake, we all liked him. But the standards had just got too high. He just wasn't in that league, it was as simple as that. Then, a couple of nights later, Robbie, Jake's producer, sends this song over, this ghost song, with the lyrics and a few of lines of text that were to run at the start of the video. It was a story basically.

And we look at each other, Jenny and I, and I just say, you better call Blake. You can't do this. And she stares at me and says, Dad, this has to go up tonight. It has to go up tonight. And I just say to her, Jenny, pet, you know, you've been working non-stop on this thing and I know why you're doing it. I understand passion and I'm so proud of you. Then I lean down and hold her shoulders. When I was your age, I tell her, I was sitting around in garden sheds with the boys, smoking like chimneys and listening to records until our ears bled. It was harmless really. But this, this has just gone a step too far. And Jake, at this stage, he's no better than, let me put it like this, you know when you go to the greyhound races and they're parading all the dogs. And there's one poor mangy mutt there and you just know he's not a runner anymore. He shouldn't be there. He's limping. His coat doesn't shine like the rest of them and his owner, some old fellow with a cap and a stick, is beating him because he's desperate for one more win. This is desperation, that's what this is. Look, I thought playing in a school was an act of desperation to begin with, but using the death of your daughter? Jenny, you're my daughter. I love you so much that if anything were to happen to you, the lights would just go out. That's it. I wouldn't be able to go on living. But to do something like this, it's just a defilement of the little girl's soul.

Oh, come on, Dad, Jenny says. First off, you're embarrassing me. Secondly, Jake is a big boy. If this is what he wants to do, then this is what he wants to do. If something were to happen to me, and you got a sign, from me, telling you do to something, you'd do it, wouldn't you? I don't believe in those things, Jenny, I say. That's because you've never had to, Dad, she says. I know Jake. And I'm really sure he has his girl's blessing. Then she spins around on her chair and doesn't even look at me anymore. I'm putting it up and it's going to be the best video job I've ever done, she tells me. And that was it.

### *Andy Kirwan. Music writer and journalist.*

So how do you like that? Eh? I had always believed Jake was hiding something and as time went on and the more I got to know him, I began to suspect that he was actually hiding a lot. In the grand scale of things, the bigger picture, did it really matter? Probably not. But, in my profession, your suspicions are what guide you. If something doesn't smell right, you have to at least check it out. And Jake wasn't very forthcoming when I spoke to him, certainly compared with the other contestants who were delighted to talk to me. My blog was being read, every day, thousands of times. And my weekly piece for the paper went up online also and that was getting the eyeballs too. The contestants, these young whizz kids, they were lapping it up, loving the exposure.

Anyway, suddenly this skeleton falls out of Jake's closet. Or should that be ghost? Blake came over to see me and we listened to the song together before he made a call on it. He told me the story as Katie had told it to him and it was some story. It really was some story. And we talked it over. I say talked it over, Blake basically told me to write something about it in the blog the week the song was to go out to be voted on by the public. It was the penultimate round and the songs had to be online by Monday morning and this was Thursday evening. The votes would come in over the course of the week and the winners announced on the Friday morning. If that sounds like it put a lot of pressure on the contestants, well it did. It put pressure on everyone involved and it was the one real flaw. Because it meant those still in it had only three days to get something new out by the Monday. But that was the gig, you know what I mean? And anyone with the right drive and focus would be working on the next song and video well in advance, even with the knowledge that they might not get to show it because they'll be knocked out. That was just foresight. So it wasn't just about the talent and artistry, it was about hard work, graft — grit, basically, grit. That mental toughness and willingness to persevere. And I had my favourites by then. One of them was a girl who just called herself Aischa. And do you want to know something? She had a story too. A real tragic story, the type of story that, when it pops up, stops the world turning for a moment and everyone pays attention. But she didn't want to tell it. She was a refugee, from Syria, and she was living with her sister and her family, a husband and four children in two rooms. The rest of her family were dead. But when I spoke with her, she didn't want any of that on record. Apart from the fact that she was from Syria she didn't want any of her background to be used as leverage to groom the public. And she worked her arse off, wrote these incredible songs that had everyone talking, and was just blowing people away every time. In a nutshell, she let her music do all the talking.

Then Jake comes along with this ghost story and for the second time in my career I'm having to take orders from Blake. And although he's paying me well, I challenge him on the basis that it's totally biased. He doesn't want to know. All he says is, trust me Andy, you need this to happen as much as I do. And when I ask him to elaborate he just tells me this is one show that will not be over when the fat lady sings. Then he just sort of sniggers and says, come on, Andy, sometimes you have to look at the smaller picture, not the bigger one.

Whatever that meant, I had no idea, you know what I mean? No idea. And on the Monday evening, Jenny puts this song, Ghost, out there with this video and milked it for all it was worth. Jake didn't feature in the video, which was a fairly abstract piece of work and for the first time employed the use of text overlay, so the lyrics faded in and faded out throughout the song and it was all going on. Faint images of an empty house, a grave, the sky, beams of light in the dark and just about all the mawkish imagery you would expect. I was waiting for an actual photo of his daughter to appear at some stage. I mean, that would have really got them wringing their hankies, but thankfully he restrained himself. And guess what? It worked.

# NINE

# *The Final Song*

*Paul Smith (Smithy). Jake's childhood friend.*

The final for this whole charade took place in Vicar Street, a venue with a capacity of just over 1,000 people. Everyone thought it would take place in the arena, and I was pleasantly surprised. Kudos to Blake. Vicar Street might be a small space but it's a space where everyone, you know, the biggest names in music, have played. Bob Dylan, Neil Young, Paul Simon, Randy Newman, Richard Thompson, Morrissey, Dionne Warwick, Joan Armatrading, it has hosted all these massive names, legends, this intimate venue, so it was really going to put the last ten into a pressure cooker.

Up until now, they'd all been feeling the heat, but they had learned how to deal with. It was tension they had grown comfortable with after what, over two months. Recording, editing, overdubbing, all done from the safety of a studio with a green screen, lots of tools and so on. Jake was one of the very few who actually got out there and performed his songs on the streets. He had years of playing live in front of people. I wasn't worried about that. What I was worried about was his approach. I was just hoping he'd go and just play to his strengths, no stunts at this one. He didn't need to.

My real worry was the song he was going to perform. Free as a Bird, the song he had been playing for years as a closing number. Katie told me that was the song he had picked and I remember telling her to try and get him to change his mind. He had hundreds to choose from. You weren't permitted to play a song that had already been used in the heats, but you were allowed to do a cover. But it needed to be something upbeat, something that would inspire, not just the audience but the hundreds and thousands who would be viewing and voting online because the whole thing was being streamed live on the Dream website and obviously the reaction of the thousand or so people in the audience would influence the votes.

I wasn't there, just in case you're wondering if we'd kissed and made it up before the big night. Wasn't going to happen. Jake never invited me, just to get that straight. Was I disappointed? Of course I was. I was gutted. But it's what I expected. Each finalist had three passes they could use for friends or family, which was mean enough but it was a small venue. Jake invited Katie, who never actually went, Donnie and, just to add insult to injury, never used his third pass. That was meant for me. That empty space, the symbolism of it all wasn't lost I can tell you. Whatever. You know, at the time, that's all I thought. Whatever. I genuinely believed that once it was all over, we would mend what had been broke and I'd get a chance to explain.

Anyway, the tickets were like gold dust. It was a lottery basically. When you first registered to vote you were assigned a number and all those numbers went into a draw at the end for tickets to the final. Well, actually there were no physical tickets at all to stop the scalpers. You were sent a barcode to your mobile phone. So, I was at home watching the show with my wife. Jake was to come on in fourth place. But a young girl from Syria called Aischa opened it up and blew the place away with a cover of We Just Won't be Defeated by the Go Team, who you might remember as this very wacky band who were, well, I don't know what they were when they appeared in the early part of the noughties with this juggernaut of an album Thunder, Lightning, Strike. It was like they had just spread their arms and swept up every major influence in music. I mean, you heard Motown in there and you could also hear the theme to Sesame Street. And this girl opened the show that evening with just a small backing band and a shed load of gear and smashed it. The sound was phenomenal. And they all had to follow it.

The second act on was this woman who competed with Jake in the age stakes. She probably got the edge on him actually. And she sang this Dionne Warwick song, Heartbreaker, accompanied by just a piano. Grand. It was grand. But I remember watching her and just feeling so sorry for her having to follow that explosive opener. And my fears for Jake suddenly went up a notch. Then came this young girl who was a freak of nature, she really was. Sang like Dolly Parton, looked like a teen from one of those shows my kids watched, Aria Grande or whatever, and she played this big-bottomed guitar in a country style. I had always found her uncomfortable to look at, but not to listen to, if that makes sense. She did that Lana Del Rey song, Ride, with her band and it was a real band and she pulled it off brilliantly. Then it was Jake's turn to come on. And I couldn't bring myself to watch, knowing the song he was going to do. I just didn't see how he was going to do it out there.

To put you in the picture a bit, in between the acts, a screen came down, and the host came out, a funny guy who I had never heard of. He did a couple of minutes' banter with the crowd to rile them up and took the piss out of each act a bit when they'd finished and introduced the next act. And after he had finished having a laugh at the poor girl with the big voice and big guitar he went on to talk about Jake briefly for a minute as he was setting up behind the screen. I remember wondering if he would go for him, have a bit of banter with the crowd about him. But with the story of Jake's daughter still fresh in people's minds he obviously decided or was told to hold back and went instead to tug at the crowd's heartstrings than tickle their laughing gear. This next act recently opened a chapter of his past and let us all into his pain and so on, you know, that carry on. Wasn't necessary but it brought a bit of a hush into the venue and there's a warm, round of applause.

So the guy walks off, the lights go down and the screen goes up and all that's onstage is a patterned rug and a little table with Jake's bird cage on it illuminated by a spotlight. Have you got that image in your mind? Because that's all there is. Nothing else. And after all that has gone before, I'm thinking to myself, this is very, very sparse. I'm holding out for a stunt of some sort. At the very least, I'm expecting a small band, a bass and drums even, because as good a job as Jake did with that song, Free as a Bird, it was a fairly ordinary song that took Jeff Lynne and the rest of the Beatles to make it fly.

And there's a bit of a delay going on. A bit of heckling from the crowd, a few whistles. Where the hell is Jake? And there is something about watching a live stream on your desktop, phone, tablet or whatever, which tests your patience. I don't know why. But where watching TV has always seemed like this lazy, leisurely activity, where an ad break means a chance to grab a cup of tea, go for a wee, have a stretch, watching anything online is like an exercise in restraint. If something isn't happening, you want to have the means to scrobble as quickly as possible. And for a second I found myself doing that. Looking at the screen to move it forward. Where is Jake? And already I'm thinking, this delay isn't good.

And finally, he comes on, with just his guitar over his back and his neck brace resting on his shoulders. And there's a rousing round of applause and he gives this little wave and goes up to the mic. And by Jayzis, I was nervous. I don't have a nervous disposition, by nature. I don't. And as I've testified, whenever I've watched Jake play, to his Mum at home, at parties when we were kids, in the pubs when we were students and beyond, hospitals, at those parks and even watching that clip from the school, I was never nervous for him. He would always do it. He would always do it. But as he walked on, something struck me. Something wasn't right. What was it? His gait? His demeanour? The way he was dressed, all flamboyant in a three-piece suit? I couldn't place it at the time. But when I think back now, I knew what it was. It was one very simple thing he did which I'd never seen him do before.

Just before he went to play, he turned to the bird cage beside him on the table and very slowly opened the little door. I didn't think anything of it. I mean, I really didn't think anything of it. He just flipped opened the door of the bird cage. So what? I remember my wife even said it to me, over the top of the wine glass, you know. What's he opening the bird cage for, Paul? It's empty. And I'm nodding in agreement. Give her a shrug. No idea, I say. But what came next . . . I really don't think he could have done anything more spectacularly bad.

## *Miles and Jenny Adams. Father and daughter.*

So my wife and I were looking at it on the laptop, which was connected to the TV via the HDMI cable. I can't watch anything on a tablet or a PC. I need a decent screen and I need to be on the couch. Glass of wine. Cup of tea. In this case, Saturday night, glass of wine and thank God I had it in my hand and the bottle sitting at my elbow. Because Jake basically threw everything back in the faces of all the people who had ever helped him. Ever. Down through the years. Everyone. Not even the greatest magician or illusionist or ventriloquist could have delivered such a shock, a blow, in front of a live audience and hundreds of thousands of online viewers. This was career suicide. Right there on the stage.

And, of course, my first reaction was, this is an act, this is like a warm-up sketch and any minute now, the backdrop is going to just come down and there's going to be a full choir or an orchestra or some killer rock band to deliver something that will raise the roof. But it didn't happen. It didn't happen. And the crowd, the people in the venue, were stunned into this silence for about thirty seconds. Then there was this one guy, you could hear him very clearly, and he just shouts out DO ME PROUD JAKE! YEEHAAAW and erupts into a peal of laughter. But he was the only one laughing. Because very quickly there came a few heckles, then the booing started. It was hard to listen to. And it grew louder and louder until even my wife and I, sitting at home, had to put our hands over our ears to drown out not just the noise but the shame.

Then Jenny calls me, poor soul, she was backstage, and she calls me before Jake had even finished this sham performance and she's actually crying. She was in tears.

Dad, she says, what's going on? And I'm watching Jake finish, take his usual bow and stroll off the set, with a wave, like he had always done. And I say to her, Jenny, was this planned? Did you know anything about this, it's a joke, please tell me it's a joke.

And she's sobbing like a child. No, Dad, she says. I just don't understand what's happened. And you can hear, wherever she's standing it must have been out on the corridor back stage, because there's a lot of shouting going on, a lot of voices, a lot of confusion and someone is just saying, get the next act on, get the next fucking act on, quick!

And I try talking to her again, and she interrupts me suddenly. He's coming, Dad, hang on. And I hear her calling him. Jake! Jake! And there's a lot of people shouting at him by the sounds of it. Then I hear Jenny again. Jake, it's Jenny, remember me? Jake, talk to me. What happened? And I can just make him out, saying, Jenny, my little star, and then the phone is muffled for a second. It's chaos. A lot of noise. Jenny, what's going on? He's gone, Dad, she said. He's just left. He hugged me and he left.

## *Brian Blake. Promoter and manager.*

Did I know anything about it? LIKE FUCKIN' WHAT? People have really had the nerve to ask me that. Even asking me is a fucking cheek. Let me tell you where we were at. Jake had stormed into the final ten with that Ghost song. It even took us by surprise. I mean, Jenny called me within a couple of days of it going out and the figures spoke for themselves. He just spiked. Soared right up there. It was an unbelievable result. And the potential was now actual, he'd done it. Whether or not he went on to win didn't matter. People were going to remember him, that song, that tragedy, his whole background, the reclusive years, the Fly-in gigs, it was just a great story. The whole package was there. All the other contestants, they were great but they didn't have this persona that I had succeeded in creating with Jake. Fuck it, it was going to be big. Within weeks he could start releasing material properly, start performing in proper venues not park benches. It was all there for him. We had viewers logging in from the UK and Europe. By week five or six this thing had gone way beyond our expectations. And I remember, I called him. Even before the official results had come in, I called him. And I was buzzing like a fucking wind-up toy.

Jake, I say, we've done it. We've done it. You're in. And there's this pause, good, Brian, he says. That's great news. But he's not sounding particularly excited. Do you know what this means, Jake? You should see the figures. They're the best you've ever got. That little girl of yours, Jake, she's smiling on you today, my son. Beaming like a little star, I say.

I'm sure she is, Brian, he says. And we discuss what song he wanted to do at the final. I had grandiose notions of him recruiting a band, backing singers, this was live now. There was no hiding place and in Vicar Street, people can see the whites of your eyes. That's why I chose that venue. It's a gladiatorial slaughterhouse for something like this and all the acts needed to feel that crushing, creeping sense of dread. They had a break of four weeks to feel it build. They wanted their dream, well, let them see it coming, over the horizon like a great Biblical storm. Jake, I say to him, go out with a BANG. Do you hear me? This is it. This is where it's been going. Go out with a big fucking bang that will blow their minds and the world is yours. I intend to, he tells me. But when he discloses the song he wants to sing, solo, with no accompaniment, I say, you're fucking shitting me. Just you, I ask him. Because I know he had been working with a couple of musicians over the past few months recording. And it doesn't make sense at this stage not to want to go out and put on a show. Jake, I've been getting specs in from some of the acts, I say, and you are going to be like a tug boat up against the Titanic if you do that. And he just says, well, maybe, but the Titanic sunk, Brian. Listen, I don't feel threatened by big productions. It's an intimate venue. It suits me, I'm going to feel right at home there. It'll be me and the audience, I'll look them all in the eye and I'll sing to them. They're going to love me, Brian. This is my moment and I don't intend sharing it with anyone else. Brian, he says, do you remember that day, what was it, must have been six months ago now, you call me up to your house? I do, I say to him, you behaved like an arrogant little shit, Jake.

And he laughs at me, I didn't mock you, Brian, I mocked your ostentatious surroundings. If you recall, on the table that day, in your home, there was the offer of an instant, bogus happy life or the authentic one that you had to achieve yourself, with failure being a real possibility. Yeah, yeah, I remember all that, Jake. So what did you decide? And he says, well, we're about to find out.

And that was that. The last conversation I ever had with Jake. I didn't see him the evening of the final. I was in the production booth with the team most of the time anyway and we had a stage manager looking after the running order and a production manager looking after the set, I'd no reason to be back there and I didn't want to be. I didn't want to be seen mixing with any of the acts. And it started so, so well. That kid, Aischa, Jesus there was a star. Explosive. On the night, she was the winner for me. Clear winner. Next two acts, maybe, maybe. Then it was Jake's turn. And I had a thumping going on in my chest before he came on. It was like a basketball banging in there it was that loud. And do you know why I was worried? His confidence. His confidence when we spoke had me worried. Confidence is great but you need to feel the fear going into something like this. Fear is good. It gives you an edge. It reminds you that you are human, vulnerable. Jake, he sounded like he was just playing in the park all over again.

So the first thing to send that shiver right down my spine was his tardiness, right. Where the fuck is he? There's the mic stand on the stage and a high stool with his bird cage on it and a rug. I mean, all he had to do was walk on and I could see him, in the wings, wavering, holding back. Come on, Jake, what the hell are you doing? And a bit of heckling starts and he lets it build a bit and you can feel the intensity out there and then, only then, does he stroll on. And there's a big cheer for the guy and I'm thinking, well, they do love him. And he goes over to his bloody bird cage and pops open the door. I'd never seen that before. And somebody shouts out, really loud, DO ME PROUD, JAKE. And I remember looking down into the crowd, wondering who that was. Because they had said 'me' not 'us'. Usually you say, us. Am I right? When you're supporting someone at an event? Do us proud. And Jake just grins, waves, goes to the mic, adjusts the brace around his neck, good evening, he says. And he plays this one chord. One chord. And it's an alarm bell. Straight away it's a fucking big clanger. That shiver I had? It was turning into a lightning bolt. Right into the bowels. Something wasn't right. I had heard him play Free as a Bird on countless occasions and I knew how he played it. I knew the very first chord and even from one chord you can tell the tempo and this was not it. And I looked around the booth and nobody else seemed to be unnerved at all. But then he starts playing and very quickly it's clear what he's up to. And the team in the booth with me, they're looking at each other then they're looking at me. Then their heads just go down. And after about thirty seconds, when it's obvious it's already over, one of the guys, he just sort of whispers, Brian, what do you want me to do? Because, we could do nothing about the crowd in the venue. They would have to just wait it out. But we could pull the plug on the live stream. Throw something in and save our blushes.

And then, all of a sudden, this sense of calmness comes over me, just descends like a little cloud and I actually feel all right. Okay, Jake, I think to myself. You made your choice. So I turn to the operator and just say, leave it. Just let him finish.

## *Donnie Miller. Record store owner, old friend.*

I was smack bang in the thick of it, right in the crowd. Jake had got me a ticket and I was hoping Smithy was going to come along with me but that wasn't going to be. They hadn't spoken to each other since Smithy had given that box to Blake. And as much as I'd have wanted to, it wasn't for me to get in the middle of them. At least not then. Let it settle. Their friendship had so much durability, permanence, it couldn't just close with an episode like that. And it tarnished any goodness that had come from Jake's victory. Because this was a triumph, however you wanted to look at it, it was a triumph. He was about to play on a stage that had been graced by the legends, the stars that he gazed at on the walls of his room when he was a child. He had bounced back from a tragedy, persisted, fought to do what he loved doing despite the odds stacked against him and I was feeling real proud for him.

And the place was jammed in there. Man, you couldn't have squeezed a cigarette paper in between the bodies down on the floor. It was heaving. But you wanna know what hit me? They all still had their phones out. Every one of them on the floor, no kidding. I must have been the only person in the audience standing with my arms folded and my hands free to applaud an act when they came out and deserved it. Everyone else was watching the live stream, on their phones, even though the goddam show was only feet away.

I tapped this guy in front of me on the shoulder just as it's about to begin, and I say, hey man, do you not think you can put that away now? And he kind of frowns at me. What are you saying, dude? Dude, he calls me. And I say, well, you're here. Do you need to be looking at it on the screen as well? And he glances at the phone and then at the stage as the first act is coming on. And then he just goes blank, says nothing, and turns back to face the stage, still with the phone in his hand. And all around him the people are doing pretty much the same thing, watching the show on their phones even though it's right there in front of them. And I just thought to myself, if the music died when Buddy Holly's plane went down, then its soul has gone to hell tonight. And I whisper to myself, Jakey, you got to come out here and show all these people just what music means. And after the third act the host comes out, this not very funny funny guy who is just there to rile the crowd. And I've got the butterflies. Do me proud, Jake. Do me proud, I say. Actually, I shout it, I hear myself shouting because it's that loud and it's coming from the echo chambers of my own heart. DO ME PROUD, JAKE! YEEHAAAWW.

And the guy in front turns and looks at me, because Jake still hasn't appeared. And I just nod at him. Wait until you see this guy play, I say to him. Then he appears, in the wings, hesitating, letting it build. He walks on. Smiles. Waves. He opens the door on his bird cage which is there next to him on a rug. Then he just says, good evening. Then something happens. It ain't right. Something's not right. He plays the first chord. And again. And again. But the rhythm's not right. Then I begin to laugh. I'm sure I recognise the song but I just don't want to believe it. Then I laugh some more. And as Jake gets into it and the whole crowd is just stunned into this silence, looking at their goddam phones, I just think back to that line in the movie of George Orwell's 1984. The people will not revolt. They will not look up from their screens long enough to notice what's happening.

## *Andy Kirwan. Music writer and journalist.*

I said it at the very beginning and I'm going to say it again. This was the strangest departure from the world of music I'd ever seen. It was shocking and it was, it was insulting. And it was downright offensive. It was tragic, actually. And it was very, very hard to watch. But, you know, I saw something like this coming. And when we all get to summarise and wrap it all up and give our final thoughts, I'll tell you exactly why. But, that evening, that final show, and what should have been something spectacular became an abomination. It was a travesty.

We, all of us back at the production booth, we were really excited about what was going on. We weren't popping the champagne corks just yet but we were almost there, you know what I mean? Those butterflies were rising up. And, when you think about it, there was really something revolutionary happening that night. Because there has, in recent times, been a great concern that streaming music, Spotify, YouTube, Soundcloud and all these digital channels, would eventually kill off the live music scene. The clubs. The caverns. The upstairs rooms in the pubs and the backrooms of the bars. And without these places bands would be steering their talents in a new direction, forgoing the live audience and concentrating instead on production values to cater solely for online listeners. But what I witnessed that evening was really something of an anomaly. You had all these people crammed into this space to watch these artists perform live, yet simultaneously looking at their phones for the live stream of the very same event. It left me totally bemused, and where before, the cynic in me might have went, you know, this is it. I am witnessing the death of live music as we know it, by the time the first act had finished I had, forgive the pun, changed my tune. Blake was onto something. He had really tapped into the zeitgeist here. But then Jake came out and did his utmost to fuck it all up.

Now, I had called Jake out some time back. He had struggled when I asked him some fairly basic questions in a very easygoing interview. I thought at that point he was out of the running altogether. And I think he deserved to be out of the running. He'd been found out. He had a small bag of tricks and he'd used them all. Then he, or at least people close to him, pulled off this miracle with a ghost story and a song that he had wanted to keep the lid on. And I'll tell you what I think of all that later. But the word was Blake had leaned on him to release that track. And that might have been true up to a point. But he didn't just use his own weight to lean on him, he used the weight of his bloody chequebook too. Jake got a six-figure sum to release that song, even though, contractually, Blake could actually have gone ahead and released it anyway. He didn't need permission. But he coughed up six figures. I was never Blake's fan, we all know that. But I saw another side to him over the weeks we worked together on the whole project and he wasn't always the bad guy. He was driven by his love of music first, business second and, okay, maybe his love of humanity came last but he wasn't a monster and Jake was well rewarded for his emotional pain, if you want to put it like that. Blake got him through to the last round, performing to hundreds of thousands of viewers across Europe. And how does he reward him? I'll tell you how.

Out he comes, onto the stage, keeping the audience waiting, and, you know, he's dressed like some dandy in a three-piece. I knew the plan was to perform Free as a Bird and he opens the door of the bird cage as some symbolic preface. Fair enough, Jake. And at that point — it's quiet, there's a hush, because all the other acts have these explosive, incendiary openings but Jake's entrance, he's like a little glow worm on that stage in comparison. Then this guy shouts out DO ME PROUD, JAKE! YEEHAAAWW! Some old guy in the audience who seemed to think it was a bit of a hoot. And it kicks off this chorus of cheers and with that, Jake grins from ear to ear and strums this one chord before going into this oompah rhythm.

And away he goes with it. Ooom-pah. Ooom-pah. Ooom-pah. Ooom-pah. Ooom-pah. And I'm thinking what in the name of good God is this. And the old guy in the crowd suddenly starts laughing, actually he's close to hysterics. And at first I just think, right, so Jake had picked up on this guy, thought he was a heckler or something and this oompah thing is his response. And he's going to stop very quickly and we're going to have one of his famous theatrical stunts. If he can do it in a school he is surely going to pull something out of the bag tonight. Because the crowd are really wondering what's going on. There are people looking at the stage then back to their screens, you know, totally confused. Is this all an illusion? Is this some bloody cyber vortex thing we've been sucked into? What's real and what's not real here?

But then, then comes the death blow. Na-na na-na na-na nah, Na-na na-na na-na nah, Na-na na-na na-na naaaaah, quack, quack, quack, quack. Na-na na-na na-na nah, Na-na na-na na-na nah, Na-na na-na na-na naaaaah, quack, quack, quack, quack. It's the Birdy Song. The Birdy Song. And as some people begin to laugh, others actually join in. Singing along. Na-na na-na na-na nah, Na-na na-na na-na nah, Na-na na-na na-na naaaaah, quack, quack, quack, quack. And there are those still scowling at their phones. Me? I was just disgusted.

I watched the whole thing, even though every fibre in my body was pulling me out towards the bar. I watched because I wanted Jake to see me watching him. My eyes must have been glowing like the devil's and Vicar Street is a small venue and Jake makes a habit of eyeballing as many people as possible, that's always been his thing. Eye contact. And he did see me and you know, he didn't flinch. And when the horror ended, he actually stood back and finished off with this little blues riff and ended on a seventh note. Just to — I don't know. I actually don't know anymore. Then off he skipped like a bloody jester to a chorus of laughs, boos, jeers and whistles.

I pushed my way out through the crowd as quick as I could but by the time I got backstage he was gone. And there were people everywhere back there tearing around in a flap and the next act was being rushed on. Clipboards were flying. Blake had come down and he had his hands wrapped tightly around the back of his head and Jenny, she was leaning against the wall sobbing. So I approached her, put an arm around her and just said, look, Jenny, move on. As quickly as possible, just move on. He'll be forgotten by the end of the show, I can promise you that. We can save this thing with cool heads, move on.

But she had always adored Jake. He was this rebel type that teenagers aspire to and boy had she been let down. Where's he gone, I asked her, looking around. And she nodded at the back door. He left, she said. Walked out with the guitar on and the harmonica hanging off his neck. He just walked out. Never said a word to anyone, except me, she said. What did he say, I asked her. And Jenny just shakes her head. My little star, that was it. Then someone said he just jumped into a taxi and drove away.

## *Katie Ryan. Girlfriend.*

Well, he left a trail in his wake, didn't he? Destruction. Who saw that coming? I didn't. Everyone said I did. How did I not know, sure I lived with him. But in the weeks leading up to that last show, he had been so preoccupied, and when we had the time together we pretty much just left the music out of it. Apart from the day the Ghost song was resurrected. But Jake never knew my involvement in all of that and Smithy . . . I feel real bad about Smithy. But Blake was right. It was best to be utilitarian about it and just let one of us take the fall. Not that it made any difference. Jake was gone. Gone, just like that.

I didn't go to the show that night. I was so fucking sick and tired of the whole thing by then. And after Ghost went out, Jake had become so morose I really, really questioned whether I had done the right thing. Jake was dark as dark can be. He had retreated into a bad place. I kept saying to myself, look, he's been there before, he knows how to get out of it. The music will save him. Then we watched. We all watched. Hundreds of thousands of us watched. I watched, sitting at home, watching him go down in flames, watching him on the screen of a little tablet which was resting on my knees. It just didn't seem real. I didn't want it to be real. But I kept watching and I knew what it was. And I heard the whistles and boos and the laughter and I thought, well, it really is all over now. But it wasn't because that wasn't the end. The end was he never came home.

# TEN

## *The Bird has Flown*

**Paul Smith (Smithy). Jake's childhood friend.**

In the months after Jake disappeared, his pantomime act became a colossal hit. I'm talking millions of views, shares, all that bleedin' stuff which I have grown to utterly detest. But we count our lives now in clicks, whether I like it or not. And out there, right now, somebody is probably doing a search for 'Jake Green Birdy Song'. And I've taken the time to think about the whole thing, going right back to Jake's Fly-in gigs, the school, Blake, the whole lot. And one question has now become crucial. And I'm going to show off the bit of Latin here now just to really stress it. Cui Bono? Cui Bono? For whose benefit? Who stood to gain the most from all of this? And if you look at the facts, you can reach an interesting conclusion, right?

    His streams, Jake's streams, have clocked up hundreds of thousands of hits. His downloads from his own website and other streaming services have soared. Ghost was downloaded hundreds of thousands of times as was Little Star, which is still used by the show as the theme. His YouTube channel, with all the videos from the ten weeks or so of that competition are getting new views daily, plus there is plenty of archived video that can be uploaded over the coming months. I know that.

    But look at what else has happened, and I had no inkling about this until I saw someone on the street the other day with a T-shirt, with this image of a yellow bird and the line 'Jake Green's Not Dead' on it. So I checked his website and lo and behold, they are now selling merchandise — who are they? That's the question — with this logo, this little yellow bird, and a choice of slogans. 'The bird has flown', 'A little bird told me where Jake Green is hiding', 'Jake Green, bird of passage' and my personal favourite, 'Jake Green never gave a flying f\*\*\*'. Music aside, this whole sideshow has resulted in the creation of a very profitable brand for them. Again, I say they and them, and of course it can only mean Blake, Andy and Jenny. Jenny, I realise now was the prodigy who became Blake's protégé. It's genius really. I mean, musicians have been trying very hard, over the last number of years, to make more from doing less. Because really they've had to work so much harder to make a living. And what better way to do that than just, disappear. Create a story, create a legend and create a brand. So well done on that one, Blake. And, well done Jake. Did they work together this whole time? Think about it.

But let me just say one thing final because it's important and it's something that has become lost in this whole sorry bleedin' mess. I miss Jake dearly. It has felt like a death in the family. We spoke every day, Jake and I. Every day, no joking. All these years. Then there was this very sudden disconnect, this very real sense of loss. Like someone just pulled the plug and he was gone. And I miss him. And what I did might have seemed wrong, but I expected to get some contact from him at some stage. Anything. Email, text, message, a postcard even. But nah, nothing came. And Jake wasn't the type of guy to bear a grudge. He did genuinely feel that life was just too short to make enemies out of people, especially the people that matter to you. He had made few enemies. But I must now be counted among them. And that hurts.

## *Brian Blake. Promoter and manager.*

Once you're dead, you're made for life. Jimi Hendrix said that, and if you look at his career, it was actually very short, just a few years. But who doesn't know Jimi Hendrix? Probably one in every five homes has that iconic poster on a wall in one of the bedrooms. He was great when he was alive, he became even better when he died. Now, let's just get one thing straight, I had nothing to do with that circus act. Nothing. No part in the planning or execution of it at all. Are we clear? It left me feeling very, very sick. And I was just so glad that the real little star of all this, Jenny, that she was there that evening. It was her came to me at the end of what was otherwise a very successful show at Vicar Street. We were able to console each other and, fuck it, congratulate each other too. We pulled it off. That kid Aischa won and by the end of the night, once she came out again to play, I thought to myself, well, they'll move on and forget. The mob's memory is short. They'll move on.

But I was standing outside afterwards having a cigarette – I gave up smoking 20 years ago, by the way, but that is what the night had done to me. I cadged a ciggie off one of the production team and stood outside in the laneway and sucked the life out of the thing. And very quickly, as people filed out and chattered and babbled I got a very clear idea of what most of them were talking about, and it wasn't the winner. It was Jake and his fucking birdy act. And I went weak at the knees. I got a dizzy spell like I'd been hit with a spade and crawled back inside to the bar and got a snifter of Brandy. And it was getting quiet, people were almost gone and Jenny came in and sat down beside me. And, I had grown to love Jenny. She just gets straight to the point, never wastes time on banter, trying to cheer you up with useless tropes or nonsense, she just says, Brian, this is the best thing that could have happened to us. We can do this all again. Only better. Watch, the next one will really take off. No pun intended. And we laugh. And she was right. We can do it all again.

No, I didn't have anything to do with Jake's vanishing act, but yes, Jenny and I and Andy and all the team will have everything to do with profiting from it. And as long as the green keeps coming in, we'll fucking lap it up. That's the business, baby. As for Jake, I'm sure he's out there and he'll be getting his share. It's going into his account. I honour my commitments. He's a fucking ghost himself now and if I'm to be honest, I'd rather deal with the ghost than the real thing. It's a hell of a lot easier and a hell of a lot more lucrative.

## *Miles and Jenny Adams. Father and daughter.*

Dear, oh dear, oh dear. I need a holiday too. I'm exhausted after all of this. I'm just glad it's all over so I can get my house back. But look, although Jenny has really gained from this experience, and she has a bright career ahead of her because of it, I know she's filled with a deep sense of regret. She was very fond of Jake, as were we all. And my hunch was right, she had been badgering him for some time before that morning in the park. She targeted him for her project. And I can understand that. There is such pressure on kids in school now that the savvy ones will have already started making inroads into a career before they've even sat their leaving cert. She wanted a career in music, production, digital media and this is what she decided to do. She had no idea it would pan out the way it did but it will stand to her, I'm sure of it.

On a personal note, I'm sorry for what happened to Jake. What his pal Smithy did to him seemed like a stab in the back. But, at the same time, can you imagine being burdened with the task of repressing someone's grief? It had dragged on long enough and, presumably, Smithy decided it was a good time for Jake to deal with it. But clearly it wasn't. And Jake's response says it all. Classic breakdown. Where is he now?

I fear the worst, I really do. If you ask me, he got into a taxi and skipped on the boat to England. He could be under a bridge now, sleeping under slabs of cardboard. And that is a very real scenario. We should actually all be worried, all of us, anyone who was in any way involved because we might be complicit in a tragic death.

And I've been onto Jenny to get a missing person's page up across social media, instead of profiteering from the poor man's troubles. But in those crucial first couple of days after he vanished, nobody thought to put the word out. No search. No Facebook posts. Nothing. And still nobody has come forward to officially report him as missing.

Katie, she still thinks he'll just waltz back in the door. But I hate to say it, it's been a few months. He would have come back now if he were able. And my worry is that, he isn't able.

## *Katie Ryan. Girlfriend.*

If I knew where he was, wouldn't I be going there? Or maybe not. Maybe he's just somewhere he wants to be. Somewhere peaceful. Somewhere quiet. Somewhere he might be left alone. Somewhere nobody will hassle him. Somewhere he can just sit on the street and play his music. Somewhere, over the . . . I'm not going to say it. Shall I say it? Over the rainbow, there you go. He'll come back. I'm sure of it. I'm still in his home and everything is here, all his things. Even that photo of himself and his mum, the one image from his life that he was prepared to leave out for people to see. He wouldn't have left that behind. One day, soon, that door will open and he'll be home. Or, failing that, I'll get a message from him and he'll tell me where he is and I'll head on over and we'll all live . . . here we go. . . happily ever after, there, I said it.

## *Donnie Miller. Record store owner, old friend.*

What a beautiful exit. Just beautiful, man. We had a long chat about what he was going to do for that final show, Jake and I. Went through all sorts of scenarios. It wasn't Jake, that whole dam thing. It never was. And we talked about how best to get out of it. We came up with the right kind of song, the right costume even, getting a band, pulling some stunt, all sorts of things and we settled on Free as a Bird because he said that after the show was over, he was done. He would fly, free as a bird. So I guess he got other ideas as the night got closer that he didn't want to share with me. That's okay. Boy, it was a hoot. So a few people got hurt. Who cares? They should never have forced him to put that song out there about his little girl in the first place, that was plain bad. That was wrong. Wrong. Wrong. That was bad karma and I know there are a few people raking in the cash right now but, watch this space, it'll come back around. The chickens, let's stick with the birdies, will fly the fuck home to roost. Jake is not done yet. He's out there now, hatching – see what I did there – hatching another plan. The Birdy Song though. You really have to just love it.

## *Andy Kirwan. Music writer and journalist.*

Well, it looks like it's down to me to drop the bombshell. To say what nobody else will say. Because, let's remember we do live in age now where to say something against the consensus ends up costing you dearly. People's careers have been destroyed because they carelessly said something that everybody was thinking but nobody would say. This is the age we live in. I'm not saying what Jake did was a scandal. But what I am saying is that people, everyone, even me, have been afraid to question that whole story. The story. The ghost story.

I mean, what kind of villain would you be to quiz someone over their little girl's death? But I began my career in the newsroom many, many years ago. And it was my job to question everything, scrutinise it, don't let it out until every possible angle is covered. And I've had a bit of time to probe that whole story. I was never sold on it. So here's the bombshell that needs to be dropped.

Jake's daughter never died. And I'll tell you why. She's very much alive and well. And do you know where she's living right now? I'll tell you. In his house. Katie is Jake's daughter. Sound implausible? Well, just think about it. A few things sounded the alarm bells for me. Firstly, he was deeply uncomfortable when I was asking him anything about his past. And that nice story about meeting Katie? On a train or something? He made it up. They made it up. It was a pleasant story. Added a bit of credence to how they got the whole Fly-in gig thing going. Fine, fair enough. But look at her. She's half his age. If you got them both to flash some ID, that's what you'd find. She's probably in her early twenties, that's all.

Next item? I never once, not once, saw a show or sign of affection in public. They never held hands. Never kissed. Nothing. Even that first day I saw them together, in the park? She just didn't look like his girlfriend. There was nothing there, no chemistry. The body language, it was all wrong. But there was something else alerted me, something more conclusive. Jake's contract was amended when he agreed to release that Ghost song. Not only did Blake have to give him a six-figure sum, but Jake insisted on what he called a 'hit by a bus' clause. Meaning should anything happen to him, his intellectual property rights and royalties would go to someone else. Katie. Come on. I mean, they weren't even married. They were 'together' what, a year or so if we are to believe his story.

So, I'll tell you what I believe happened. Jake and his then girlfriend, they had a daughter together, foolishly, while they were both still in college with no jobs, no income, at a time in Ireland, the late 1980s, when there was huge unemployment and there were people emigrating in droves. They lived, one can only imagine, in some damp, shitty hovel in bedsit land. A one-room crib that was probably badly heated and sagging at the top and sides from damp. The little girl, God bless her, was probably sick every week. Her parents, I would say because I was a student myself, were probably party animals. And one day their daughter gets very, very sick. But they're not monsters, of course they're not. They love their daughter but they're students, and they miss a letter. The hospital knows that. Come on, our health system is bad but not following up on a letter like that? Seriously. So after some time has passed the hospital wonders what is going on and calls social services and one day there's a knock on the door. It's midday. The baby is crying. The parents are hungover and still asleep. The flat is freezing. There's no food. It's filthy. And social services come in and the game is up. The baby is taken into care. Jake is distraught. His little girl is gone. She's as good as dead. In fact she needs to be dead so he can actually feel grief rather than face purgatory knowing she will be always out there somewhere in some foster home. So to cement the fabrication he makes up the fact she's dead. The girlfriend is distraught and she joins the brain drain and heads to London. Jake goes to ground, records all this music and he gives this Ghost recording to Smithy.

And we kind of know what he did after that. He became this reclusive figure who would come out of his shell every now and again to play in strange places. Really he just became something of a wastrel for years, didn't he, until he was able to find his kid again. But apart from owning the house he lived in, he'd nothing else. He needed an income to support his daughter. So between the two of them they found a way to concoct something that would take us all in and never be challenged. And so the ghost is born.

Does that all sound like a bit of a stretch? Can I prove it? I think I can. The files will be out there. The records, they have to be. Do I want to prove it? Is it in me to go and expose something like that, ruin their lives? This man, a father who just wanted to do everything for the daughter he loved. Loved so much he was happy to disappear so she could be financially secure. So where is he now? Who really knows? But one way or the other, he has finally made a success story for himself in a very extraordinary way. And as I always say, people just love that shit.

ENDS

Printed in Poland
by Amazon Fulfillment
Poland Sp. z o.o., Wrocław